White Cranes Dancing

Nancy McKnight

Published in 2013 by FeedARead.com Publishing — Arts Council funded

A CIP catalogue record for this title is available from the British Library.

Cover image © plusphoto

CHAPTER ONE

I don't suppose my relatives intended to ruin my life with fairy-tales, unsuitable though they are for children. Peter MacKenzie, my grandfather, meant to teach me to deal with bullies (he'd dealt with not a few in his time), so he stuck to his favourite; The Three Billy Goats Gruff. Over and over he'd tell it, embroidering the horrid detail till I was screaming and damp-knickered with terror. The embellishments came out of Granda's head, not out of a book, for though we were all great readers the only book he ever read from was the Gaelic bible.

These days I don't scream or wet myself, but I certainly can't be trusted to keep the promises I make on bridges. Given the option between the ugly, malevolent troll and the small sharp hooves and horns of the killer-goat, I'll say anything, just anything, to get myself off the hook.

Then there was my aunt Peigi - the educated one, the fey one, the one who's a MacKenzie to this day, and still lives on the island, in Balvaig, for she never married. The monsters in her stories were always heroes in disguise, and all the princes were charming and brave and muscular, like the ones in the films of the Kirov ballet she took me to see, or the poems she read to me as I fell into sleep.

I had no brothers or sisters to set the record straight, so I suppose I should be grateful that Frank Stuart, my father, read to me too; Kinsey and Marx and Sergei Esenin are less dangerous fodder than Bonnie Kilmeny, to an impressionable mind.

My mother read only for herself. There she'd sit hunched over her Mills & Boon, eyes glazed, strands of long, black hair sticking to her hot face, lips moving slightly. I daresay that's where she found the name she branded me with. Serena. How was I supposed to know what a 'Serena' should be like when there had never been another either among the MacKenzies or in the village of Balvaig? It wasn't the label for a person I could have pretended to be. An elegant, calm, mysterious Greta Garbo type, or a Catherine Deneuve – they could get away with "Serena". But she wouldn't let me change it; she didn't care that I loathed my name, because she didn't like hers either. Morag; the name you might give a pet sheep.

So Morag named me, and Peigi taught me to believe in fairies, but Frank sealed my fate, because it was his own religion he gave me, handing it over on my fifth birthday. He pressed the picture book he'd brought home from the International Youth Festival into sweaty, dubious hands that would have preferred a toy. 'That's my most precious possession I'm entrusting to you, sweetheart,' he said, 'so that you'll grow to love the place as I do.'

And he added that no matter what others might try to tell me, no country could be evil where books cost less than bread. 'A beacon to the rest of the world. If we still had men like John McLean, Scotland would have followed her lead long since.' He'd written his name and the city's name carefully inside: Frank Stuart, Leningrad, April 1957. Exactly a decade before I was born. I traced the elegant Cyrillic script alongside the English with my finger, and knew in my heart I'd be able to read it one day (though Frank never learned to). Then I opened the book at random, to a panorama of river and bridge and steeple: View from the Lieutenant Schmidt Bridge. Love hit me like a train. I recognised the place where the Prince would find me - on an iron-lace bridge over the Neva, in the city that was originally named for a man called Peter, like my Granda, but had been allowed to change its name. There I'd wake up, and live happily ever after.

'That's one of the ones they open up at night, to let the ships through,' Frank said, looking over my shoulder.

'What – when people are on it? Like the bridge of San Luis Rey?' (Another of the volumes on Peigi's shelf.)

'No, they warn you first, silly.'

I kept the book if not the faith. I reached the age of thirty still imagining the bridges of St Petersburg are made for love, and Prince Charming is a Russian with perfect cheekbones and very tight tights.

CHAPTER TWO

Love was the last thing on my mind when I agreed to cross the Baltic with an old school friend last summer. Dee had suggested the trip because we had decided we were both sick of men. She'd been jilted three weeks before her wedding; I was in the final stages of divorce.

Dee's an orthodontist. Money's no object, as far as she's concerned. But I'd had to convince myself I deserved a treat.

In any case, it was only three years to the Millennium, and I was well past the stage where I could think of myself as a 'girl' any more. I needed an adventure. I needed to lay some ghosts.

The first day was almost gone already; the following one would be taken up with a full-day excursion to Pertodvoretz and Oranienbaum. All my chores were complete; the picture postcards were bought and written and mailed – though God knows if they'd ever reach their destinations. The tawdry souvenirs had been acquired. I had only one evening to say goodbye to Peter's city for a final time. I didn't really expect to be back.

We'd arrived at the height of an unaccustomed heat-wave, but it had rained two days before, so the air had the soft, fresh-washed texture of swansdown – subtly different to home, where the breeze after rain is like a silk chiffon scarf drawn gently across the skin. West Highland summers and Baltic ones; sweeter because they're nearer the bone. I wanted to rest my cheek against the night air of St Petersburg, and suck my thumb and cry.

Time didn't stop when I was eighteen. A dozen years on, there I was, crossing the bridge where the first man (perhaps the only one) I loved completely and without conditions proposed to me, though as a proposal it wasn't quite what I'd been expecting. He'd be the same age as me now. We could have passed in the street and not recognised each other.

'Wait here a mo,' I said to Dee. 'I want to look at something over there.'

I'd had an urge to stand on the exact spot again. Perhaps I wanted to check if Sergei Timochenko had been back to carve our initials in a heart on the lamp-post where we'd stood locked in each other's arms on a June night in 1985. We'd gazed at the romantic vista of water and bridges and elegant buildings, and basked in the glow of young love.

'I have a book at home with this exact same view in it,' I'd said. 'I wish I didn't have to go home so soon.'

'If we can't live together, perhaps we should die together,' Sergei announced, out of the blue. 'We could jump, in each others' arms.' His breath was warm against my cheek, and he wasn't joking. That bridge, or any of the others.

'We'll live together, Seriozha, pet,' I replied quickly, still reeling after my first spin on the roller-coaster of the Slavic temperament.

'Promise you'll come back to me, then,' he said. 'We'll marry at once. We're both old enough. I'll wait for you, I'll never marry anyone else, I swear it. Promise?'

'I promise,' I said dreamily, revelling in how blessed I was to be engaged and have my future mapped out just weeks before I finished school.

As I began to cross I assumed the river of traffic would slow, or swerve, or take some action to avoid running me down, the way it would in Princes Street. But I found I had to gallop heedlessly because it didn't. Since I wasn't paying attention, the right heel of the uncomfortable sandals Dee had persuaded me to buy for my holiday wedged itself firmly between the inner edge of a tram-line and the decrepit tarmac.

Then I heard the tram coming. Clickety-clack. Who's that trip-trapping over my bridge?

My name rang in my ears, as if someone was calling me. 'Ser-eee-na.' My mother's voice. It's run in my head, an endless-loop tape, all my life. Its batteries didn't run out when hers did. 'Can't you do anything right? What a stupid, ugly way to die. Who's going to weep over your warm, mangled body, or remember that your eyes were still open and go off to war to forget? Come to me. You'll be better off here. It's hot all year round.'

I stood up straight, wiggling my foot frantically as my greasy bell-clanging Nemesis trundled and scraped towards me, rather than risk the indignity of dying with my arse in the air if I bent to unfasten the buckle.

My tramline thoughts were no orderly re-run of my life either: Will the others go on with their holiday as if nothing had happened? What will Fergus put in the paper – 'Suddenly, in St Petersburg, as the result of a tragic accident, Serena, beloved almost-ex-wife'....? Perhaps he'll have me cremated out of spite, for who's to stop him? He's still technically my next of kin. Who was Lieutenant Schmidt anyway? Naturalised German? You'd think he'd have changed his name. Bet his descendants did, in 1941. Wonder why the

8

Communists left the name in place? Strangers will root through the stuff in my bag..... And I wondered if tram-wheels are smooth and burning hot with the friction or sharp and cold as Lizzie Borden's axe, and thought about life's small missed opportunities.

Above the din of traffic on the bridge, before I'd started to cross, I'd heard a man whistling, a sweet, pure, limpid sound that reminded me of my father. Morag used to yell at him for whistling indoors, as unlucky as bringing in hawthorn blossom or peacock feathers. So I'd hear him whistling down the street, then the sound would stop, like a doodlebug bomb. Sometimes there'd be an explosion, sometimes not. Well, Frank would be with her, wherever dead folk go and he'd have been proud to die in St Petersburg, though he'd never have agreed to call it that. He was whistling me to him.

I closed my eyes and waited to be mashed to pulp. I've no knowledge of how he arrived beside me, only the sensation of strong arms that gripped me, swung me round and over the edge of the metal track, snapping my foot free of the flimsy leather strap, and clasped me tight against a pale-blue-shirted chest that smelt of clean laundry and fresh cigarette smoke. The tram passed so close it brushed against my hair, and I felt the draught of the driver's breath as she swore at me – 'Cretin! Do you want to get yourself killed?' (And who has the correct answer to that one?).

I clung to the edges of a leather jacket. 'I've got you,' he said. 'You're safe. Keep still.' A deeper voice than I'd expected in an angel, with a rough edge to it, a husky quality like Marlene Dietrich's.

For I was in no doubt who'd saved me. My guardian angel. I've known him since I was seven, standing at Edinburgh's busiest crossing at the top of Leith Walk: A man plunges suddenly into the tide of cars and taxis and buses to grasp the arm of a blind woman who's marched purposefully off the kerb. People on the pavement scream. Possibly I scream too. Afterwards, the hero melts into the crowd of shoppers and I'm left wondering if the woman wanted to die. Perhaps she cursed and swore at her rescuer. 'Her guardian angel was watching right enough,' says Aunt Peigi.

I'd decided there and then I'd like one of those. I called him Gabriel, because it sounded sunshiny and wholesome, like the adverts for Comfort fabric softener. I didn't tell my Granda, because he didn't hold with angels.

I'd never touched Gabriel, far less spoken to him, though he'd saved my life twice before. Angels speak Russian. Eat your heart out, Diana Cooper. This was no feathery, supernatural creature in a nightie, but then my Gabriel had always been indisputably male. He wore leathers and rode a Harley-Davidson and had a muscular body and a gun instead of a sword. He needed to shave twice a day. I was an unnatural child.

He hugged me to him as if I'd been there most of his life too. Then he scooped me up and dodged between cars till we reached the pavement.

Perhaps this is the second part of my inheritance, trickling down through the matrilineal line from my ancestors in Skye? I never understood why God squandered the gift of the Sight on pessimists like the Highland Celts in the first place. Maybe he has a sense of humour. They love nothing more than a good tragedy, so he's given them two bites at the cherry. My grannie's mother was cursed with it; they say she'd cry out in anguish, so vivid were the pictures in her head. The same way her own great-grandmother, the legendary Sarah, fell down in a fit, seeing the thatches of Suisnish in flames, years before the bailiffs laid a torch to them.

'Excuse me,' he said, setting me down on my feet, holding me steady. 'You were so scared I didn't know if you'd be able to run.'

'Probably not. It hurts.'

'So you do speak Russian. I wondered if you understood what I was saying. I figured even if I broke your ankle it was better than your neck.'

He kept hold of me. The feel of his hand was familiar; the warmth of the skin, the way his palm was firm and smooth and without hint of sweat, and his long fingers curled round my bare wrist.

I thanked him for saving my life, and he said sternly: 'I was watching you. I couldn't believe my eyes when you just stepped off the pavement.'

He'd had to take a risk too. 'I should have used the proper crossing,' I said humbly.

Moments earlier, I'd been ranting to Dee that nowhere feels foreign nowadays; it's all Coca-Cola signs and black and white striped street crossings.

'Worse. That helps them take aim,' he said. 'Do you feel calmer now? Can you put your weight on that side?'

'Why were you watching me?'

'You're beautiful.'

Dee arrived precipitately beside us.

'Stand right here,' the stranger said, 'Promise me you won't do anything silly.'

I nodded obediently, and he dodged back into the traffic to haul my shoe from its grave. 'It's scuffed, but only the strap's broken. I have a pin.' He knelt on the pavement and fastened the thin leather to the side with meticulous care, then ran competent, professional fingers over my ankle. I decided he must be a doctor. 'I don't think it's even sprained,' he said, 'just bruised. You'll allow me to buy you a drink.' Even allowing for the fact Russian speakers place the stress differently, it wasn't a question. 'My name is Maksim Grigoriev. Most people call me Max.'

Well, of course. I always knew in my heart it would be like this. It's not the angel Gabriel, it's my prince. He extended a much more formal hand. 'And you?'

Cinderella. 'Serena Stuart MacKenzie. And this is Deirdre McCulloch. Dee.'

'I need a drink,' Dee said, 'after watching Serena's party trick. Where's the Nevsky thingie? We wanted to go to the Literaturnoe Café.'

And even before we reached that, I'd wanted to check if they'd still left the blue and white stencilled notice on the wall: *Citizens! In the event of artillery fire this side of the street is the most dangerous.* Lest we forget.

Max shrugged dismissively. 'It's obscenely expensive and it closes early. Let me take you to a bar where you'll meet real Russians.' He'd switched casually and unobtrusively to English. As we began to walk, he fell into step beside me.

'I should really go back to the ship and put on some sensible footwear,' I said unconvincingly.

If I went back so early, its captain Paolo Conti would be waiting, of that I had no doubt. He was too self-assured to make the type of mistake that could cost him his career. It wouldn't have gone further than kissing, but matters would have progressed irrevocably. 'If this is not meant to happen, block it,' I'd chanted earlier, inside my head, while Dee and I wandered aimlessly among Vasilievsky Island's sinister streets-with-no-names. 'Let everything turn out for the highest good of all concerned, as recommended by Shakti Gawain. Amen.'

'Anyway,' I said, 'we need to get back to the other side, before they open the bridges.'

Max consulted an empty wrist. Careless! Forgotten his watch.

'It's just after ten,' said Dee.

'Plenty of time,' he said. 'Several hours. Isn't the river beautiful, with the moon almost full and the daylight still with us? I often walk across to the Strelka, just to savour it. That's the scene the ones who've left dream of.'

And even with the Communist paint flaking, it was. Numinous drifts of amethyst mist over the Neva, the elegant three-branched streetlights on the bridges and along the embankment casting pools of tawny light as atmospheric as anything you'd see in Paris, lacy bridges and clipped limes silhouetted against a peach-and-lemon sky. It would take a Philistine to notice the rusting sub moored opposite us. 'Our White Nights,' the locals say, as if they'd invented the endless twilight, getting-out-of-school sensation the Scots call the simmer dim. But Max didn't see what's underneath any more than I see the rash of ticky-tacks that's swamping Balvaig.

'You'll be fine with these shoes,' he said. 'It's not far. Your injury is slight.'

'Are you a doctor?' I said. I'd noticed his preternaturally fine hands and elegant fingers. Musician's hands.

'No! But I have healing hands.' He smiled down at me, a sweet enough to eat smile that made the earth spin beneath my feet. 'I'm a cellist. Did you know – it's Stravinsky's birthday tomorrow?'

And today's the anniversary of the day they hanged Imre Nagy.

'For Christ's sake!' said Dee. 'Get a move on, Serena.'

Max didn't quicken his pace. 'Although you speak my language with an excellent accent, I can tell you're not from here,' he said. 'You're on holiday?'

'A cruise. There's the ship across there. The Fortuna. We're only here till tomorrow evening. Not really long enough. I'm glad I've been before.'

'She picked up a man that time too,' Dee snapped, over her shoulder. 'She only looks the quiet type. Captain's had her lashed to the wheel since Copenhagen. But don't get your hopes up. She doesn't go for fair men, no matter where they're from, though she's always had this thing about Russians. Since she was in primary school.'

Max was pretending not to have heard Dee, or not to have understood her.

'Dee's not rational,' I said, just in case. 'She's had a fright. We both have. We got lost down the side-streets earlier.'

That afternoon, we had strayed into a time warp of 1960s Leningrad. There were few people around, and those we met sized us up like cannibals. The buildings I remembered were faded to water-colour-left-in-sun shades even the classiest paint firms couldn't reproduce: only time and climate. Every available wall was covered in peeling posters, advertising long-finished theatre performances, circuses, and English classes, dozens of these. Everyone wanted to learn English, to get out.

It reminded me of pictures in the old National Geographics Frank insisted on keeping. The Red Menace; the Enemy. 'He only gets them to look at black women's tits,' Morag used to say, thumbing through them for pictures of big brown men with small loincloths. She was wrong. They were the backbone of Frank's collection of Reasons to Loathe the Americans.

'You couldn't get lost in Peter,' Max said, 'the streets are all on a grid.' And he caught my hand again, drawing me back from the path of a speeding car. 'Careful! They'll hit you rather than risk getting rammed. Less damage to the bodywork. Don't they have traffic in England?'

'Scottish drivers aren't homicidal.'

He gave me that oblique and secret smile again, while I registered that he had the most perfect teeth. No sweeties when he was young.

'So – Serena Stuart MacKenzie from Scotland. That's a beautiful name. Serena.' And in that sexy accent, indeed it is. 'Whereabouts in Scotland?'

'I was born in the Highlands, on an island in fact, in a tiny village called Balvaig. But now I live in Edinburgh.'

'I'm not really Russian,' he said, 'but I was born in this wonderful city. It's marvellous that you speak my language. You learnt when you were here before?'

'No, at school. I was only here for a week, a dozen years ago. Leningrad.'

'Is it any different?'

More run-down. Still beautiful. In 1985 it was austere and scarcely free, but the paint wasn't flaking, and people had work. There was more grace about it. Strangers, even young people, didn't call each other 'ti' from the first meeting, and they still used the patronymic. But the city's heart was the same as ever. Fabergé and shit.

'The churches are churches again,' I said.

The women can get religion while the men hit the booze. Just like home. Superstition masquerading as religion, fatalism, cruel gods, hospitality that verges on masochism.

None of it makes sense. The answer to it all is a message at the bottom of a bottle, if only you could find the right one. Best drain them all, just in case. I'd had a fright too.

We caught up with Dee, and Max took us to a shabby pub along from the Gostiniy Dvor. I could see from the way he flicked the notes surreptitiously between his fingers, that he could ill afford to be hospitable. Dee downed her first glass in one gulp. She'd been on the booze since we left Leith and I'd suffered guilt-pangs over neglecting her while she went through the trauma of being dumped by a banker five weeks after reaching her thirty-second year and deciding maybe she'd better have some of her eggs frozen. Stupid drunken bitch.

I studied Maksim Grigoriev, closely and stealthily. Tall, muscular, slender. Wrong word - thin. Very blond hair, with a forelock that fell across his eyes, and a mannerism of sweeping it aside with the

16

back of his hand, like a wee boy needing a   trim. Nose a shade too large to be classical, but it suited his lankiness and made him look distinguished.   A sensitive mouth – no: sensual - and lacking the sullen down-turn I'd grown accustomed to over one short day in Peter.   Eyes the colour of a peaty burn in spate; warm brown with gold flecks.   Dangerous eyes. A narrow, high-cheekboned Byzantine-icon face with the most exquisite ellipse of jaw line, the curve Burne-Jones gave his knights. I had a powerful urge to trace it with my finger. I clenched my hands under the table. Max smiled at me anyway. He knew.

I was being inspected too. Men gawp at me and notice my hair and my eyes and my fashionable lack of boobs, and my neat wee bum. Maksim looked into me rather than at me, as if he could see through my skin. I couldn't have been offended.

'You want to go on to another bar? Maybe this one isn't very smart,' he said anxiously.

'It's fine,' I said.

Dee was halfway to the door. 'This is a dump. Let's go somewhere we might meet interesting people.'

'We'll walk a little first. Let you work up a thirst again.'   That's how we ended up in a larger, noisier pub near the Mariinsky. 'Stop fretting,' Max said,   'it's only three minutes to your ship from here.'

It was a bad move all the same.

'Ah, Grishkin!   You'll introduce me to your friends?'

The man who elbowed his way through the crowd towards us wasn't so tall as Max, but more powerfully built.   Black hair, black eyes, luxuriant moustache, a wide face that had more than a touch of Asia in it; an artist's impression of Genghis Khan. Although he was smartly dressed he had an aura of thuggery and I registered that Max wasn't deliriously pleased to see him.

'These are my guests, Zhenya,' he said. 'Visitors. Behave yourself.'

'Don't be greedy, you dirty bugger. You can't screw two women at the same time. I'm getting hard just looking at the dark one.'

'The dark one speaks excellent Russian. Yours is the blonde.'

Genghis blushed, and I could see then that he was handsome, or at least striking. His almond eyes glowed like coals. 'Sorry. I only meant to be friendly. Joking with my old comrade-in-arms.'

He seized Dee's hands in one of his paws. 'I like very much to practise my English. Yevgeny Kutozov. Zhenya. But my friends call me Kuzkuz.'

'The stuff they eat in Morocco,' said Dee.

'That's me. Wholesome and filling, but you won't put on weight unless you're greedy.'

Canned laughter from a greasy, weasel-faced spiv at his back indicated that he'd not arrived alone. The hair on the back of my neck prickled. I pressed closer to Max, and he didn't draw away.

'Tourists!' said Zhenya. 'And what have you found to gawp at today, my lovelies?'

'The Biggest Museum in the World,' said Dee. 'And a turquoise palace. The one where they keep going on about who stole their bloody amber.'

They all laughed. It had made me sad, though. Yes, they've brought back all the treasures they'd carried away for protection, and they allow the herds of tourists in to graze on them briefly, before they're shepherded back onto their buses. The guides brandish folding umbrellas above their heads like crucifixes. So many tourists, so many guides, so many umbrellas all

18

the same, so many buses parked in Palace Square, such a risk of getting lost. Most don't. They're safely decanted back at their hotels, their cruise-ships, the airport, and they go home to bore their friends with stories of: "when I was in Russia." But they're deluded. St Petersburg's not Russia, any more than Balvaig's Scotland. It's all veneer, the lapis lazuli and malachite and amber and gold, gold, gold - everywhere you look everything drips with gold (even the smiles). It doesn't do to believe it's part of Europe either, though it pretends to be.

And the Catherine Palace! Couples in eighteenth-century gear strolling in the gardens. What would they have next – Nicholas and Alexandra on ice? I'd read that factory workers were being paid in anything from rat poison to jars of pickled gherkins. How many gherkins to dress up and pose for photos with the tourists?

When the Hazelpark party visited Pushkin all those years ago, our bus broke down halfway, and KGB minders' cars circled it like sharks. Might as well toss a coin to decide which was the better outcome.

I refused Zhenya's offer of a drink, and demanded coffee. One of us had to keep a clear head. Max's frown subsided. He stretched his elegant legs under the table, so that I could feel his warmth. His aura.

I watched Kuzkuz. An old friend, he'd said, and Max hadn't denied it. Dee's thigh was pressed against his, and her skirt had ridden up so her knickers showed. Gagging for it. Fergus says there's a point with women like her when it ceases to matter: animal, vegetable or mineral.

She was babbling too, because she was jealous.

'The girls here are smart. Quite fashionable.'
The sole female in Kuzkuz's entourage was dark and
handsome rather than pretty, but the passing blondes,
perched on their stiletto heels, all high cheekbones and
elegance, had the colouring Dee's obliged to buy from a
hairdresser and the Estee Lauder counter in Jenners.

'It's another baby-pigeons mystery,' she burbled.
'These dreadful old women in black coats, and the
young girls. No gradations between.'

'What did you expect?' asked Zhenya.
'Deformities because of Chernobyl?' The alteration in
his voice made my throat constrict. 'People dressed in
rags? In your country, do the girls not have pretty
dresses? Very good, Catherine's Palace. No matter that
the people have no food. They've repaired it for the
western tourists who come to stare, even busloads of
Germans. You know how many millions of our
civilians died in the Occupation? And we've repaired it
for the Germans to see.'

'You'd repaired it anyway,' I said, hoping to
defuse a fight, 'out of cussedness.'

He grinned and became affable again. 'We
repaired it? The Russians repaired it. We're just
mongrels, Max and me. Not pure-bred. Anyway, no
need to fall out. Why don't you come for a drive with
me? I can show you the sights. Take you to a night-
club. You think this is the third world? Of course we
have night-clubs, excellent ones. I'll give you a good
time, Dee-Dee dentist.'

'Only if you have a decent car.' Car-daft. She'd
agree to copulate with Jeremy Clarkson if the deal
included a spin in something fast and dangerous. But
surely even Dee would balk at a madman?

Zhenya jerked his thumb carelessly towards the silver 600 Mercedes parked at the door. I'd had a good look at it on the way in. 'My company car.'

'No chance.' Max's voice was angry. 'You can play that game on your own.'

'What's the harm? He wouldn't mind. Maybe he's left the keys in it for me. Anyway – your girl can come too. I won't invite you, since you're so critical, Grishkin.'

'Come on Serena – it'll be fun.'

'It's too late. We have to get back to the ship.'

'Bollocks. Your pal said it's hours yet. Anyway, Kuzkuz can give us a lift.'

'No way you're getting in that,' I said. 'Have you seen the tyres?'

'That's the problem with these foreign models,' said Zhenya. 'Can't get the parts. If you find a single car in this city with tread on the tyres it'd be a miracle. The wheels'd be worth more than the entire article. It's the same as the dodgems, sweetheart - safe, because we all know it's dangerous. Come on, Serena, or whatever your name is. I can satisfy two women. I'm not a cello-player.'

'No thank you. Dee – you don't have time to go for a drive.' Round the back, up against a dustbin will have to do. I might as well have tried to reason with a gerbil on heat. I couldn't believe she'd be so foolish, this so-called health professional who wears rubber gloves to poke around inside the mouths of douce middle-aged Edinburgh lawyers.

'Serena's in a hurry to get back, ' she said. 'Hot date with a sailor. I thought she was going to get more than her dinner at the captain's table tonight.'

She put her fist under the edge of the café table and lifted it an inch or two. She can make folding a hankie look obscene, and people always laugh. Even Max smirked. 'She's desperate to be there when he gets his anchor up.'

Then she was out to the car and snuggling into the leather seat. God be with the days when Dee would have halted a rapist in his tracks with: 'When did you last floss?'

I sighed and put my hand on the door-handle.

'You have to play what Deirdre wants to play, said the Morag-tape in my head. 'We owe the McCullochs so much.....' As long as I could get out and walk while he serviced her.

Max's hand was on my arm, a firm grasp that was designed to persuade. 'If she's determined, let her go. I'll walk you back.'

'I'm completely sober, and I'm capable of looking after myself.'

'All the same, I'm not allowing you to get into that car.'

I forgot I'd been wishing he'd touch me. Bastard man, acting like any other, thinking he could tell me what to do.

'Please, I feel responsible,' he said. 'I brought you here as my guest.' And he looked so troubled and young and sincere the resentment evaporated and I stood back from the Merc. Dee's a big girl now. I wouldn't have to explain to her parents.

'That's really a dentist?' he said dubiously, watching the tail-lights vanish at the corner.

'Even better. She's an orthodontist. Fancy stuff with twisted silver wire, fees that'd make your eyes water. She's a very successful businesswoman. If we get our Scottish Parliament she reckons she's made because the new MPs'll want their teeth fixed for TV.'

('My future's secured,' she'd said, 'because most of them will be ex-councillors from Glasgow.')

Max led me back into the bar. 'And she's your friend? Close friends, I think, to vacation together.'

'She only brought me with her because I speak the language. The last time we went away together we were still at school.' Almost true. 'She's had a very distressing experience recently.'

'Jesus!' said Max. 'Anyway, it's you I want to talk about.'

'Explain the joke about cello players.'

'He's being vulgar. Zhenya plays the violin. They claim to have more stamina with women.' He blushed. (That was the first time I saw how easily that happened. It made me want to kiss him, to redden his cheeks even more.)

'So where is it?' I pretended to look under the table.

'Sold, years ago. I couldn't afford to keep it.'

'Cellos are so expensive to feed.'

He shrugged, but his eyes were sad. 'The problem is, I have to eat, occasionally. It's a pity. I could have made money busking in the streets with all the others for tourists like you. I was good. I trained at the Leningrad Conservatory.'

'What did Zhenya mean, you're both mongrels?'

He gave that lop-sided grin (the private one that would be only for our jokes).

'He's just babbling. He's Siberian, I'm half-Ukrainian. Anyway, tell me what work it is you do.'

The standard glazed expression as I told him what I do to earn a crust. I wanted to slap him. Please don't be so predictable.

'You're on TV?' he said.

'It's no big deal. It's only the news. I'm rarely seen. Just the occasional read. It's only a commercial channel called Albion. It's not as if it's the BBC. It's a boring, tedious job, not at all glamorous. The Merc – it's not Zhenya's, is it?'

'It'll be fine. You must meet famous people though?'

'Minor politicians, middle rank policemen, local businessmen, the odd footballer. Very occasionally some celebrity or science guru who's visiting. All very mundane.'

Weasel-face had disappeared. The dark girl stared morosely into her glass. Down a side street I could see the elegant rake of the Fortuna's bow. Less than five minutes it would have taken to walk across.

'I think I should start heading back,' I said.

Another endearing smile. 'There's no rush, surely.'

Grishkin, the others called him. A sweet, innocent name; a child's name from a fairy tale. Deceptive, like the city. The sinews on the backs of his hands were symmetrical as the spokes of a wheel; strong hands too. I knew instinctively he was no angel after all.

'So – the car - is it Zhenya's?'

'It belongs to a man called Mayakovsky. Local businessman. You want me to arrange an interview with him?'

'So he's stolen it?'

'He's – borrowed it. He only wants a little fun.'

'I've let Deirdre leave with a mad rapist in a stolen car.' (Oh God, what will I tell her mother?)

'Rapist! She'd have lain down on the floor with him here if there'd been space.'

'The car – what will the owner do?'

'Shoot the pair of them. I'm teasing you. They'll be back before he ever finds out.' He lit a cigarette, stubbed it out again after one drag. I expect I slung him The Look I'm accused of zapping smokers with.

'Zhenya knows him?'

'You're bored here? Let's take another walk.'

'Where is this man? He must be nearby. Or did your pal steal his car elsewhere?'

'Who knows? Zhenya has the sense not to stay away too long. Fuck!' He hauled me to my feet so fast I stumbled, but he held my hand firmly. 'Inna - shift your butt.' The dark girl leapt up and ran out with us.

I'd formed the cloudiest impression of three men in sharp suits swaggering into the bar. 'Right – what comedian's taken it?' one of them said. They were wearing shades - to hell with the White Nights; it must have been two in the morning.

Max kept his fingers laced through mine, as he hauled me down one side street after another, Inna on his other side. I wasn't afraid the way I'd been while we were lost, just glad humans don't have shells, though I used to think it must be a fine thing to be a crab and have carapace and pincers both.

After we'd sprinted down half a dozen streets he slackened pace, and squeezed my hand. Inna had left us at the previous corner. 'You weren't frightened were you? Your poor feet in these stupid shoes. Shall I carry you?' He gathered me up effortlessly, and my arm found its way round his neck as if it was familiar territory. 'Come home with me for the rest of the night,' he said. 'You'll feel better when you've slept a little.'

'I can't do that.'

'The bridges are open. You can't get back over for hours. Look.'

There was my suicide bridge, upended, street-lamps at a crazy angle, like the freeway in a Californian earthquake.

'What about Dee?'

He shrugged. 'Perhaps they'd crossed the river anyway. Zhenya'll see she comes to no harm.'

(That Russian shrug again. It drives me mad. I thought I'd forgotten it, the way they'd act thoughtlessly, leaving doors open so all the heat got out, and shrug: 'Nothing to do with me, comrade.' The paradox is the love I feel. Damn Frank. Damn the Soviet-Scottish Friendship Society that fed his illusions.)

'Don't frown. You'll get wrinkles. You'll be safe at my home.'

I became optimistic. 'You live with your parents?'

'Of course not. My father died ten years ago, and my mother went back to work in Kiev, where she comes from.'

'What does she do?'

'Doctor,' he said casually. 'Women's reproductive problems. It's quite a large hospital. She's pretty senior. She delivers babies too, if there's a hitch.'

'She's a consultant?'

'You assumed I was from an uneducated family?'

'I was surprised.'

'What age are you?'

Have to get used to that again too, the directness. Next he'd ask me what my salary was. I toyed with the idea of lying because I hate the finality of it.

'Thirty. And you?'

'Twenty-nine. Well, nearly. September.'

On my birthday in April, I wrote down a list of all my fears, ranked in order of magnitude. I discovered that finding myself in a falling plane or a sinking ship was a less scary prospect than another three decades with no change, skating on the thin ice of my life till it was over. I resolved then that I'd not let another chance slip. Next time, I was climbing out of the rut, no matter how unlikely the candidate proffering a foot up. I was going home with a stranger, and my mother could get lost, dead or otherwise.

'So you live on your own?' I said.

He hit me with that attractive naughty-child's giggle that could break my heart. 'Yes and no. Reserve judgement till you see it. You weren't really going to bed with your ship-captain tonight?'

'Only in Dee's fertile imagination.' (God! I hope she isn't. That'd upstage the frozen eggs idea.)

'But you have someone special at home?'

'I used to be married.'

He stopped walking and stared at me. 'What happened – he died or he left you?'

'I'm divorcing him. Well – the divorce is just newly through.'

'MacKenzie – that's his name or your own?'

'Mine.' Though not my father's. 'His is Learmonth. Like Lermontov.'

'And now you have a boyfriend. Will you marry again?'

'Certainly not him. I don't have anyone I intend to settle down with. Do you?'

'No, I'm the same; there's no one.'

I began to panic. I've never experienced a full-blown holiday romance, the one where you don't learn his second name, possibly lack a common language or any more enduring liaison than a quick and casual copulation in a doorway or on a beach. Sand in your knickers, unspeakable horrors in your bloodstream and no clear memory of what he looks like in daylight. Dee would do it on a whim, unnecessary for the man to buy her a drink, never mind a meal. 'I can't be bought for the cost of a fancy fish supper,' she'd say. 'I am a virtuous woman, and my price is above Harry Ramsden's.'

'Maksim, I know you reckon Dee's an easy lay, but I can assure you I'm not.'

'What a high opinion you have of me. If I thought that I wouldn't have invited you home. You know I wouldn't take advantage.'

I wasn't so sure whether he was safe with me.

'This Mayakovsky, what sort of business is he in? I thought the Mafia hype was only in books?'

'Some of it's true. He runs what the Western media – you – choose to call a protection racket.'

'So he takes money from the bar owners – or were his people just looking for his car?'

'He takes money from anyone who's raking cash off the tourist trade. That's what gets Kuzkuz so wound up. Mayakovsky is a rich man because of Westerners. Even the stallholders in the street. I bet some had set up beside your ship before the gangway was down – how do you think they managed to be there when the police move the others on all the time?'

'They were no more than seventeen or eighteen most of them. It's small change they get for their junk.'

('Bet there's not much these girls wouldn't do for dollars,' Dee had said. 'Probably the boys too. A few of the old geezers off the ship might get lucky. That's why they call it hard currency.')

'A cut out of enough change adds up. And he supplies the crap they sell. You don't imagine there's a posse of craftsmen making matriochka dolls of Clinton and Yeltsin, or that all these Red Army hats came off real soldiers?'

'So how does Zhenya know him?'

'Used to work for him, so did I. We were musicians, in one of the big hotels. Not the sort of place I could have afforded to have a beer, never mind eat there. But the western tourists wanted Tchaikovsky while they stuffed their mouths.'

'And you quit on such a promising career?'

No smile. 'Mayakovsky owned the instruments. He wouldn't let us practise. Said the punters wouldn't know the difference if we played a few bum notes. I wouldn't work that way, neither would Zhenya. We cling to the remnants of pride. We graduated from the finest music school in the world.'

'So that's who you sold the cello to? If he'd let you practise you'd still have been working for him?'

'Don't take that tone. You'd have done the same. It's not fun to be hungry, Serena. Let's change the subject. We're nearly home. Are you cold?'

And Seriozha – what did he need to do to survive?

CHAPTER THREE

Casually Maksim put the question, as if he could read my mind, not breaking his stride nor slackening the grip of his arms.

'You met someone when you were here before, when you were a schoolgirl?'

I'd hoped he'd have enough delicacy to leave it alone.

'Your friend mentioned it. Was he handsome?'

Was he ever. Sergei Timochenko was – is – the most aesthetically perfect human male I've seen: exquisite cheekbones, delectable nose, luscious sloe-dark eyes, lashes like a Vogue model (only his were real), and hair as black as mine, with a crisp wave to it. He was tall and slender and muscular. The other girls drooled over him, but from the start his rare, slow smiles were aimed at me. He didn't conceal his delight when he found I was the only one who spoke Russian – but then that was the sole reason I'd ended up on a Hazelpark geography trip; the school had discreetly paid my way.

Seriozha, his workmates called him. A pretty name. The name of Anna Karenina's son. I spared no effort to let him know I was smitten, because I recognised, with absolute clarity, that he was the love of my life. Had the staff roster worked out differently, my future would have been altered too.

The hotel was at the cheap end of the tourist market: spartan and ill furnished. Scary, hatchet-faced concierges supervised each floor. No giggling in the corridors. In 1985, the cracks in the veneer were still painted over. Visitors see what they want to see, and I wanted to see the Promised Land, even though it had lost my father his job.

'I had a crush on one of the waiters in the hotel,' I said to Max. 'We were both teenagers. Absolutely nothing happened.'

'A *waiter*?' As much of a snob as ever Fergus was.

'He was only a kid. He planned to go to art school. He was exceptionally talented. He wasn't stupid.'

'I'm sure he wasn't. And you had an affair with this handsome, talented waiter, or so your friend said. Dark haired, I suppose?' Max gave a wan smile.

The first three days in Leningrad it had been no more than looks and smiles, because Seriozha was agonisingly shy. Then I'd contrived to let his hand brush mine as he handed me a plate and his fingers against my skin were like an electric shock. My hair should have stood out round my head in a halo.

Two days before we were due to leave, he was loitering in the corridor after breakfast.

'Don't you ever get any time off?' I asked in what I hoped was a bantering tone.

'I have a half-holiday today,' he said.

'You could show me the city. The parts the tourists don't see.'

He was nervous. I understood this was a risky business. But I was in love, and I'd as soon have mutilated myself as betray him.

'You can manage to get away from your teacher? Then meet me in the Summer Garden. Here I'll mark it on your map. I'll wait for you at the embankment gate at three. You'll come alone?'

We strolled for an hour or so in the stately park, under the clipped limes, talking in soft voices, holding hands. His English was archaic but precise – he said he read Shakespeare and the Bible for practice.

Later, we sat on a dark green bench close to a weird statue that looked like a woman suckling a pigeon. Seriozha kissed me, timidly and inexpertly at first, growing bolder till we twined in a paroxysm of fumbling lust. He undid my plait so that my hair fell round us like a cloak, and he groaned with desire.

'Never cut your hair. I want to spend the remainder of my days running my hands through it, feeling it against my skin. It's darker than the night.'

Then he slid his hands under my tee shirt. He might as well have flicked a lighted match onto dry whins. I thought I'd pass out with the need to have him make love to me, so that I could twist and writhe and squeal in his embrace, like a green bough in the fire.

But there was the damned eternal, infernal daylight and nowhere we could have found privacy. I was in a room with three fifth years. Seriozha had to share too. The only one with a room of her own was the geography teacher.

' 'scuse me, Miss Galbraith, can we borrow your bed for half an hour?' Not a perfect idea.

Two women stopped and stared. 'At it in full daylight, in these enlightened times,' said one. 'The police should move them on. Why do respectable citizens have to look at whores plying their trade?'

We stood up unsteadily and walked, walked, walked for hours to cool down.

We told each other the secrets of our future life histories. Seriozha would become a successful artist.

'I'll paint your portrait, over and over,' he said. 'Like Chagall and his wife, you'll be my only muse, both naked and clothed I'll paint you, only you, for the rest of my life.'

We stood with arms locked round each other beside the second lamppost on the east side of the Lieutenant Schmidt Bridge; that was when he proffered the invitation to a joint suicide, unless I promised to come back to him and be his wife and bear his children; tall, black-haired children with solemn long-lashed eyes like his, the colour of liquorice. We parted at the corner of the street. We were very late and I'd have been missed. Nothing in the world mattered.

'Tomorrow?' he said. 'I have no time off, but I have to see you. I love you, Serena. We were born to be together. There must be empty rooms – I'll find out which, I'll get a key. Don't be afraid, I'll not hurt you. I'll look after you.'

'I haven't done it before.' (Even in those days, Dee was forever assuring me I was a statistic, and not an admirable one.)

'Neither have I. This is the most important lesson we'll learn in our lives. We'll learn it well, because we love each other.'

In a grey room, with grubby windows, I'd give myself to him, and his seed would take root in my body, and I'd never be alone again. I've not been that certain of anything since.

'Goodnight,' he murmured, burying his face in my hair. 'Soon I'll be able to say that every night, our heads on the same pillow.'

How lovely the Russian words are, spakoynye noche, peaceful night, and how peaceful it would be to fall asleep in Seriozha's arms for the rest of my life. By the evening meal next day I was miserable enough to sidle over to dragon-woman who was in charge of the dining room.

'Where is Seriozha?'

'Sergei Ivan'ich had some leave due. He's taken it.'

'But where is he?'

She pretended not to hear me.

'He hasn't gone home to Odessa?'

'You're too bold with your questions, miss. I think I'll tell your teacher about you, slut, Western bitch trying to corrupt our boys with your loose behaviour.'

I'd been too naïve to realise that getting away from my teacher had possibly been the lesser problem.

I was on the bus, ready to leave, when I spotted Seriozha. He was waiting thirty metres along the pavement, miserable and nervous. We gazed into each other's eyes through the grease and grit of the coach window. I should have leapt up, run into his arms, to hell with everything else. My legs were lumps of ice. Cold feet.

As the bus pulled away we exchanged an imperceptible wave, a mere curling of the fingers. I knew in my heart I'd never see him again.

I arrived home distraught. Seriozha had probably lost his job because of me. The only honest and responsible act was to go back and look for him at once, and bring him home to Glasgow.

Morag blamed Frank. 'It was him was so keen she should waste her time learning that useless language, otherwise she'd never have been there at all. Imagine. All that cash in fees, and she plans to throw herself away marrying some wee Commie skivvy without a cent to his name. Well, you can forget that, madam. You've your university to go to, then a job to get. I've more to do than work my butt off supporting you and your fancy ideas. I hope you haven't let this wee nyaff knock you up. We can't afford a Sonia Finlayson in this family.'

Sonia had been let loose in the Algarve with her cousin at the end of fourth year and brought home a handsome bartender's child in her belly. Her folk had cash. She and Ferdy had a fancy wedding and were set up in a hotel on the Clyde, another baby on the way ten months later, contented as mice. How I envied her.

I don't recall why I expected moral support from my father. You shouldn't miss what you never had.

'I have to go back for him,' I said. 'I promised I would. It was all my fault. We were followed, and I was too stupid to notice. He'll be punished. He's a good Communist, Dad, and a hard worker. You'd like him.'

'Your mother's right,' Frank muttered, staring out of the window. 'You've your uni to finish.'

Then he turned on Morag, smirking over her ironing. 'She's your problem,' he yelled. 'You sort it out. Like mother like daughter.'

I lost what vestiges of faith were left over from childhood. I had no more luck trying to confide in my best friend. 'He'd have been a lousy lover anyway,' said Dee. 'Russian men are. I read in Cosmo ninety per cent of their women have never had an orgasm.'

Morag searched till she found my diary. 'When are you due? I thought you marked it down when you get your monthlies?'

'A couple of weeks.'

'Jesus! You'll kill me so you will. My nerves won't take it. Mark it here on the calendar. You let me see when it comes. I can't be doing with something else to worry about.'

'See what?'

'Your sannies. Blood. I want to see, to be sure.'

'You think I'd let that happen to me?'

35

She thrust her hot face close to mine. 'You've been a wee slut since you were a child, haven't you? Even when you were a baby you'd be forever touching yourself down there. Then there was all that fuss you caused at home, displaying your wares to the loony.'

Sins of the flesh. That's what the MacKenzies called the impulse for loving.

Morag had a Cairn terrier bitch when I was young, Terry she called it. She'd not have her spayed, so the creature came into season every month or two, and all the dogs in Balvaig would arrive at the house, howl, pee on the walls. They'd smell her on me too, if I went out. When I was four or five a collie set its huge black paws on my shoulders and humped my leg. I screamed louder than ever when I saw white globs running down over my sock.

'Mammy, the poor dog's burst, its insides are coming out.'

She told all her pals, and I heard them snigger together. But clearest of all I remember the wee bitch herself, rubbing her belly along the carpet with her inflamed crotch stuck in the air. Morag the man-hater would kick her hard and say: 'Stop that, you disgusting brute.' And she'd lock Terry in the cold, dark shed.

'I'm a virgin, Mammy,' I said.

'What is you have down there then? Velcro? You'll let me see when it comes, my girl. If it comes.'

She lifted Frank's washing into the twin-tub with wooden tongs and a viciousness that made me wince. She wasn't even thirty-six then. I should have realised she knew better than I did that a bitch on heat has to be shamed for her lewd behaviour.

I wrote to Seriozha every week for months but never had a reply. I imagined dragon-woman intercepting the letters and reading them salaciously in her room, her hand in her knickers. Then she'd burn them. Since then, of course, I've read about their postal system. The truth would have been less dramatic - either they never arrived, or his replies went missing.

I wonder how long his dream lasted? There was hardly a day between that June and this I didn't think about him at some point. Such a fire he lit in me that everything since had been a damp squib. When I was first married to Fergus, I used to shut my eyes and try to imagine it was Seriozha. It didn't work.

Over the years, I've found myself thinking it would have been easier to bear if I'd known he was dead. Easier than imagining him seeding another woman with his child.

'We didn't keep in touch, Maksim,' I said. 'I'd completely forgotten him till Dee mentioned it. She needs to get out more.'

All that time, and I betrayed Seriozha after all.

CHAPTER FOUR

'Home,' said Maksim, setting me down at the doorway of an exquisite Empire-style building with faded primrose walls. I'd become increasingly dismayed as we got closer. It was in a slum, not at all what I'd expected, so close to the centre. At least there were people about. That had troubled me earlier, among the deserted streets of Vasilievsky Island, the feeling nobody's at home, or if they are they certainly won't answer the door; they watch, from behind half-closed shutters. That too had bred dreams.

He led me through the street door, the posh entrance, into a soot-dark hallway. 'Rape, abduction, white slavery, embarrassing diseases, you know nothing about him, he may be a criminal, an anarchist-communist-drug-dealing-abortionist, filthy creatures, blah, blah, blah,' said Morag-in-my-head.

Max released my hand, and moved away from me.

'Don't leave me here in the dark,' I squealed. 'Where are you going?'

'Out the back. Call of nature.'

'Isn't there a toilet?'

He was laughing at my panic. 'Of course there is. It keeps it cleaner for the women if the men pee outside.'

This is Russian chivalry. When he came back he drew my fingers into his, and must have felt me recoil.

'It's all right,' he giggled, 'I used the other hand.'

Another of my mother's phobias: ice cream that wasn't from a shop. 'Where do they do their business when they're out in these vans all day?' she'd say. 'They pee in empty lemonade bottles and throw them out the window. And do they wash their hands? You're much mistaken, my girl, if you think I'm letting you put anything in your mouth after they've touched *that*.' Frank would buy me the forbidden food, and make a show of wiping the outside of the cone with the serviette they'd hand out. 'Quite clean now. But don't let madam know. Our wee secret?'

I switched Morag's voice off. Maksim and I weren't strangers, never had been. It was only that I knew nothing about his background, his health, his bank account, his politics, his religious beliefs, or his views on his country's history.

'It's so dark. Isn't there lighting?'

'People borrow the bulbs. You're not afraid of the dark, surely?' He held my hand tightly while we climbed four flights that smelt of cooked cabbage and raw tomcat. At the triple-locked front door he produced a jailer-sized bunch of keys. Once inside it was a haven of panelled mahogany and parquet floors. Max took his shoes off at once, and I padded along the corridor after him, giggling. Memory sinks its claws in small details; Proust and his tea-dipped madeleines, soft footfalls in Russian homes.

'You live in a mansion and I live in a wee house built for artisans,' I said. 'Communism's alive and well.'

But Max's territory was rather less than half of a larger room, partitioned with plywood, austere enough to make me shudder. A mattress on a wooden frame - you couldn't call it a bedstead, but it looked clean - and two insubstantial blankets neatly folded on it. A narrow cupboard, a small table with a lamp, a wooden chair and a dilapidated armchair. No source of heating that I could see. Numbing to think that was all he had.

'Don't you like it?' he said. 'I am a free man. There's nothing to steal. In the suburbs I could have had a flat of my own. But I love the old city. Life must be about more than living space. My home has soul.'

'It must be freezing here in winter. How do you keep warm?'

'We're very civilised. We have central heating. Look.' He tapped a set of hideously corroded pipes. I hadn't noticed them because they were at his head-height. They didn't look as if they'd retain liquid.

'I wouldn't like to be near one of these with hot water passing through it,' I said.

'It's quite safe. They test them every few years, under pressure. Usually only a handful of fatalities.'

I knew he was teasing me, but it made my flesh creep to picture him there in December, shivering under a thin blanket, or scalded by a boiling jet from a burst pipe.

'My feet are filthy,' I said. 'Where's the bathroom?' I'd discovered it was a Virginia Woolf loo, with a Room of its Own.

'I'll bring water.'

He knelt on the floor and washed my feet gently, stroking my ankle. 'It's only bruised,' he said.

'Have I got tar on my toes, from the tram-line? I used to all the time when I was a child, off the road. My Aunt Peigi would rub my feet with butter, the same as she'd do to the cat's paws.' ('Tinker's child,' Morag would say. 'Do you think I want the whole village saying I can't afford to put shoes on you?')

Maksim kissed my feet fleetingly as he dried them. 'No tar. You have very pretty toes,' he said. 'All yours.' He gestured to the bed. 'Make yourself at home. Take both blankets. I've slept on a chair often enough, I'll be fine, I'll put a jacket over me.'

'Who's next door?' I could hear them talking quietly to each other, a man's voice and a woman's. The walls must be the thinnest ply money could buy.

'Oleg and Maria, ordinary people, about our age. Brush out your hair. It's bad for you to sleep with it plaited.' I've never grown out of wearing it like that, even though Fergus used to say we looked like Willy and Colette.

'Have you a brush?' said Max.

I grabbed my bag from him. 'Yes. Here.'

He knelt on the bed, and brushed my hair, the way no man had done since I was ten. He ran his fingers through it, weighed it in his hands, stroked it. I was choked with conflicting emotions.

'Serena,' he said huskily, 'I love the sound of your name. Serena with the mermaid's hair. Did you know that's what it means in Russian? Mermaid.'

Does it hell. There's a world of difference between a siren and a mermaid. I lure sailors to their deaths, whatever. Even Max's thumbs are beautiful, not spatulate or coarse, but slender and shapely with perfectly oval nails. The sight of his right thumb curved along the brush-handle made me want to slide my lips and my tongue round it. I was trembling. I was afraid he'd notice. He stopped brushing.

'Lie down now,' he said sternly. 'Take off some of your clothes, or you'll be uncomfortable. I'll leave you for a moment.' And he left abruptly, while I struggled to think what I'd done to offend him.

41

When he came back, he switched off the lamp at once. I tried to sleep, but the neighbours were still jabbering. Besides, I felt guilty and miserable. 'You could lie down here too, Maksim,' I said in a small voice. 'There's plenty of room.'

'You wouldn't mind?'

'I'm stealing your bed. You saved my life. How could I mind.'

I heard him unbuckle his belt in the darkness, and remove clothing, then he stretched beside me gingerly, on top of the covers. I turned my head to try to see him in the dark, very close, for there was only one pillow.

'You know what,' he said, 'if you save someone's life you're responsible for them. Do they believe that in Scotland too?'

'We just pass by on the other side to avoid thinking about it. Goodnight. I'm tremendously grateful to you.'

There came a disconcerting scrabbling and rattle of claws on wood, loud in the darkness. 'Is that a rat?'

'It can't get inside the room. It's in the wall. It's only a small mouse.'

I know a rat when I hear one. But I lay down again, and he settled at my back.

'You'll be cold,' I said. 'Please – you must get under at least one blanket.'

I wanted him to cuddle me; unfair, as I didn't require any more intimate services. I was strenuously resisting the temptation to snuggle against him when he wrapped his arm round my waist, in a way that invited no argument and held me tight and secure.

'There. No mouse can come near you.' He sighed a little, wondering, no doubt, who decreed it was his duty to snatch me from the path of trams, protect me from rodents, give me his bedclothes. Suddenly he sat up, leant over and kissed me gently and chastely on the mouth. 'Good night,' he whispered.

My hormonal system got stuck in overdrive. Spontaneous human combustion. All that'd be left in twenty minutes would be a wee pile of ashes and my feet, which are always too cold to burn.

I don't know which of us was more startled when I squirmed round to kiss him back, not a friendly kiss or a grateful one, but a hungry, thirsty, first-white-man-in-years one. I sought him the way fire-lighters seek flames, craved the sensation of his bare skin against mine, all over, outside, inside, everywhere. I whimpered with desire.

He'd possibly been a little excited already when he lay down; by then he was so hard I'd have been frightened if I hadn't wanted him so badly. I arched my body to let him slip my pants down. The couple next door chose that moment to begin. Squeaky bedsprings and heavy breathing I might have coped with, but not running commentary peppered with exhortations.

Sweet God, I thought, I'm about to seduce the archangel Gabriel in his monk's cell, and it'd sound like *that,* they'd hear us too. The entire building must be able to hear. Probably my impromptu bout of lust had set them off. Oleg had just been faster on the draw. An alternative version of the gunfight scene from High Noon began rolling in my head, and I drew away from Maksim so precipitately I rolled off the bed and lay there, knickers round my ankles while Maria caterwauled and yelped. I stuffed my fist in my mouth to drown the laughter.

Poor Oleg didn't get any good lines, just stage directions. 'Slower. There. Yes! Yes! Hold onto it. Don't come yet. Yes, yes, yes!' Making up for lost time, if Cosmo had its facts straight, I thought. Or else she's popping her cork for the entire Russian nation. Russian brothels must be something else with walls that thin.

I adjusted my clothing and sat up, struggling to fight down the vibrations in my throat. Max leant across without speaking, pulled me back onto the bed, swaddled me as if I was a baby, and lay cuddled against my back. Even through layers of bedclothes I could feel he wasn't horny any more.

He drew his fingers gently over the side of my face. When he realised I was giggling it set him off too. 'Joke,' he whispered. 'The police arrest a man, and say: "Are you going to come quietly?" "I always do," he says, "I live in a communal flat." '

What a man. All that expensive education, and there's no way my command of colloquial Russian holds a candle to his of English. How on earth did he manage to learn so well? We lay like naughty kids, blanket stuffed in our mouths. I could never laugh in bed with Fergus. It's more intimate than sex. After that, anything other than cuddling would have felt like incest.

But I grew sad imagining how it must be to lie alone night after night, listening to the neighbour having her pipes reamed less than a yard away. Men don't cope well. I never suffered from penis envy. I'd be terrified of having an appendage equipped with a mind of its own, sharp hearing, imagination.

'Are you OK?'

'Yes,' said Max sleepily.

I lay awake wondering where Dee was - back on the ship, cursing me for a double-standard slut, or lying with Kuzkuz in another bed, crushed under the weight of his big body, or astride him, a mad horsewoman, acting out one of her fantasies, the sex-goddess who couldn't get enough of it.

'Do you think Dee's gone home with Zhenya?'

Max grunted.

'She would, you know. She has exceptionally enlightened attitudes to sex.'

'You came home with me.'

'That's different.'

'I know. Sleep now. We'll find them later.'

I dozed, in the warm circle of his arm, letting my fickle, treacherous body mould itself against his, while I imagined I was home in Kingdom, Granda's house, in my own bed, and this man with me.

Granda wouldn't let my mother sleep with her husband. Better to marry than to burn, is it indeed? Well, Peter MacKenzie was the man who knew all about putting out fires. So in my earliest memories, when my father visited he was banished to a narrow iron bed in the wee back room where Grannie usually slept. Morag and I slept above with her sister Peigi, across the landing from Granda's room. Even once we moved to Glasgow, Frank's periods of residence were sporadic. It wasn't till I was transformed into an urban child and befriended by Deirdre McCulloch that I learnt other people's parents slept in the same room in the same house, never mind the same bed.

I don't blame the old folks. The tenderness had been bred out of them from the days their ancestors were herded like beasts and their homes burnt over their heads while the police looked on. If the politicians trying to get their heads around Northern Ireland and Bosnia could have talked to my Grannie, then they might understand.

A raw religion, theirs, and its kirks nearly empty now, though it still has its claws in me. What mattered most in those days was that I didn't get an Easter egg when the kids whose grandfathers weren't Free Kirk catechists got theirs.

'It is a solemn time,' Granda would say. 'Your Saviour has spent His death-agony for you, His precious blood running down, and you wheenging for sweeties to rot the teeth God gave you.'

And I knew if I as much as opened my mouth to protest he'd lock me in the old shed that used to be the toilet and still smelled of it, so I wouldn't grow up thirled to the sin of anger.

I know fine what they said in the village when Fergus and I parted, though Peigi, her face white as bone, tried to make me believe it was someone else they were sniggering over. Old Peter put a hex on his daughters, they said, he cursed them so they'd never find happiness in a man's bed. And there's Morag's daughter gone the same path. Even unto the second generation.

They pulled down his tinpot church years ago. Possibly he did the best he knew how. He wanted a tranquil life and sound teeth for his daughters. No sex, no sweeties.

Lying there in a stranger's bed, I decided I could murder a bar of Dairy Milk. Max slept so silently and still I'd wakened from drowsing more than once and laid my hand across his chest to reassure myself he was breathing. But I could sense he was awake then too.

'Max – I don't suppose you have any chocolate?'
'Chocolate? No, sorry.'

Then I remembered I'd half a bar hidden in my bag, because Dee doesn't let me eat sweets either. I slipped from the covers and fetched it. 'Want some?'

He giggled. 'You can't eat chocolate in the middle of the night.'

'I'm hungry. Do you want a piece?'

He nuzzled my fingers as I slid the chunks into his mouth, and I found I'd managed to burrow under his bit of blanket as well as my own. He turned his back to me, and drew my arm round his waist, clasping my hand. So very thin. His bones were like the ribs of a wrecked ship. We dozed again with our heads pressed together on the pillow, united by the safe, comforting taste of milk chocolate.

Max shook me awake softly. 'Come with me. We'll get clean before the others are up.'

In the kitchen, we washed and dried each other as innocently as cats, still half-clothed. He cleaned his teeth, and proffered the brush hesitantly. 'You don't mind?'

'Certainly not, if you don't.'

Not another person in the world I could share a toothbrush with, not my mother, not my friends, never Fergus or any other man. That's how it was from the start with Maksim. Closer than lovers.

'You have the most beautiful eyes,' he said. 'They're like flowers.'

I revised my opinion of the colour of his eyes. Warm amber. Even his skin was far too smooth and beautiful and tawny golden to belong to a man. 'How do you keep so clean in a place like this?' I said.

'Bathhouse. The one Russian tradition worth keeping. Shall I take you there later? Surely you have them in Scotland. Saunas? The best thing in the world for your health. That's where the babies would be born in Karelia. The cleanest place in the village.'

I grinned to myself, thinking about the alleged health benefits of Edinburgh's saunas.

He dressed modestly, with his back to me. Watching him slide his jeans over those narrow hips, and tighten the belt, gave me intense stomach-cramps. If I'd still kept a diary, I could have noted it down. Five minutes and thirty seconds past eight, their time, on Wednesday the eighteenth of June, 1997, fell in love definitively with Maksim Stepanovich Grigoriev.

'Max - suppose I stayed on here?'

'How can you?'

'I have enough money to last for a few weeks.   I could get a job teaching English.'

'Where would you live?'

I tried not to hesitate or show disappointment.

'I'll find my own flat.'

'Without me? Who'd protect you from mice?'

'Well, we could get a better place together, if you'd like to.'

'This is what I can afford,' he said stubbornly. 'If you stay with me, it'd be here or somewhere like it. I couldn't expect you to live this way. It's awful. I'm used to it, but you couldn't stand it. You'd be ill for weeks till you got used to the food and the water, then you'd go out of your mind trying to live in this dump.'

He was right. I couldn't survive in a room where I didn't know how you'd get out in a fire. But I refused to become depressed.

'I'm not putting this well,' he said. 'If I could provide for you, I'd like nothing better. There's no future here for a girl like you, no opportunities for you to use your talents. You'd be wasted.' He slapped my bottom lightly. 'Get dressed, hussy. I'll be back in exactly five minutes. I've no food in the house. We'll go shopping.'

He padded off, to give me privacy. He knew that matters to me.

CHAPTER FIVE

'Ah, Katya, welcome home!' Last night's neighbour breezed in without knocking. I recognised her throaty voice. 'Oh! Excuse me. I thought you were someone else.'

Then Max was in the doorway, glaring at her, white-faced. The girl gave me a gap-toothed, knowing smile. 'I thought Katya had come back, when I heard you had company. You've heard from her recently, Max?'

He shrugged. 'She's still at home in Odessa, I suppose.'

'Please,' he said as soon as she left. 'It's not what you think.'

'So her name's Katya, this person who doesn't exist. This no one special.'

'She isn't anyone special.'

'She lives with you?' The margin for dignity-retention had been narrower than the bed. Small wonder he got by with a smile on his face and few bedclothes.

'She has slept here, yes.'

'You have a woman you live with, and you brought me back?'

'Nowhere else to take you. Unless you wanted to swim the river.'

Mortifying. I'd read too much into it. 'You could have taken me to a hotel. I mean – you could have shown me one, pointed one out to me.'

Damned inconvenient language to get angry in, Russian; separate irregular verbs for too many nuances of meaning.

'You imagine a respectable hotel would have let you in at that time of night? I wanted you to come home with me so you'd be safe. It's not important who's visited before.'

'You'd have shagged me, and all the time your woman's only away for a day or two?'

'She's been away for months. Anyway – if that's what's worrying you, I'm perfectly clean. I'm careful in these matters.' Not much indication of that last night. I'd wanted to believe we were both swept away by passion, so it didn't matter. Lunacy

'This Katya's expected any day, apparently.'

'She may come back to Petersburg, but not to me. There's no sort of understanding between us. It's not important.'

'She lived with you, she slept with you. That's important.' I couldn't prevent my voice trembling.

Max shrugged. 'I didn't tell you I was a monk, Serena. You have had relationships too.' He stood behind me and wound his arms round my waist.

'At least I told you. I should leave now.'

'You have nothing to be jealous of.'

'Why should I be jealous? You're just some guy I met on holiday.'

'Pity. You are important to me.' He rested his chin on the top of my head. 'You are a special person.'

'I don't enjoy finding I've slept in another woman's bed.'

'You haven't. You slept in mine. I'm glad you did.'

'What would you have done last night if she'd turned up?'

'Slept in the middle, to avoid arguments. It would have been cosy, but we'd have needed to borrow another pillow.'

Frank could always do that too. Make me laugh, when he was in the wrong.

'Show me a photo of her.'

'Why does it matter? I don't have one, truly. I think you find it difficult to understand the way life is here, for most of us. It affects relationships, families, love. She'll have met someone else many weeks ago. Sorry. I told you, I don't express myself well.'

'I suppose she's a musician too?'

'She's a violinist, yes. I know her from the days when we were students at the Conservatory.'

Wonderful. What did she holler in bed? *Allegretto ma non troppo - Ritenuto*!

'Why don't you get married?' I said bitterly. 'Found a string section.'

He shrugged and tutted. 'I don't suppose anyone would want to marry me. I have little money, no prospects.'

A Ukrainian fiddler's reject. That's what I was reduced to fancying.

'Anyway,' he said, 'you were married before. I suspect you weren't thinking of him last night. It's the same, except I never believed I loved any woman enough to marry her. I'm not good with commitment.' He pulled me round to face him. 'If I'd brought you home because I was without a woman for the night, you think I wouldn't have taken what I wanted? That's not what it was about, and you know it.'

I'd practically raped him. 'I'm sorry,' I said, 'I don't want you to think I'm into casual sex with someone else's man.'

'I think you're a very lovely girl and a very moral one, and very honest. I respect you, as well as lusting after you. And we only have today to get to know each other a little better. Let's not waste it on silly talk. We'll have breakfast, then you'll fetch your other shoes and I'll show you this marvellous city I live in.'

Dee hadn't been back to the ship; it was eerie to be in our cabin, like sifting through a corpse's possessions, the way I'd had to do with Morag's. This time there was no guilt. I had done all I could to avert disaster. Automatically, I replaced the top on her pot of Guerlain Hydrabella, which I knew had cost her more than my mother ever earned in half a month's work, lying open as usual. I had to wipe my eyes as I surveyed the collection of shoes. I put on my own comfiest pair, after toying with the idea of borrowing some of hers. Twelve pairs. On school trips, when pupils were restricted to one case each, Dee would make everyone pack a pair of her shoes, and she'd be late down every morning, deciding which to wear. She'd rate a change of shoes higher than clean knickers. Morag was just as bad, obsessed with anything that came in pairs – shoes, earrings, ornaments.

I let Maksim Grigoriev take me walking, as if this was any other holiday. We visited Peter the Great's log cabin. I should have been able to predict that this was his hero.

'He married a woman who'd been a slave,' said Max shining-eyed. 'And he was miserable if he wasn't working. Kings, diplomats, no matter who, they had to talk to him while he worked in his shirtsleeves at the lathe.'

I smiled politely, caught up in how clever I was to have bitten my tongue before I said: 'I know'. (I see the mobile phone ads on TV nowadays, and each time I say to myself: That's who Max would want his one-to-one with. Big Peter. I should have paid more attention. Stubborn bastards, my Russian menfolk.) Leningrad couldn't fool me by changing its name. Peter's city. Its citizens call it that again - they always did, in their hearts. "Peter", they say, and there's devotion in their voices, laced with cynicism. Not another city on earth so entrancing, though as many people live in it as in the whole of Scotland, and its maker was no saint. The new brides still lay their flowers at his feet, Peter, the rock, on his high rough plinth of granite, his horse rearing, trampling the serpent for ever and ever and ever, as he gazes out across the Neva at what he started.

I used to dream about him as well as his canals. Big Peter. A huge man with coarse, calloused hands and a coarse, callous sense of humour, but oh God, he was sexy, I feel it in my bones, an enormous, perambulating stick of testosterone. And he was a cruel man, but then that's part of the attraction, always has been. I've read about the Polish officers at Katyn, and the collaborators at Babi Yar, and I know what they did in Hungary, in Czechoslovakia, in Berlin, and I've seen the documentary pictures of the German prisoners face down in the mud with their balls hacked off, and I know it's bad still and there's worse to come. History judges them harshly; in my eyes, they can do no wrong.

'Frank Stuart must be the only man in the Western hemisphere who gets a hard-on reading about Stalin's purges,' I overheard my mother say to Peigi when she believed I was too young to understand. Mine is a dangerous heredity on every side.

Max and I climbed the three hundred steps to the viewing platform of St Isaac's, and studied the old city spread beneath as intricate as a tapestry - it's possible to avert the eyes from the drear grey high-rises beyond.

So much silent water, where Peter made them manhandle the Neva into an elegant open granite coffin, and all the other water of the swamp too, until there are fifty artificial rivers, somnolent and vindictive and trapped in prisons whose walls offer no grip to the nails. How can you contain the waters that lie under the earth? Fifty waterways, forty-two islands, with almost three hundred and fifty bridges tying them together like rafts. So many bridges, so much misery, so many ghosts.

'Built on bones,' the geography teacher from Hazelpark told us in 1985. 'Peter the Great, Stalin, the war. Built on bones.' For years after, my dreams swam in canals filled with enormous blind carp which had gorged on eyeballs and human flesh. No good can come from imprisoning rivers.

A suicide's paradise, as long as you weren't wearing anything that'd catch on the wrought iron as you clambered over, trapping you like an inept acrobat. You could stand swaying on a parapet and no one would intervene. It's not London where a stranger might cajole you down and buy you a cup of tea, or Amsterdam where a jovial Dutchman would fish you out with a boat-hook, or Bruges, where Japanese tourists would click cameras while you drowned; 'Look – a pageant. A re-enactment of the tragic lovers in the Minnewater.'

In St Petersburg no one would push you. They'd pause a moment to give you that opaque, calculating, sideways glance - same as New York; no eye contact. Then the shrug. People with money in their pockets don't jump in the river. They'd walk on. Not a head would turn when the splash came.

And I used to wonder why no one prevented Anna Karenina from going too near the edge in the first place.

Max's fingers were warm as life round mine.

'It's so beautiful,' I said. 'You love this city, don't you?'

He picked up the regret in my voice, and smiled wistfully. 'I adore it. I was born in it and I've never lived anywhere else. If it doesn't break your heart you're lacking one. Built in heaven and dropped on the earth in one piece, that's what they say.'

'It's not healthy for you, living here,' I said. 'And I don't rate your friends. I suppose you know Zhenya from the Conservatory too?'

He looked surprised. 'No, he's a lot older than me. We met in the army.'

'You were a soldier?'

'For a little while. Practically all of us were, in Chechnya. We weren't given much choice.'

'I wouldn't have thought you'd approve of that war.'

'I love my country and I'm not a coward.'

'So Zhenya and you had a merry little time killing people?'

'Nearly getting killed, most of the time. He helped me out of a few unpleasant spots, before we both took ourselves the hell out of it. I owe him. OK? Let's change the subject.'

'How do you mean "took ourselves out of it"? You mean you deserted?'

He glowered at me, squeezed my hand so hard it hurt, and told me to shut up. We walked on till I was exhausted. So many walled-up, hopeless faces, such contrast between the bleakness of ordinary lives and the

56

gold leaf dripping off the palaces and museums. Nothing changes. Maksim deserved better.

The ship was due to sail just before six. By five, there was still no sign of Dee.

Max and I strolled back and forth across my suicide bridge till I could see them starting to untie one of the gangways.

'Go,' he said. 'You can't do any more to help. I'll find her. There's only five million people after all.'

'I'm afraid I might not see you again.'

'You'll forget me once you're home.'

'Don't say that, Max! I'll never forget you, I promise.'

He laughed and squeezed my shoulders gently. 'You believe I'd let you get away from me so easily? You've cast a spell on me. There's a thread between us that won't be broken. I can get a visa and visit you, if you'll let me.'

We'd discussed that earlier, in a bantering way, and he'd carefully written down my address. This time I required a guarantee.

'I want to stay.'

'I haven't the means to look after you in Peter. '

'You don't want me to, in other words?'

He groaned. 'This isn't a romantic movie. I can't conjure up a happy ending here for us, sweetheart. Before you know it, you'll get a call from Edinburgh airport to come and fetch me. And you'll have to bundle this person you don't mean to marry out of the house pretty damn quick and tell the neighbours to keep quiet about him.'

'I have to go back on board for a minute or two. Promise you won't go away.'

'I'll be here till the ship sails.' He kissed me hard; a farewell kiss.

'Let me have one last try at persuading them to wait,' I said.

I packed a bag quickly with essentials, then trotted back and forth between the ship and the passport control shed, trying to get bored officials to help. The surly green-uniformed dame in the booth with its stupid slanting mirror still made a three-act pantomime of gazing carefully at my passport photo, then at me, each time. Madwoman! I wanted to club her over the head. Police were summoned, but they didn't bother to take off their sunglasses and the tour manager was too nonchalant for his own good. 'We have a schedule to keep,' he said, 'and so does the port.'

My knee twitched with desire to make contact with his groin. 'You're not proposing to leave her behind?'

'She'll turn up in a few hours. She should have her passport. She can fly on and rejoin us at Tallinn.'

'She's been kidnapped, you moron.'

'What nonsense. We've been bringing tourists for years. I've never heard of a single one having that sort of problem.'

Paolo Conti appeared then, laid his hand on my shoulder in an avuncular way, and spoke to me as if I was a naïve five-year-old, addressing me throughout as "Miss Stuart". Never got round to having my passport altered to either Fergus's name or the one I'd decided to use professionally. I wanted to tell him to fuck off, but instead I smiled enigmatically, made the purser cash the largest cheque I dared write, and tottered down a gangway already half-untied. Men on ship and dock yelled and swore at me in a variety of languages.

Max grinned and shook his head.   'Idiot,' he said. 'Incurable romantic, I thought you were sure to fall in the water. I'd have had to rescue you again. And I can't swim.'

'What do you mean you can't swim?'

'Some old witch – a fortune-teller – told my grandmother I'd die by drowning. So she wouldn't let me learn. "It'll be a quick, gentle death this way," she'd tell me.   "It's the swimmers who drown slowly in agony." '

'What a silly idea,' I said. 'I'll teach you.' But where? Not in a swimming pool, because anything with that smell of chlorine makes me throw up, even after all these years.

Max's eyes were warm, and he hugged me so hard I knew he was glad in his heart. We sat on the embankment wall, watching the Fortuna get under way. Paolo was on the bridge, of course, and he didn't so much as glance in my direction. I'd been daft to expect anything else. He was playing a part. The company presumably paid extra to get a handsome man, to keep the women passengers coming back for more. In another year they'd all queue again to have their photo taken with him; he was probably on commission from the photographers.

Captain. I used to find the term reassuring - a captain is guaranteed to look after you. The bastard didn't look my way - lying about being apart from his wife too, no doubt.   Peigi was right, railing at me when I had my wee fling after Fergus left.   'I can't be doing with all this "separated" nonsense,' she said. 'You're either married or you're divorced. It'll end in tears.'

'Poor Serena,' said Max, ' you could have been sailing home with a handsome man who has a well-paid job, and you came with me instead.'

Oh no, I couldn't. I don't know how it had happened in the first place. I'd let myself get too lonely. Or perhaps I'd been trying to match Dee drink for drink. All I know is that I found myself in the wrong place at the wrong time long before we reached St Petersburg. The first night out of Stockholm, there I was alone on deck with Paolo Conti – Paolo; a name as warm and sensual and sophisticated as its owner – and I took my eye off the script for a moment too long.

He certainly was attractive. Dee had her eye on him before ever we set foot on gangway. He'd been out on the docking bridge, checking to see if he'd scratched his boat parking, and he glanced down at us with those deep, dark eyes and smiled. It'd have been no surprise if Dee had shinned up one of the mooring ropes, like a hungry rat.

When the gold-embossed invitation was delivered to the cabin (a very expensive cabin; Dee doesn't do things by halves) she was beside herself.

'They're not allowed to fraternise,' I said. 'All you'll get is your dinner.'

Sleepy sea, rolling ship, velvet sky, false security. I tried to forget Dee's reply: 'I bet they do it all the time. Specially the married ones who're used to getting it every night.'

To take my mind off that, I watched how quickly the Fortuna's wake vanished behind us. No one would know we'd been there.

'You're always so sad,' said Paolo, 'I noticed this about you from the moment I first saw you. What can I do to make you smile?'

'I was thinking about the Estonia. It can't be far from here it went down.'

'A little further east. We don't pass directly over it.' He gave me a quick, reassuring hug. 'You knew someone who was on it?'

'I was on it, with my ex-husband. Well, nearly.'

Fergus had been researching a documentary about the vice bosses in Riga and Tallinn. 'Do you realise,' he'd said to me, eyes gleaming, 'most of these girls they send to Frankfurt or Dublin are only sixteen or so? If that.' He'd only taken me with him to save on the cost of an interpreter.

'We'd got on for the return trip, but I panicked,' I told Paolo.

That's when I'd begun to believe I might have inherited my great-grandmother's gift after all. For the matriarch from Skye apparently refused to get onto another boat, well over a century ago, the one the landlord had laid on to take them off Skye and off his land and off his conscience, all the way to Adelaide. She marched south to Glasgow instead, her four children at her heels, and her man and dozens more were dead of the smallpox and typhus before the Hercules reached Cork to pick up its next passengers.

Fergus hadn't been best pleased when I balked at the last fence: 'It's because you're too hysterical to go on the sodding plane like a normal person we're on this tub to begin with. Piss off then. Walk home for all I care.' But he was spooked too, so he followed me down the gangway willingly enough. We trailed back into town and had to take a room in the most expensive hotel because it was so late. On the way to the airport next day we heard what had happened. That was the first and only time I knew Fergus speechless. The police pulled us in for questioning, because survivors had mentioned hearing an explosion, but I managed to convince them I wasn't a terrorist. Nothing incriminating on the hands.

I've never been confident it was anything more than coincidence. Almost one in ten made it, and it isn't the cruellest death. Water is the enemy of flames. And for what, in the end, had I saved myself?

'They persuaded me to get off without making a fuss,' I told Paolo. 'I've always felt guilty about that. If I hadn't been so willing to go quietly, someone else might have been saved.' Instead of lying curled like larvae, deep and dead in their cabins.

And he drew me close and kissed me, a significant kiss, not a perfunctory or sympathetic one. He twined his hands in my hair, and kissed me on the mouth and the shoulders, it should have been exciting to be necking with an experienced man, a man who still wore his wedding ring though he'd separated from his wife, ('Insurance policy' he'd said, laughing), and was handsome and debonair. I allowed him to kiss me because I'm a fraud. He believed I was weepy at the thought of the hundreds who'd lost their lives. The truth of it would have scunnered him: my pity was all for myself.

I slapped Max playfully. 'I don't fancy sailors,' I said.

He pulled me round to face him and laid his hand behind my head and kissed me, till I could think of nothing but the blankets he'd folded so neatly, waiting for us. There's not a man in the world with such a mouth as his, and his way of kissing that makes me want to die rather than stop. We dropped my bag at the flat. I hoped he'd suggest we went to bed.

'Let's eat. You said you had some cash?' he mumbled.

I made him take more than half of what I had.

'For safe keeping,' I said, hating Russia for humiliating him.

He ate like a starved wolf at first, scarcely chewing the meat before he swallowed it. Then he looked apologetic. It broke my heart to see it. I had an urge to look after him I never experienced for Fergus or any of the others. The next day he could teach me to haggle for food in the market. There were supermarkets too, the same as home.

'I'll get a job,' said Max. He had cheered up enormously. 'I'll start looking tomorrow. Employment that'll bring in enough to keep us. Honest work,' he added, seeing my frown. 'I've been foolish, wasting my life and all the training when I should have settled down to my métier. I should have joined an orchestra. Perhaps it's not too late. We have to extend your visa too.'

'I can work as well. It won't be so bad.'

'We'll make a new life together. Even here, it must be possible.'

If Katya showed up, she could sling her hook. Under new management. It wasn't too late to do what I should have done a dozen years before. All I'd missed out on was having a stake in a few years of momentous history.

CHAPTER SIX

We were less than a hundred yards from the restaurant, when I spotted the car, and its driver.

'I never thought I'd be pleased to see that oaf.'

But Zhenya was alone. 'Can't tear yourself away?' he said.

'What have you done with Deirdre? Because of you, she's stranded. The ship's sailed.'

'Because of me? Don't worry, she's safe enough.'

'Where is she?'

'My dacha at Pushkin. She was delighted to drive out there with me. Maybe she thought I lived in the palace.'

'Why didn't you bring her back with you? She'll have to catch a plane.'

'The state she's in they wouldn't let her near a plane. I'm damned if I was having her in this car either, I don't want her throwing up all over the seats. Get in. '

Zhenya adjusted the driving mirror so he could look at me. 'So - Grishkin kept you well entertained?'

'Where did you and Dee get to?'

'We tried a couple of clubs. God in heaven, she can put away the drink, your friend.'

'So you left her alone in the middle of nowhere while you came swanning into town.'

'Inna's with her. Poor Inna.'

He turned off the main road after half an hour, bumping a couple of hundred yards down a rutted track towards birch-woods. The house was disappointing. Not one of the quaint wooden ones I'd seen in books, but single-block construction, with an ugly felt roof.

Inna appeared in the doorway. 'You should have arrived sooner, to mop up after your drunken-bitch friend. That's not my job.'

Dee couldn't even focus her eyes.

'Take us back to town now, Zhenya,' I said. 'She's better. She won't throw up.'

'Grishkin'll take you. There's not enough gas anyway.'

'Marvellous. You need to get some. I'll pay.'

'Go yourself.' He chucked Max the keys, over his shoulder, without looking. Unerring aim. Everything about the man was scary. I'd figured out what his eyes reminded me of: photos of Rasputin in history books.

Max hesitated. 'For God's sake,' I said, 'I have to get her away tonight. It's all right. Inna's around.' He left hurriedly.

'And you, you mother-fucker – why did you get her in this state?' I yelled in Zhenya's face.

He snatched me off my feet. I thumped his chest as hard as I could.

'You learnt Russian at school?' His laughter sounded as if it came from under a great depth of water. 'Progressive school! Still, I prefer a woman who fights and curses. You and I can have fun together sweetheart. We'll fight without our clothes. See the size of my butt? Takes a big hammer to drive a big nail. I daresay the cellist's rosined his bow.'

'Maksim's a gentleman.'

'Just as well I'm not. Your friend had her face in my flies before we'd driven out of the city. She's not choosy which way up she is. Don't worry - I'm not too keen to grease my axle anywhere I might catch a dose. I watch myself with the ones that have the front door open after a couple of drinks. You know what I love best, Serena? To do it in a woman's hair. Protein conditioner. Safe sex too - the worst I'll ever catch is dandruff. You have beautiful hair, haven't you, sweetheart? Lovely long thick hair. And eyes the colour of ice-flowers. Calm down. I'm teasing you.'

He flopped into a chair and drew me onto his lap. His grip felt as if it was cracking my bones and he'd a scar across the palm of his right hand that cut into me like a leather strap. Utterly foreign, he seemed to me, in a way that Max never could be.

God, was this the level Dee had descended to? Mind you, the last time I tried to lecture her on treating men as nothing more than sex objects, she just shook her finger in my face and said, 'Pot, kettle, Serena. Nothing I've seen indicates you're one iota different. Name one male *friend* you have?'

'Why were you in Petersburg?' Kuzkuz said, in a new tone.

'On holiday.'

'I'm not an imbecile. Why here – why not France or Spain or Italy or Greece? That's where your breed pass their vacations. Why here?'

'Because I love this country. I used to love what it stood for.'

He yelped with laughter. 'It stands for fuck all now. This is 1997. Nobody has ideals any more – we just want cash, a job, a place to live.'

'You have your freedom now. Isn't that good?'

'Sure – we're free to beg.'

'I don't want to see kids and old women begging,' I said. 'But your own people have caused that.'

'As long as they make money from parading us, nothing will change. You need a real fright, you lot.'

'Why don't you mug a few tourists? That'd scare off the rest.'

'You get that in any city now. Madrid, Paris, even London. I bet they warned you that'd happen to you here. You still got off the boat. The West forgets quickly. They've repaired the palaces and they serve food you could eat in the foreign currency restaurants. Our people stand in line to sell the clothes off their backs. But not in a spot the tourists might see. The police keep moving the poor bastards on. You think giving us Big Macs is enough to make us forget?'

His eyes were blazing, spinning in his head. Dee seemed to have fallen asleep, and there was no sound of Inna elsewhere in the house. I was being allowed to peep through a window that had been sealed up for many years, and any minute it could slam shut again, trapping me by the fingers.

'You have visited Kronstadt?' Zhenya sounded moderately sane again. 'I'll take you to see that tomorrow, sweetheart. Warships, hundreds of them, tied up and rotting. People went hungry so these could be built, to protect us from the Americans, because the Americans could afford to buy the whole of east Europe, tell them we were their enemies. They didn't need bombs, the Americans. Hamburgers and dollars. So the ships can rust to buggery. No money for fuel for them anyway. No pay for the crews.'

'I'm no friend of the Americans. I was raised believing you were the good guys.'

'You're sweet,' cooed Zhenya, 'the first decent Westerner I ever met. Don't you want to love me? I'm descended from royalty. My mother was a Tuvan princess. I'm from an older civilisation than all this crap.' He waved his hand dismissively in the direction of the Catherine Palace. 'But we're all half-breeds now.'

67

I saw that the ring finger of his left hand was missing above the middle joint. Why hadn't I noticed that before? I began to feel a little sorry for him, and I preferred maudlin to violent. I stroked his hair tentatively, and allowed him to hug me. It felt no more threatening than passing the knots of elderly winos on the Royal Mile. 'So you've fallen for little Grishkin?' he said.

'But he already has a girl, hasn't he? Katya.' How low could I get? Tapping a fruitcake for the dirt on Max.

'She's not his girl. He uses her when he needs a woman, the way we all do from time to time.' He gave a greasy sob. 'Your Max who's such a gentleman – and he is, Serena – if you've nothing extortion's no crime. His father was a party man, strong principles, afraid of no one. We need men like that. Yeltsin should have had a bullet in his gizzard long before this.'

'I thought people our age were all for Yeltsin? The tour guides think he's wonderful.'

'That's because they've bought into the system.' Then he was rambling again. 'Bloody Europe. They're so busy with their snouts in the trough they don't give a toss about anyone else. Look at Bosnia. Look at the whole mess, they'll let all the rest go to buggery while they worry over their eco-fucking-nomic union. All I ever wanted to do was fight for my country and earn my bread playing music. You want to see my guns? I have quite a collection.'

I heard the car coming back and Zhenya set me gently on my feet again as Max came in, rubbing his hands.

'Let's get the girls back into town. They have to go home.'

'We could make us some cash, Grishkin. We could get their people to pay a modest finder's fee.'

'We could get ourselves killed. Are you driving?'

'Stay tonight. They can't travel anywhere at this hour.'

'Now, Max,' I hissed at him, 'you and me and Dee.' We heaved her into the back seat. 'Go, go, go! He's deranged, your pal.'

Max laughed mirthlessly, as he started the car. 'He saw things in the war that'd drive anyone out of their mind. His kid brother blown to pieces right in front of him. Can you imagine that? Your brother's brains and guts spattered in your face? I have nightmares about it still. You kill one of theirs, and they'll find you. I used to wake up wondering if I was dead.'

'Is that when he lost his finger?'

'Hell, no. We both came through the army unscathed. Relatively. His wife did that, when she flipped.'

'He's married?'

'Was. She tried to knife him while he was sleeping.'

'So what happened to her?'

'He wakened and grabbed the knife by the blade, pushed her arm round and cut her own throat with it. After that he called the police.'

'Why isn't he in prison?'

'No case against him. Self defence. Enough of their neighbours testified they'd seen her with the knife - it's not unusual you know, plenty cases of that here, women murdering their husbands. She had the knife, she started it, no one disputed that.'

'She cut off his finger?'

'Silly bugger wouldn't have it seen to. It turned septic and started to rot.'

He was driving faster and faster, but I wasn't afraid. It put the miles between us and Pushkin. 'And this paragon's your best friend?'

'Christ, Serena, I'm not condoning it, but the man lived for music. His hand was so badly damaged he can't play properly. That affected his mind more. He had a great gift. Just coming into his prime.'

'You left me with a sex-crazed maniac who cuts up women.'

'You were safer with him than in a stolen car with me. He'd not have allowed anyone to come near you. If you want to worry, start worrying now. If Mayakovsky's thugs are around we'll see about getting cut up.'

'Zhenya needs treatment.'

'I know that. The only treatment he'll get is a bullet in the back of the head.'

'Why do you associate with these people? You're not like them.'

'More than you think. I daresay I'm not much use to him. He fed me though.'

He braked abruptly. 'You can't know what it is to live in this country, Serena, with too little food, no real home, no one to help you. It's a wonder more of us aren't criminals. They're the ones with money. The rich pay no taxes in Russia. That's nothing new, corruption, every last Communist official was crooked. But not the ordinary people. We've all been forced to be that way now. Jesus, what I've done, merely to live.'

He laid his head on his hands on the wheel and wept. I was so taken aback I couldn't say anything; I stroked his neck till he cheered up, just as suddenly, and giggled to himself.

'Maybe I'll end up dying for stealing a Mercedes Benz motor. Excellent car. I prefer this to a BMW. Last time a mafia boss got blown away hundreds of these at turned up at his funeral. Imagine that, downtown Petersburg gridlocked with fancy cars, and old women trying to sell the shoes off their feet on the pavements.'

Jeez! It was going to be an awful come-down when he discovered all I have is a Peugeot 205. But of course, I hadn't told him my plans for his future yet.

We deposited Deirdre on the steps of the British consulate, then drove a few few blocks away. 'Serena, you've found your friend,' Max said. 'Now it's time to go home. I have to leave and dump the transport while I have the chance.'

'Let's dump it then. I'm staying for a while.'

He shook me by the shoulders. 'You need to be born to it, the way Zhenya and I were. You think this is the chance to make a TV documentary? Fashionable now, isn't it - smug people can sit in comfortable homes and bitch about the Bloody Reds, perhaps pretend to pity us. Sweetheart – I know you're not that type. But it's best you leave, and I'll visit you.'

I wanted to get back to his narrow bed and the warmth of his skin. 'Please don't send me away.' We were still locked in a clinch when they appeared from the twilight, torches shining in our eyes. It's the noise I remember most - harsh voices, shouted commands I only half understood – total confusion. Who were they? They had camouflage gear and guns but no uniform I could recognise. I caught a glimpse of Max's face, sickly-white, before they separated us.

They spread-eagled me against a wall, while a lout ran his hands all over my body, up between my legs, over my breasts. He took his time about it. Then he started going through my bag. He was disconcerted when he found my passport and then my press card. That made me want to giggle with nerves - all the years I've carried the damn thing, and never once had to show it. And thank God, it took his mind off rooting among my things before he reached the small, heavy objects.

He allowed me to stand up and I glanced round. They had Max face down on the potholed roadway, his beautiful, fragile fingers laced behind his head, the bones delicate as a bird's. Just one casual blow from a rifle-butt, and he could end up as damaged as his friend.

One of them stood over him, a gun pointed casually at his back. The angel in my head who rides a Harley-Davidson, and chases ambulances to see the accident, kicked in. I could picture bullets ripping into warm flesh, splintering bone, spurting blood; special bullets, crimped in six places along their edges. Lives still fall light as leaves in this place, even now. It was enough to make me forget that the creep beside me had a gun too. I dug my elbow in his ribs so hard I bruised myself.

'Is this the way you treat your city's guests?'

'Foreigners shouldn't be out in the middle of the night. Who are you anyway? Why do you speak Russian?'

'I'm a journalist researching a documentary on your tourist industry. That's why I was lent this car, and this driver. You'll surely get promoted for your contribution to encouraging visitors.'

He faltered. No turning back now. 'You were lent this car?'

'Why else would I be in it? You think British journalists steal cars?'

They let Max stand up.

'Now,' I said, 'if you'll permit us to be on our way, we'll forget it. You made a mistake.' I'd fifty dollars loose in my blouse pocket. I pressed it into his hand, while I fantasised about spitting in his face. 'Thank you for your assistance.'

He half-saluted as we drove off. We had to stop the car after a couple of blocks while I was sick. Max had told me how his father died, a car spinning off a straight road with no obstructions, no ice. A stroke while he was at the wheel, or else he was so drunk he lost control. That was the official version. Max had never believed it. The body had been too badly burnt to tell. 'The forces of evil,' he said. 'That's what killed him. Bad things happen to good people in this country, and no one cares.'

He got out and stood beside me, absent-mindedly kneading my shoulder. He hadn't stopped trembling. 'Bastards,' he kept repeating, 'I wanted to kill him for putting his filthy hands on you. Shit! I should have killed him. What the hell. I should have grabbed a weapon and let him have it. I'm a good shot. The Russian army gave me that at least.'

'It was no worse than I've had at airports. Don't dramatize. I'm not getting in that car again.'

He went to the boot – he said later he didn't know what impulse he was acting on – and opened it. The two green canvas sports bags inside were stuffed with cash, notes that spilled over the top, dollars, roubles, Deutschmarks, a numismatist's stockroom. There were taped-up plastic bags too; they could have contained anything: drugs, body parts, trash. I wanted to throw up again. We slammed the boot shut. It didn't occur to either of us to help ourselves. Max's face was a death mask.

'Let's get the hell out of this. We need to get you away. You see now why I said you can't stay?'

'And you? '

'I'll lie low for a while till they forget.'

'Your mother?'

'She has her own life. She'd be really happy to see me, specially if I'd a few thugs at my back. Mayakovsky won't hurt me, not much, just amputate a finger or two. Serena - I'm teasing you. This is a large country, plenty of places to hide. I'll be all right. I'm a survivor.'

That clinched it, the memories of being told that as another man abandoned me in Bruges on the pretext of a sensible career move. 'You'll get by. You're a survivor.' He'd meant it as a compliment. I'd taken it as the pronouncement of doom because it decreed I had to spend the rest of my life abandoned and helpless and tired, rescuing myself, like the relic of a nuclear holocaust, or my gassed-population dream.

Maybe Russia won't rise again, it's been counted out this time, all the years of history, the stylish buildings, the bridges and canals. All gone the way of their literature and their sportsmen and their dancers and musicians, even their circuses, damn it. Max had become inestimably precious, as if by saving him I could save a species on the brink of extinction.

'I want to get my bag from your flat,' I said as nonchalantly as I could.

'It might be unwise to go back there.'

'Give me your keys. No one knows me.'

I climbed the stairs two at a time, emptied my stuff on the bed then chucked every item I didn't absolutely need for the next few days at Maria's door. I took as much from Max's cupboard as I could stuff into the space. I had plenty of clothes at home. This was all he possessed. There was an old shoebox containing a few letters and photos. I resisted the temptation to rifle through them for the one of a girl, and dumped the lot in.

He drew me into the shadow of a doorway and kissed me lingeringly.

'I brought some of your things too,' I said. 'A few clothes, and papers that looked important.'

'I shouldn't have let you do that. Brave as well as beautiful. I won't let you take any more risks. I'll get you to the airport and you'll be safe.'

'You're coming with me. I can't leave you in this mess.'

'I have no visa. It'd take too long to get one.'

'You told me you can buy anything here, with dollars. Can you not buy a visa?'

'It's your people who issue them. They know exactly who my father was.' He shuffled his feet awkwardly. 'And anyway, I'm not properly registered here. I haven't all the documents I should have, even for our own authorities.'

'Finland isn't far. We'd could get home from there.'

'You think they would let me into Britain, if we reached it? They'd stick me on the first plane back. Mayakovsky could send a welcome committee.'

I knew he was right. I've seen too many documentaries about airports, where hunched men and women with gaunt faces are herded down the long corridor to a sinister plane waiting on the tarmac. Their passports would be stamped: "Deported". Not a chance of ever getting in again. We prefer to believe we don't do that.

'Can't you buy a marriage certificate, Max? They'd have to let you in if we were married.' The words flew out of my mouth like hornets, stinging him so he winced.

'I don't believe they would. Anyway, I can't marry. I can't support a wife.' He didn't forget to be polite. He omitted to say he didn't like me enough. 'Suppose I managed to get out that way, where could I go, where could I live?'

'With me, in Edinburgh. I have a house.'

'You mean really married? Living together? I don't see how this is possible.'

'Listen Max, the marriage thing works just fine the other way round. Your women come to Scotland to marry men they've hardly met. I know two men in the University with Russian wives. They'd hardly known them more than a day or two; the only difference was they had visas. They're perfectly happy.'

Bad choice of argument. 'The visas weren't the only difference.' His face grew sombre. 'Women can expect the man to support them. I will not be a burden to you or take advantage of your generosity.'

I looked down at my hands, determined not to cry. 'No need to make excuses.'

'You'd really do that, to get me out?' he said, tipping my face up to look at him. 'You've nothing to gain from taking up with me. You'd do this for me? I want to, Serena. Jesus, yes, I want to. You're pure and brave and beautiful. You'd actually marry me?'

He kissed me till I was trembling, because I loved his mouth so much, so warm and alive, with a rounded firm lower lip that drove me crazy.

'If you change your mind, if it's not what you'd hoped – you can end it, when we're back in Scotland. It's as easy there as it is here, I'd think,' he said.

A few meetings with lawyers, half a dozen terse letters, an official document that should arrive any day now. Probably lying waiting for me at home. Easy peasy.

'Could we organise it quickly?' I said.

'With enough money, possibly. We'll try tomorrow. Tonight we'll stay with Edouard and Anna, friends I can trust, over beside the Finland Station. We'll be safe.'

CHAPTER SEVEN

We spent an uncomfortable and chaste night on his friends' floor, and next day I gave Max most of the cash I had left. He looked miserable.

'It's only bits of fancy paper,' I said. 'Use whatever you need to. However much it takes, if it gets us both home safely.' Jesus, how much *would* it take? You usually have to wait ages here.

Max never could make me understand how he knew which one to bribe. They both looked formidable to me, battleship women stuffed into navy blue suits two sizes too small. He walked confidently and casually up to one of them, while I dithered in the background. I didn't see the cash change hands, though I was watching with the concentrated attention terror brings. He beckoned me across.

'Lucky girl,' cooed the official, 'to be marrying a wealthy man who's so desperate to have you. Ach, to be so much in love you can't wait.'

She pinched my cheek, and flashed a mouthful of gold teeth, while Max wrote Anna's address under my name on the form and I signed it in my childish Russian handwriting, using Frank's old Parker 61 with the gold cap he gave me when I was sitting my Highers. He'd have liked that, to see me set down a Russian name, with his pen. Serena Lermontova. The first and last time I ever used Fergus's surname. It seemed a good idea at the time. God knows what address Max gave. Not where he'd been living, anyway.

'Beautiful pen,' gold-teeth said bitterly.

Max took it gently from my hand, and put the cap on it. 'Here,' he said, holding it out to her. 'For you. A gift.'

I opened my mouth to protest, but he glared at me so eloquently I shut it again.

'I'll get you another,' he said once we were out of earshot.

'That's not the point.'

Max shrugged. 'She was going to start making problems for us. You think she doesn't know what's what? She wanted it, and I wanted to shut her up. It's only a pen, Serena.'

'It had sentimental value.'

'And won't this have?' he said, with that endearing smile. 'In a few hours we'll be man and wife. Wait for me here.'

He went to a street-phone, while I nursed a vague hope he might be phoning his mother. I could picture her; tall and elegant like him - a strong personality, not much time for men, a MacKenzie woman in disguise.

'Zhenya will come and see us married,' he said quietly.

The sorcerer at the feast. I resolved to be polite to him.

Anna lent me one of her dresses – rainbow-striped flimsy cotton, with hundreds of tiny pleats; it was too wide, so she pinned it in at the back - and they borrowed a suit that almost fitted the groom. Zhenya bought me a bunch of blue scabious from a street stall, holding them up beside my face. 'They match your eyes,' he said. Pity they clashed with the rest of the ensemble. He counted out the blooms carefully, throwing one away to leave an odd number, for luck.

Superstitious people, even Max's generation. I stored that nugget of information away.

A couple of hours later, our ill-assorted party stood in a dingy, dank, magnificent office while I stumbled through my answers. 'They thought you were just nervous,' Max said later. 'Weren't you? I was. It's not every day you get married.'

With borrowed clothes, and paperwork that wasn't on the level, like Ferdinand and Isabella. He slid Morag's ring – the one I'd worn since she died – back on my right hand, and we sashayed out, clutching the paper that proved I was Maksim Grigoriev's wife.

'I'll buy you another ring, I swear it,' he whispered against my hair as we trailed down the steps. 'I'll work till I drop to get you a new one. Expensive wedding, all the same. And this was without a decent dress for you. We should have helped ourselves from Mayakovsky's savings. Perhaps it was his present. Never mind. We have the certificate.'

I had ten exposures left in the camera. Edouard fooled around, pretending to be a photographer, then took the film out carefully.

'Keep it in your bag for safety,' he said. 'For your children and your grandchildren. I can tell. You'll have half a dozen.'

We all drank sweet, lukewarm Russian champagne, standing there in the dusty sunlight, and after a few glasses Max was misty-eyed over this farcical event. 'I'm a married man,' he kept repeating. Then he took my face between his hands and kissed me, but he was laughing, we all were. Play-acting, kids who've found the dressing-up box while the adults' backs are turned. I should have had a net curtain for a veil and a ring out of a Christmas cracker.

'Now we have to cross town to let you lay your flowers at Peter's statue,' said Zhenya

But the symbolism of that other custom's not lost on me, or the nightmares I had when Frank read me Pushkin's *Bronze Horseman*. Even now, Peter gets the first flowers.

'That old lecher has as much chance of droits de seigneur with me as you have Kuzkuz,' I said. 'Anyway, the tourists take photos of the wedding parties. I thought you disliked that?'

The idea appealed to me though. Tourists from Morningside taking pictures of Serena MacKenzie as a Russian bride, with safety pins all down the back of her gown.

'They only take pictures of the ones in fancy white dresses,' said my husband bitterly. 'Handsome couple, aren't we? Neither of us in clothes that fit.' He'd been so happy a few moments before. Now he was morose and weepy, his friend's arm round his shoulders.

'I have to make you a gift,' said Zhenya, sliding his hand into Max's pocket. Wonder whose wallet that came out of? Perhaps Dee's. The two men embraced.

'You'll look after him for me?' Zhenya hugged me tightly. 'You're a sweet girl. He's made the right choice this time.'

I became weepy too. He liked me better than Katya. We'd all drunk too much. 'I wish we could take you with us,' I said.

'Deirdre didn't get around to proposing. You must visit me one day. I wanted so much to take both of you to my homeland. We'll go for a long journey into the forests, just the three of us, to look for the white cranes. We might see a pair of them dancing together, Serena, their courtship dance, that's such a good omen,

81

it'd mean we'd all live happily for the rest of our lives, we'd never run out of good luck.'

Then he was gone.

The others wanted to throw a party for us.

'Afterwards, we'll move out till tomorrow,' said Anna. 'You want privacy on your wedding night.'

But Max wasn't up for that. Another round of drinks and we were back into our everyday clothes, everything else packed in my bag and an old rucksack of Edouard's.

We laid down our pathetically inadequate luggage at the door, and we all sat silently with bowed heads. 'For luck, for an untroubled journey' said Anna. We could have been posing for a refugee relief poster.

They walked with us to the Finland Station. 'Too risky by road,' Edouard said.

'Police?'

'Bandits,' said Max, 'long before we get to the police or the border guards at Torfyanovka. We'll be safer in the forest.'

We got off the train at Vyborg, and walked out of the town into thick conifers that stretched as far as the horizon.

CHAPTER EIGHT

Fifty metres into the thick Russian forest, it was already dusk. The sweet yeasty aroma of decayed vegetation was as fragrant as bread, and Maksim's fingers were strong and comforting. The antique scent of woods fills me with nostalgia as well as fear. I forced my eyes wide open, to drive away the vision of Donald John Munro with his trousers round his ankles and the blood running down his thighs.

'You're not afraid?' said Max.

'There aren't wolves?'

'Wolves, bears, snakes, and monsters.' He laughed and shook his head. 'I'll protect you. That's my duty now, for the rest of our life together. My grandparents' home was only a few kilometres away. All this used to be Finland.'

I might have guessed that, from the height and the blond good looks. But for an accident of history, he'd have been born in a country that wasn't suspect.

For the first few hours we walked on mossy ground beneath a canopy of mixed birch and pine. We didn't meet another human being, though I could feel animal eyes watching us from the undergrowth as we twig-cracked our way across the deep silence of star-strewn clearings. I'd not known such skies since I was a child.

'You can hardly see the stars properly at home any more,' I said. 'There are only a few street lights in the village, but even that's enough to spoil the sky. As for Edinburgh – forget it.'

Max looked vaguely upwards. 'They're pretty,' he said.

'Don't you get depressed, thinking about how the stars are rushing away from us? One day people will look up, and it'll just be unrelieved black. Then we'll be sorry we didn't look lovingly enough while we had the chance. They'll all be gone.'

Max squeezed my waist. 'Not in our time, Serena.'

I believe we were safely into what's now Finland before we lay down to sleep the first night, for the nature of the trees had changed, and I felt relaxed. The police – anyone in uniform, from a postman upwards – they obey the rules once you're over the border. Even the ones with guns don't point them at passers-by, or rake your crotch with stubby fingers.

Max gathered wood and built a substantial fire in a clearing. 'That should frighten off the wolves,' he said, grinning. 'Our midsummer bonfire. Hold my hand. I'll never leave you, I swear it. The fire's my witness.'

Then he made a quick ring in the grass with his cigarette lighter, scorching a circle round where we were to lie. 'To stop bugs and ticks crawling in. My grandfather'd always do that.'

I smiled to myself. It was sunwise Max made his circle, deiseil. Merely stirring a pan of tinned soup, I have to stir it the correct way too.

'We didn't buy chocolate,' he said. 'If you get hungry you'll just have to chew birch bark.'

'I won't be allowed to forget that, will I?'

'Of course not. I love a woman who'll eat sweets when she fancies them. I can't be bothered with the ones who're always dieting. Here. I have an apple. It's better to peel them, but I didn't bring a knife.'

'I have one.'

He pulled a face at me. 'That's quite a beast. I didn't realise women in Scotland carry knives as weapons. I suppose it's better than guns.'

'It's not a weapon. You never know when it'll be useful.'

'We'll plant the seeds,' Max said, 'then a whole grove of apple-trees will grow, and everyone who passes by will know two lovers spent their wedding-night here.'

I sat on the woollen rug Anna had given us, leaning against the homely bulk of an old pine. My husband sprawled beside me, his head in my lap. 'I knew something marvellous would happen to me this year,' he said, 'because of the lights in the sky in February. Everyone said it was UFOs. I knew it was a sign.'

Then we talked of our parents, ill-assorted pairs that they'd both been.

'Oh God, my parents!' Max said. 'He had a responsible job – he was an engineer – but she despised him, never let pass a chance to belittle him. He took it out on me, wouldn't let me start on the cello till I was too old. He only gave in when he saw I wouldn't put my mind to anything else. I'll never be as good as I could have been because I was late starting. It takes twenty years to train a cellist. Same with Nureyev. They didn't let him start to dance till he was well in his teens. He was never that competent technically, I've heard dancers say that. I don't have his brilliance though, to compensate.'

I knew better than to mutter platitudes. I played with his hair, where it lay long against the nape of his neck.

'You and I have more in common than our parents did,' he said. 'Although we hardly know each other, I feel that.'

'Mine certainly had nothing in common,' I said. 'And my aunt's been more of a mother to me than her sister ever was.'

'This is your fault, Peigi MacKenzie,' chanted Morag's voice in my head. 'All your primping and vanity, filing and painting the child's nails and putting ideas in her head. You've taught her your filthy ways.'

'It's sad to part with a parent on ill terms,' Max said. 'You and I now, we must learn from their mistakes. Tell me why you studied my language at school.'

'My father. He was besotted with your country. He idolised Yuri Gagarin, of all people.'

'Did he look like you?'

'Not at all. I take after my mother's side. He had reddish hair and brown eyes. And I can't pretend he was an engineer or anything clever. He was a newspaper printer. What they used to call a compositor. A real dyed-in-the-wool party member, same as yours. Much good that did him. They sacked him at the first opportunity.' On principle he'd have set his mind against every single piece of new technology anyway. 'And an alcoholic,' I added.

'Mine was the same,' Max said. 'Always swimming against the tide and always on the booze. I think our fathers were brave men.'

I never thought of it that way. Always put it down as selfishness.

Frank gave me my love of words and my obsession with Russia. He gave me my brief and heady spell of popularity at Hazelpark as the daughter of the man who said the c-word to the headmistress. I shouldn't have been there at all, because he disapproved of private education, but Morag had been hell bent on sending me, and Peigi paid the fees. No compromise would satisfy him.

'You've got it in the prospectus,' he'd said to the Head, his tone still reasonable.

'Serena won't need the Higher to take it at university. They provide an intensive course in first year.' That was her first mistake, the condescension in her voice.

'So what do you want her to take instead – German, I suppose? You've forgotten who was the ally and who was the fucking enemy, haven't you? What do you think we pay your extortionate soddin' fees for, if the girl can't take the subjects she wants? She could take German at the local school without all the fucking expense.'

I tugged at his arm, hissing: 'Dad! Dad.' I was sure I'd be expelled that afternoon.

'At least we shall do our best to discourage Serena from learning Anglo-Saxon, Mr Stuart,' she yelled, puce in the face.

'Maybe you think we send our lassies here so they can wear your scummy uniform? Fetish-fodder for all the dirty old men in Glasgow, like that perverted cunt who followed Serena and her pal round Marks and Spencer waving his dick at them? You'll get one of the girls raped, making them wear these stupid wee kilts.' ('He's going to slap it on the counter,' Dee had said. 'Maybe she'll put it in a bag.')

Frank prevailed over Higher Russian; the Head got her way on the rolling-over of our tartan skirts at the waistband and the trips to Marks and Spencers.

In the end I took English and History at university, but the obsession had put down roots, for I'd grown up with the books Frank left behind when he moved out, specially the poetry. Pushkin and Esenin and Akhmatova (such a strange choice that!). He took the Communist Manifesto with him - no loss, for it was boring. The Kinsey Report disappeared too; it had proved incomprehensible even in consultation with Black's medical dictionary and Dee, who came from a liberated family. It was Frank himself who tried to make me read it.

'He's a doctor,' he said. 'He knows what's what. Read about it and learn to enjoy it, Serena, so you won't grow up like your mother, bitter and wizened, making some man miserable.'

I think of my father when I find articles about Kinsey in women's magazines; the plastic sheeted offices, the earnest white-coated attendants, the careful tabulation of percentages of squirters and dribblers, and the exploitation of children. Frank was so hot on exploitation, you'd have thought he'd see through Kinsey.

'I was certainly on bad terms with my father at the time he died,' I said to Max.

Frank turned up at my graduation blootered out of his mind, so that I was ashamed in case anyone suspected I was related to him.

'At least he came,' Dee said, trying to cheer me up.

'Yeah. Big deal.' But I felt a little guilty.

He was in hospital three weeks later. Not cirrhosis as my mother had gleefully predicted; subdural haematoma. He'd fallen, hit his head, and been carted off to the Southern General to have a blood clot removed. He took himself home five days later, head still swathed in bandages.

'I always said he'd kill himself, smoking when he was drunk,' said Morag. 'Imagine that. The whole building a heap of ashes, not a damn thing left that was saleable.'

Kinsey and Marx; the incongruous record-cover signed by Gagarin; the set of bowls with his initials inlaid in silver; all the crystal and tea-sets he'd won in tournaments, that Morag-the-hoarder hadn't taken out of their boxes. All incinerated, like the man himself who was never there for me, not even once.

No chance of a damages claim due to negligence either, because he'd signed himself out of hospital, to spite my mother. And worse than that, the fire hadn't been quite hot enough; there was still a body for us to identify, and deal with.

'What on earth can we do?' said Morag. 'I suppose we have to have a funeral, and all the expense of a grave.'

'We could have him cremated.'

'Maybe they'd give us a discount, in the circumstances,' she said. And we giggled together. I'm hot with shame to think of that even now. It's the only memory I have of both of us laughing at the same time at the same thing. Hardly anyone turned up for the funeral. After all his union meetings, comrade this and comrade that, losing his job over it, he was just a political dinosaur.

'You must find me cowardly,' Max said suddenly, 'to flee from my country because life's difficult. I don't want to die. I always felt I was put into the world to accomplish a worthwhile task, not merely to survive.'

I could relate to that. But wasn't it, a little, to be with me? They're a pragmatic people, so brave as to be foolhardy, and wasteful with it.   Look at Gagarin himself, dead at thirty-four in a clapped-out MiG-15. All that way out into space and back, the whole world watching and listening and cheering him on, and they set him to being a test pilot again. The best scientific minds they have, ploutering about among the dust of Chernobyl in the type of protective clothing you'd put on to sand your floor. Men sent to face German tanks with no weapons.

And I wanted Max to say he'd come with me for love?

'You're a precious, wonderful girl, Serena,' he said, reading my mind. 'No other woman ever put herself out for me, or made any effort.'

'What about your mother?'

'My mother never gave herself the slightest inconvenience. I daresay when I was born she took herself into an empty room, dropped me, hitched her skirt down and hailed a passing nurse. 'Here – attend to this child, will you?'

At its worst, I'd never felt quite so detached from Morag. 'You must send her our address, all the same.'

He shrugged. 'Perhaps. She won't care.

'And your grandparents?'

'They were happy together, my father's parents. I never knew my mother's. My grandfather still thought of himself as Finnish. They used to have religious services in their own language. A priest who could speak it travelled out from Petersburg. They were old-fashioned people.'

'Your voice changes, when you speak about them.'

'The happiest times of my life. I was with them every available minute. It suited all of us. My father thought it'd spite my mother, but she was delighted to have me off her hands. My grandparents loved me. I wish you could have seen their house - like one in a fairy-tale, with carved wood all round the eaves and the most beautiful porch, shutters with hearts and flowers cut out of them. Surrounded by birch woods where you could gather mushrooms, and all sorts of berries, black ones, red ones, purple ones.'

Blaeberries and cloudberries, perhaps. The climate's not so different. Brambles - my favourite taste of all, like eating the earth herself, and the smell of bonfires is the same as that taste, and the autumn mist's the colour smoke from the berries would be. I love to crack each seed individually between my teeth, and savour the sensation. (Grannie used to say if I swallowed a plum stone it'd grow into a tree in my gut and burst my insides open. Perhaps a bramble seed slipped through, and what lies tangled in my innards is a briar patch.)

'We have berries at home', I said. 'I'll take you there in autumn, we can pick brambles.'

I wish I could have told Maksim I loved my grandparents too. I have no memory of Frank's parents. I assume they were dead before I was born. Grannie I just pitied - they used to call her the Spanish Lady for her black, black hair and exotic looks, but all she got was forty-one years of Granda. You don't get that even for murder.

And Granda himself - my strongest memory of him is fear, even before I was disgraced. Bog cotton for hair he had, and eyebrows so long they blew in the wind like a terrier's, for he was an old man by the time I knew him. He'd not married till he was forty, and it was another fifteen years before Morag was born. His eyes were the grey of a winter sea, and as merciless, and his frame had shrunk from the six-foot-four he was in his prime, so that the skin hung on him like a rumpled candlewick bedspread.

He lingered a year after I killed him, more fearsome than ever with his hair whiter than the pillowcase, and his good eye roving maliciously while his mouth dribbled prayers and accusations. We weren't a demonstrative family. My mother didn't say: 'Kiss your grandfather', the way Deirdre's did when her uncle Billy was dying. We were, however, assembled at the deathbed. I saw his soul drift up through the ceiling, blue-grey and insubstantial as peat-reek. No more Granda. No more prayers. No more hope of salvation. Doomed.

'This autumn, we'll go over to Balvaig for a long holiday,' I said to Max, twining his hair round my finger. 'We can gather as much fruit in the woods there as you want.' He was silent for a while, but his eyes were brimming. 'We'll come back here too one day, Maksim. You can take me to see their house.'

He smiled up at me and slid his hand over mine.

'It's gone. The people who took it after my grandfather died burnt the old place down and built a concrete shack as ugly as the one Zhenya has.'

I wondered if he'd had the chance to say goodbye, either to the house or to them. We all need roots if we're not to end up as restless ghosts. I'd make sure he contacted his mother as soon as we were home.

Another long silence. I could hear scuttlings and rustlings in the undergrowth, but I knew it was only benign animals. Nothing could harm us.

'Anyhow, tell me the story of your husband.'

'He's lying with his head in my lap.'

'You can't expect me not to wonder how you met, why you parted.'

'I met him by accident, in the middle of Edinburgh. He works in TV. He's quite well-known, in Scotland.'

He sat up. 'You don't still work with this man?'

'I never see him. He was with the BBC.' Just a white lie. No need to tell him yet that Fergus had moved to Albion, as their senior anchor-man before I met him.

Max didn't lie down again, but sat cross-legged opposite me, studying my face.

'He found you this work?'

'Why should you think that?'

'You told me you met him by chance. If you'd worked there you'd have known him.'

'I got that job after I met him, but it was on my own merits. Because I'm classed as a native Gaelic speaker. They couldn't throw enough cash at Gaelic broadcasting a few years ago – it wasn't hard to get a job. I've hardly done anything in Gaelic since I went. They only need one newsreader, and they had one already.'

Reclaiming my inheritance. I used to believe that's what justified my work. I was misled. They would have hired a talking dog as long as it could manage *Ciamar a tha thu*, so they could claim the subsidy. Runrig and the Gaelic mafia'll get no thanks from me for raping our culture, then hacking it to death.

'I only asked.'

Stupid to be so snappy with my new man over it.

'Hardly anyone speaks it nowadays anyway,' I said. 'Like your Finnish church services, I should think. Granda used to preach in Gaelic.'

'Your grandfather was a priest?' Max said with rekindled interest.

'Not a real one. What they call a lay preacher, in the Free Presbyterian Church. Very much a minority movement.'

And damn all I could ever find free in it. No proper music, or rousing hymns like other churches, because that was sinful, and the old ones hankered after the time they could get away with chaining up the kids' swings on a Sunday, and preventing folk going in bathing. You couldn't hang washing out, and when my mother was young the strict ones refused to cook. Cold food every Sabbath in the depths of winter, to humble the spirit and crush out sin. And sin was everywhere. They excommunicated one of their own elders for attending a Catholic funeral. Even the old Gaelic rhymes they used to croon to bless the boats and the cattle were anathema to Granda, because they'd the reek of papacy. Paganism it was, reverence to fire and sun as well as Bride and Columba, but I didn't recognise that till I was grown up, then I laughed to think the whiff of incense worried Peter MacKenzie more.

It wasn't a real church anyway, but an uninsulated corrugated iron shed painted a dismal dark green, with no organ or any other instrument. That's what I hear in my head when I look at the sea though, Gaelic psalms sounding older than time, the precentor's voice spare, pure as salt-bleached bone, and lonely as a tern headed into the wind. I'd look in his face, and it was transfigured, like the faces of saints in paintings. The face of my people, judging the sinners.

'I'm not a believer,' said Max, 'not really, though my grandmother had me baptised. Secretly. My mother would have killed her. Our women get religion when they're old. The men just take to drink.'

'So you have a baptismal cross, and all the trimmings?' I'd not noticed anything of that sort among his possessions.

He'd sifted through the papers I'd saved, and shown me his certificate from the Leningrad Conservatory. 'You precious angel, to have known that was important,' he'd said. I could see it was the only item that really mattered to him. He'd not shown me the photographs.

'I suppose there was some sort of cross. It's been lost.'

'Won't your mother have it?'

He only laughed. At Kingdom there are boxes and drawers stuffed with my teething ring, my first real shoes, all my school reports, photos; my entire life wrapped in tissue paper. I resolved to give Maksim memories from that point on. Everything of our life together I'd treasure, starting with Edouard's pictures, I'd save it all for our old age and make it up to him that he'd abandoned his history to come with me. I forgave him in my heart for the pen.

'All right,' he said, shaking me gently, 'so this husband, this Fergus, didn't get you your job. Why did you stop loving him?'

'I don't know that I ever started.'

I used to believe I was the only woman in the land who'd ended up married because she couldn't think of anything better to do. Even in our times of ultimate free choice, when I needn't have married at all. I couldn't tell Max that one of the more esoteric qualities that had attracted me to Fergus was that he looked the part for Balvaig. I'd pictured him standing down at the pier in the evenings, with the other menfolk, smoking a pipe and discussing the price of fish.

'I suppose I was flattered that a man who's famous – even if it's only in Scotland – would want to marry me. He can be charming when he wants to. It was a mistake anyway, OK? And we both realised that, so we split up.'

'You didn't have a child?'

'Of course not. Neither of us wanted children. I wasn't his first wife you know. He'd been married twice before and never had any, so I assume he never wanted them.'

'How long were you married?'

'About a year. It'll have taken about three times as long to get to the stage of a final divorce.'

Max moved closer and laid his arm round my shoulders. 'Poor Serena. But you had another lover afterwards to console you?'

'Not a lover,' I said. 'A friend. Roderick. He's an architect. We were company for each other, for social purposes. I'd known him for years, even before I met Fergus.'

'All these men with well-paid jobs. So you didn't sleep with this architect? You must tell him, though, as soon as we're home.'

Yeah. Same time as you send Katya a short, explanatory note.

'And this Deirdre, this woman you call your friend?' He'd made not the slightest attempt to conceal his contempt. 'How can she have been your friend since childhood? She's unworthy of you.'

96

'When I was nine, and dumped from a tiny Highland village school into the posh kids' one in Glasgow, she rescued me. She was in the class above me, and she stopped the older kids bullying me. Her parents were kind to me too. Her mother'd buy me new clothes, then make flimsy excuses she'd got them for Dee and they didn't fit. Eva's a saint. Dee's just over-exuberant.'

My compassionate husband snorted, while I realised that I've never liked Dee much, in my heart. She's the type who believes the folk begging in Princes Street should be grateful to live in Edinburgh. 'They make plenty,' she says. 'They're probably better off than a lot who work.'

'You must have met other men, on holidays?' said Max.

Strangely enough, hardly ever. There was the trauma of Nice just before I married Fergus, and the regrettable incident in Bruges two months after I split up with him. The only people who knew about these were my aunt and my friend Carla. ('He only wanted to fuck your heritage,' said Carla of the latter. 'He never had any intention of taking you back to Boston with him. Professor of Celtic Studies! Pooh   – every last one that can read and write is a professor in America. Such a big head, and so stuffed with its own importance. He was not a kind enough man to love you, Serena.' Leave aside the thought that my closest friend believed a man could only love me out of charity.)

'I told you, I don't go in for holiday romances,' I said. 'Did you?'

'No. Never.'

I knew he was lying. All these wealthy women tourists in the exclusive hotel where he'd played for Mayakovsky Maybe that's why his English is so good......

'But the other man.' Maksim's voice was husky. 'Your little waiter, that you loved so much. Will I do instead?' He held me tight and rocked me in his arms till I stopped sobbing. 'I'm so sorry. I didn't mean to upset you. You're tired and overwrought. It's time to sleep.'

We snuggled together, our jackets over us.

'You're not getting off the hook,' I said. 'Do you think I'm not still curious about the woman you lived with?'

'I didn't live with her.'

'I want details.'

'Same age as me, about your height, a lot plumper, black hair, not nearly so long as yours. She's a violinist, not as gifted as Zhenya, by a long way. I haven't seen her for months, and I'll never see her again. End of story. Goodnight.'

'Why didn't you marry her?'

'I already told you. Didn't want to.'

'And the others? I'm sure you've had dozens of women.'

'So many I can't remember. Lie down properly.'

For a moment he did more than cuddle me, then he sighed and drew me against his body spoon-fashion, tucking his arm round my waist. We might have been Hansel and Gretel. To hell with Billy goats; that was my favourite story, the brother who looks after the sister and risks his own life for her, pure and innocent. I don't rate the allegory-for-incest view. It'd take a twisted mind to get to the Babes in the Wood fornicating while the small birds dropped leaves on them. Unsuitable material for panto – though I've seen worse on the Festival Fringe.

'I'm sorry,' said Max. 'I shouldn't have to ask you to lie down in such a place, on your wedding night. We should have had a room with a huge, comfortable bed.'

'There's a big bed at home. I don't mind this.'

'It should have been in a church, our wedding,' he said. 'Perhaps you feel this wasn't good enough?'

'It was beautiful. It doesn't matter where it was.'

'Serena – you do want children, don't you?'

'Of course I do. With you. But not immediately. Eventually.'

'You have to let me take care of that, then – I don't want you taking pills.'

'Well, there's other ways. I'll see the doctor when we get home.'

'You're not having one of these things fitted inside you either, I've heard my mother talking about that. They don't always work, you can get a baby in there as well. What a mess.'

'The time to talk about all this is when we're home. We need to slow down and get to know each other.'

He sighed again.

'Max, I wish we could have seen the white cranes.'

'We will. One day.'

We settled to sleep.

I didn't want the forest to end, so we could linger for years in the shadowy places. But by noon the next day the trees thinned then stopped and we saw red roofed houses. Max sighed with relief.

'I was afraid I'd get us lost and we'd run out of food,' he said.

He asked directions fluently. 'My grandfather never forgot it. He taught me.'

I thought about the tour guide in Helsinki less than a week before. She practically spat venom every time she mentioned Russia. Her face contorted with loathing, she told us to relish the last time we'd be able to leave our jackets safely on the bus. 'You won't be able to do that in St Petersburg. Nor eat the food nor drink the water.'

Another who'd been born into the double bind. I wondered how well Max had coped. So little I knew about him. Not his shoe-size (other than "huge"), or what his favourite foods were or which side of the bed he preferred. But I knew he slept so silently I'd wake wondering if he'd died, and that his skin was always warm, even on a chilly night, and that he'd hated maths at school. 'I never gave a fuck what x equalled,' he said. I knew I'd done a worthwhile thing.

To save money, we lay down in barns or under the stars to sleep, though I knew Max was alert as a fox for a sound of anyone sharing our space. I was still worried about getting across borders, even now we were inside Europe.

'Don't worry. I have Kuzkuz's wedding present,' said Max.

'You can't bribe officials here.'

He drew his hand out of his pocket. A perfectly ordinary-looking British passport, not a new one either. He flicked it open. Even the photo was obviously a few years old. The name hadn't been altered. David Henderson. Place of birth: York. Height: 1m 89. Hair: Fair. Eyes: Hazel. 'He thought of everything,' Max said. 'He took the picture off an old student card of mine he had lying around. That's the only thing that doesn't look perfect, because of the part over it. As long as they don't look too closely, it's OK. If anyone starts to speak to me so I have to answer, walk on ahead. That way if I'm stopped you don't get into trouble.'

From Helsinki we travelled across Sweden to Norway, with no trouble. We were on buses and small boats for what seemed weeks though it was only three days.

I hadn't been so happy since I was a student, backpacking round Europe.

'It'd have been quicker to fly, but this is nice,' I said. They check passports too meticulously at airports.

'Fly? Never. I hate flying.'

Fate. When you get to sharing irrational prejudices, it's proof.

'It's strange,' I said, 'There was a Russian pilot who died in a plane crash near Balvaig. He was flying with the British air force; it was during the war, 1944. I'll take you to see his gravestone when we visit my aunt. It's interesting. I suppose that was the one of the first places I ever saw Cyrillic script. The odd thing is, his name was Max too. I heard people say he was a White Russian, so I thought that must mean he had very blond hair. Like yours. He was a prince. They say in the village that his people came for him after the war, and took his heart and buried it in Paris where they lived. I always thought that must be nonsense, how on earth could they find his heart after all that time. But right enough, I found another gravestone in the Russian cemetery at St Geneviève-des-Bois; he's near Nureyev.'

'Just proves flying's dangerous,' said Max. 'And sorry, but I'm no prince!'

I'd totally run out of cash by the time we reached Oslo, and we still had to get to Bergen. I tried Dee's home number. Answering machine. Hugh and Eva? I didn't want to alarm them; maybe Dee hadn't been in touch yet.

I phoned my aunt. I knew how hurt she would have been if she'd got a card telling her I'd married abroad. As bad as her pal Jean MacPherson's daughter who'd gone on holiday to Rhodes with her boyfriend and sent an ordinary picture postcard: *'Ross and I got married out here yesterday. See you soon. Love Nicola.'* Any ruse to prevent her mother from attending. Peigi deserved better.

'I wish you could have been there, but it was kind of sudden,' I said.

A stinging silence at the other end of the line. 'But you'd known him longer than that, surely?'

I prevaricated. 'He plays the cello. Like Bonnie Prince Charlie. Only Maksim's good......'. And brave. He'd never flee and leave his followers to lift the tab.

'Serena – you'd known him longer than a couple of days?'

'Circumstances weren't normal. You'll like him.'

'Och, child,' she said, 'why couldn't you have found yourself a nice Scots boy your own age who hadn't been married before?' I knew she didn't mean it, she was thinking aloud.

She and Fergus had hated one another on sight. 'A cruel mouth, that one had,' she said, the day the divorce papers were lodged. She'd come to Edinburgh to lend me moral support – not that I needed it. She took me to Jenners to buy me a bottle of Givenchy Organza, then to the Carlton Hotel for afternoon tea. 'These fleshy little lips pouting under his dirty big beard. And he liked to make it obvious he considered

102

he'd married beneath himself. Well, Serena, I think it was you that did that. Thank God there are no bairns to fight over.'

'He tried to get custody of the cat,' I said, and we laughed so raucously I thought the po-faced waiter would throw us out.

'Max is my own age, Peigi, in fact, he's a year younger. A toy-boy. And he's not been married before.' Two out of three ain't bad.

But I wasn't going to ask her to send me money. One bank supplies the entire district with coin and gossip. Carla and Dougal were in France. So I called Fergus.

'Can you wire me a hundred and fifty quid? You'll get it back as soon as. Can't explain now. Have you heard anything of Dee? No – I'll explain when I get home, should be tomorrow.'

The last ferry was tremendously crowded. In no time at all, we were at Newcastle.

'Walk. Look normal,' I said. 'We have to stick together. I won't leave you. I won't let them separate us.' Too bloody nervous; they're trained to look for such signs.

Max didn't look nervous at all. He strolled casually into the line for a female officer, and treated her to an endearing smile. Shit, I thought. Big mistake. Wrong country. But the nature of his smile always made anything permissible. He coughed, and put his hand to his mouth. 'Excuse me.'

'Summer cold?' she said sympathetically.

'Froat,' he croaked, gesticulating.

That'd blown it. Any minute now, she'd say: If you could just step this way a moment, sir -

'You want to get home to bed.'

He grinned and nodded. It was my turn. She gave me a much harder time.

By the time we were on the train to Edinburgh my head was splitting; I couldn't believe we'd managed it. Max leant against my shoulder and dozed off, but I was too keyed up to sleep. We were safe; we'd be home in a couple of hours. I shook him awake at Haymarket. He automatically lit a cigarette the minute we left the station, while I tried to bite my tongue. He found it amusing that I believed it'd harm him.

'Russian men don't live long enough to worry about what they'll die of,' he said. 'The booze gets us long before the fags do. I don't mind that. I don't want to live to be old and worn out. I'll go while I still have my faculties and my appetites intact. You've only another twenty years to put up with me, at most.'

'Don't joke. It's bad for you.'

'Life's bad for you at home.'

'This is home now, and I don't want to nag you. But I wish you'd stop.'

He kissed the top of my head. 'Soon. I promise. Let me get my nerves back.'

CHAPTER NINE

The Stockbridge Colonies. Edinburgh's Chelsea. The house I took Max home to was an upper flat in a terrace built more than a hundred years ago. I suppose the half-dozen streets, with their small strips of garden, were the work of Victorian do-gooders. Working-class housing. But by the '90s they've become trendy. An upper one with converted attic – almost identical to mine – sold for over a hundred and twenty K just before I went on holiday.

Some of the streets have upper flats accessed by an external stair. In others, the stair's inside, off a postage-stamp hallway. My first reaction to the house, trotting hot-eyed through the dusk with Fergus Learmonth a few years before was to think: Ah, this is a cut above the other streets. The truth of it may be that I wouldn't have married him if the steps had been on the outside.

The phone was ringing as I unlocked the door, so I left Max to follow me up, in case it was important. It was only Fergus himself, and he was deliciously angry.

'I'm going to have you sectioned,' he said. 'For your own safety and the public's.'

'I'm newly home. What's wrong with you?"

'Dee says you tried to throw yourself under a train in St Petersburg, like Anna Karenina. "Not Serena's style," I told her. "She'd pick something easy like pills." But now I hear it's just social and professional suicide. You've brought some stray tomcat home, have you? Is this what you needed the sub for?

Trifle pricey, was he? Love lance in good working order, I hope. Hate to think you'd been diddled.'

Ah, yes, that Dee. I'd left a message on her answering machine when I tried to phone her from Oslo. I hadn't suspected those two spoke to each other; never used to.

'Don't be childish.'

'You stupid, stupid bitch. I suppose he hasn't any of the relevant papers? That takes months. How do you know he doesn't have a notifiable disease? You're priceless, Serena. You're the one who was always so keen we keep our quarantine laws. Met his folks did you? Don't try to lie to me. You wouldn't buy a kitten under these circumstances.'

'I happen to be fond of him. Not that that'd make much sense to you.'

Max was standing in the doorway, looking awkward, too polite to barge in, though I was trying to gesture: 'Make yourself at home'.

'I have to go,' I said to Fergus.

'Knickers off and ready, is he? Well, don't let me detain you from sexual ecstasy – you remember what that is, do you? Damned if I do. I'll have that money back, by the way, I'm not into subsidising illegals. You know you'll lose your job over this, if not end up in the clink. Serve you right.'

'You'll get it as soon as I can get to the building society.'

'Jesus wept, he's waded through all you had in the bank has he?'

'Actually, Dee's brilliant fucking holiday plans went through all I had in the bank, and more. How is Dee, by the way? I assume you've heard from her?'

'She's still in the clinic in Perthshire, as far as I know,' he said.

'Clinic? What sort of clinic?' The one thing Dee and I feared more than anything else.

'Och, Pitlochry Hydropathic establishment, or some such joint.'

'Idiot! Is she all right physically?'

'That rattled you, did it? As far as I know she is. I haven't had the pleasure of knowing the lady that intimately.'

Dee and Fergus? As nauseating as the idea of picking up a stranger's gum from the pavement. But open warfare's not a good tactic. I was careful to maintain a civil tone as I bade him goodnight. Bugger it, why was he being as bad as Peigi? Why couldn't anyone just be happy for me?

I started to look through the mail I'd swept up from the mat. It was there. I recognised the longer-than-usual legal envelope. Nothing else should have mattered. But it was all ruined. I'd dreamed of letting the surprises unfold gradually, showing Max his new home, the tiny garden that burgeons into its neighbours so that passers-by gawp into our small enclave with envy and lower their voices to whispers. I wanted him to savour the way a summer twilight blurs the boundaries, so that the leafy green tunnel to the river melds into darkness till it expands to meet the stars. If you could see them. Now all I could think about was how long I'd have to keep him shut in so he wouldn't run away.

All the way across Scandinavia I'd honed the mental image of our sanctuary snoozing in the hazy sunshine, the light slanting across the polished wooden floor – from the kitchen side in the morning, the sitting room in the afternoon. The cosy evenings Max and I would have beside the dark red Vermont woodburner I stubbornly retained in the centre of town and fed with precious tit-bits of driftwood carried from home. We'd lie cuddling one another on the cobalt blue and red Qashquai rug with its small woven-in mistakes to remind the faithful only God can make perfection.

'Look at the dust!' I said. Edinburgh dust's like love. Golden and glittery as it falls, even in weak Northern sunshine, dead and grey as sloughed skin once it lands. 'Wouldn't you wonder where it comes from in an empty house, in only a week?'

I'd wanted to create an impression of being house-trained. It only served to frighten me. Jesus, it really has only been just over a week, I thought.

'I must be careful to keep your house tidy,' said Max.

The junk was Morag's, the result of welding atavistic memory of failed harvests to proximity to the Barrows. A burden I hadn't known how to lay down. Just as well he couldn't see the tiny attic. My Feng Shui book says the state of it shows why my head's cluttered. And if I'd had a basement..... but a shed stuffed to the roof was even worse. Detachment.

'Our house,' I said. It sounded unconvincing. It'd have been better left unsaid. Max gave the small irritable click of the tongue that's half gesture of impatience, half sigh.

He prowled softly from room to room, touching things in a tentative way, a small boy in a china shop, then examined my pictures quizzically enough to make me nervous. Dee disapproved of the print I'd brought back from Nice. To her the couple on horseback represented abduction or rape. I've always perceived it as rescue. Fergus says anything painted or composed this century doesn't merit the name of art. 'Hang it on the stair, if you must,' he'd snapped, when I moved my few possessions from my own flat. 'I suppose I have to thank Christ it's not Kandinsky.' But I'd had to live with his damn photographs of nude women who had bigger breasts than me.

'Chagall,' I told Max shyly.

'I know.' He gave me the slow, sweet smile that twists my heart. 'Is that you and me?' He studied my print of Gustav Klimt's Fulfilment. (Holiday in Vienna, years before Fergus.) It's not a particularly good example. In the original, the woman's hair is red, but in my print it looks almost black. 'Now, I can see that's you, wrapped in your bride's quilt.' I was so happy he'd noticed. I've always believed she *does* resemble me. 'But who's the man? He has dark hair. You have to take this one down, or I'll be jealous.'

He looked at my smallest painting for a long time. It's a tiny pastel drawing of a darkened hillside with three low white cottages.

In the gable windows of the first two, the roseate glow of a lamp.

'Your home?' he asked.

I know from the label on the back that it's Donegal, but to me it was always Balvaig. I used to pray that the unlit window wouldn't be mine.

'I want you to be supremely happy in this house, Maksim.' How I loved to say his name, roll it off my tongue.

He embraced me awkwardly. 'You've always lived here alone?'

'Since Fergus left.'

The smile froze. 'It's your husband's house?'

'It was, before we married. I bought his half.'

One of the few fair things Fergus had done. He gave me the confidence that I could cope with the mortgage and he asked only half of what he'd paid for it in 1986.

109

'I won't live in another man's house.'

'It's all mine now. I've lived in it alone for ages, except for the cat.'

He jumped. 'There is a cat?' I hadn't considered that. Perhaps he hated cats, the way Frank did. They're not exactly noted as animal lovers, despite the vogue for gigantic dogs Dee had remarked on in St Petersburg.

One of Morag's first acts when Frank left was to bring a cat down from the croft, not because she wanted one, but to spite him. See? I have a cat, and that's better than a man.

Fergus and I had stronger words over Gorby's future than over mine.

'Don't you care for cats, Max?'

'I never had one. Where is it?'

'My neighbour looks after him when I'm away. I'll fetch him tomorrow.'

His frown relaxed. No need to tread carefully for fear of a desiccated heap of fur and bone lurking behind a sofa.

'Fetch it now. I want to meet your cat.'

I'd contemplated some emergency re-naming when we got home, but Max thought it was funny. He ruffled the ginger splodge on top of the cat's white head. 'Gorbachev. That's apt.'

'You don't think it's disrespectful?'

'Only to the cat.'

'Aren't you tired? I'm terribly tired.'

'I don't suppose you've anything to drink?' he said. 'Whisky? That's what Scots drink, isn't it? I have to learn to be a Scot.'

I left him with a full glass and sprinted upstairs to haul fresh sheets out of the cupboard. I carry the weight of my grandmother's superstitions too: leaving a house with the bed made up tempts the devil to sleep in it, and he can never resist temptation.

Max was reading a comic Roddy's brat had left behind. 'Why do you have a kid's magazine?'

'I do have friends with kids, you know.'

'You and your husband don't have a child?'

'Of course. I leave that for the neighbour to feed too. You're my husband anyway.'

'You know what I mean. It might live with your husband. That happens.'

'I told you, I have no children. Do you?'

I had managed to get my head round the reality he'd had a woman; a sprog would have been a tougher gig. On our first night in the forest, he'd said he'd never bring a child into the world to grow up in Russia.

'You know I don't.'

It was going to be all right, he wouldn't rush me, so gentle and tender he was, so loving. I wanted to drift into sleep with his arm round me, his hand stroking my hair, nested together the way we'd spent all our nights thus far. But he reached for me, drew me round to face him, almost roughly, and began to kiss me in a different way, possessively. I was suffocating, hyperventilating, my heart beating so harshly it felt as if it would rupture; they must be able to hear it next door. Max was growing impatient. He seized my hand and drew it down. I pushed him away and leapt out of bed.

'What's wrong?' he cried, sitting up in alarm.

'I don't want to do that.' I tried to conceal the nausea catching my throat.

'You're my wife. Husbands and wives make love.'

'I'm sorry, I'm tired.'

'What do you want then? I don't know what use I am to you otherwise. How else can I repay you for all you've done for me? I thought that's why you wanted to marry me.'

'For sex?' Jeeees*us*. Have I brought home a Russian gigolo after all?

'Not only that. I know you meant to help me, but I didn't expect a white marriage, a pretend one. I misunderstood. You want to sleep in the same bed with me and not make love?' He sighed, flung himself down flat on his back, the covers pulled to his chin, and glowered at the ceiling.

'I want it to be perfect, the first time,' I said. 'It's only that once. You can never get it back.'

Always the same. Ever since I was a child, I never want the fireworks to be lit, and I'd save my piece of icing till last, afraid to eat it because after it's gone the plate looks so barren and hopeless. My life's left a trail of sad little heaps of melting American Frosting and marzipan. It's an unnatural instinct - other animals guzzle the best first as a survival tactic.

'It was daft thinking I could sleep beside you tonight. I have a single bed in the room downstairs. I'll sleep there.'

'This is your room,' he said coldly. 'I will go downstairs. I'm the intruder. In any case – I suppose this is the same bed you slept in with your husband?'

'I bought a new mattress. I didn't want to be reminded of it either. It's only the wood that's the same.' I'd presumably had to make do with the bedding he'd shagged Katya on, for God's sake.

'Stay here, Maksim. The other bed's not big enough for you.' I grabbed my clothes from the chair and fled. How Fergus would have laughed.

How Max would have laughed too, if he'd realised I believed in fairies till I was more than nine years old. He wouldn't have found it naïve and endearing, merely ridiculous, like everyone else I know. Angels are something else altogether, they're fashionable, they have a public, they have a shelf to themselves in Waterstones. But I'd been brought up with Aunt Peigi's poetry books, and till I was nine I wanted nothing more than to be like Bonnie Kilmeny. I wanted to saunter out after tea one evening, up the long glen, and find fairyland, and a boyfriend who was neither flesh nor blood nor bone, and never have to go home.

So when Donald John Munro told me he knew where the entrance to fairyland was, I begged him to take me there, even though he was thirty-four, and I knew in my heart men that age have no truck with fairies. He drove me to the woods at Ollasdale, in his father's car. I was aware even as he started the engine that I wouldn't have been allowed to go if I'd asked. Donald John had been there all my life, except for the times he was in hospital, and his father was an elder in Granda's kirk. I knew that the other grown-ups said he wasn't right in the head, but I was desperate with longing, and anyway I'd heard my mother say it was small boys who weren't safe with Donald John.

It wasn't until we'd parked the car and were several hundred yards into the trees at Ollasdale he tied a scarf over my eyes. 'So that you won't be struck blind if we surprise them at their dancing,' he said.

It was an off-duty policeman from Aberdeen, up on holiday, who stopped for me when I found the road, and ran out blindly, waving my arms. I should have asked him to take me in the opposite direction. Anywhere but home to Granda's house.

But my only thought had been that I should have stopped to wipe the knife-handle clean.

All of that I should have been able to tell Max, so that he began to understand. What stopped me was the memory of how difficult it is to convince an adult that you once believed in fairies.

CHAPTER TEN

Another two days and it was time to go back to work at Albion. Plan A: reunite Fergus and his cash. I didn't have enough in my account to cover it till the next payday. I decided to prevaricate. He'd calmed down, and reverted to his old bantering, avuncular tone.

'You always were too soft-hearted. I suppose I'm lucky you didn't bring home a planeload of tramps. Darling witch, I can't bear to think of you with an uncouth stranger. What do you know about him?'

He's a lot less uncouth than you, I thought. But I recognise the nuances of Fergus's voice. It'd have been entirely in keeping with his nature to have the immigration authorities on the doorstep within half an hour.

'You gave me the money to bring him into the country.'

'Only because you lied to me. Anyway, I didn't give, I lent, while we're on the subject.'

'You'll get it soon, don't worry. I didn't tell you why I needed it. Could have been to buy a load of crack cocaine for all you knew. Cash transfers are easy to trace.'

'Are you threatening me, Serena?'

'No more than you're threatening me.'

He laughed. 'Touché. He hasn't broken your spirit anyway. I prefer it when you give as good as you get, it's more interesting. Why couldn't you have been more like that when we were together, kitten? Did you get your bit of paper from the Court of Session, by the by? I cried when mine came. Real tears, Serena. We were so good together.'

He's at his most dangerous when his voice waxes lugubrious. It's a thin veneer over a viciousness which alarms me more than his anger.

'Just tell me you're not sleeping with this Russkie,' he said. 'I can take anything but that.'

I wasn't proud of my reply. 'Really?' he crowed. 'Daft wee lassie. What are you playing at? I hope you lock your door.'

He remembered perfectly well how much I'd have given to be able to fit a lock to that door; the jamb's too shallow. But Fergus's voice was silky and affectionate and unpredictable. 'And not a penny to his name. That really is priceless. You married my bank account rather than me, didn't you? That and my house, so that you could paint it up to look like a Carl Larsson calendar. Jesus, what's between this man's legs? That doesn't cut much ice with you, does it? That's it. No cojones. Serena's found herself a eunuch at last.'

I went into the newsroom and slammed the door on him. I reckoned he'd had enough interest on the loan.

I tried to put on a fresh-back-from-holiday face for my colleagues. I knew I should have been grateful to be there, because nearly everyone I knew envied me. It's my own fault that I didn't take to it; I lack the media mindset, as Fergus never tired of telling me. 'Face up to it, why don't you, kitten,' he'd say, 'your days in this game are numbered. Not cut out for it; need to be more assertive. The sparkle's missing. Speaking a language both outlandish and antiquated isn't enough.'

I find it boring. There, it's said. It's incestuous. Everyone chases the same stories, ourselves and the BBC and the papers, then we drop them the next day. It's all beginnings and no endings. And when a juicy lump of genuine news drops in the pond, there's feeding-frenzy, blood on the water. Nauseating, and dishonest too. As often as not we write the cue before we do the interview, so we know exactly what we want them to say. That's why Paxman's a genius - he excels in situations where they won't co-operate.

I wasn't particularly fond of the people I work beside either, except for Nick, and he's not typical. He's not into Feng Shui and he hasn't got an altar and he wouldn't dream of having his clutter professionally cleared. He is an expert falconer, and has a licence to keep peregrine falcons.

Anita Forrest, my boss, I couldn't work up an enthusiasm for in those days. A callous bitch, she seemed to me, who didn't care who she trampled on, but Fergus maintains she's just marvellous at her job. 'She's focussed,' he says. 'And she had the savvy to get onto the production side well before her sell-by date. Though she could have gone for radio instead. It wouldn't matter there that you can count the rings on her neck. Best microphone voice I ever heard, though she's done her best to ruin it with smoking.'

Katie-Mary MacDonald I'd have liked to kill, if I could have found an undetectable method. A genuine native speaker, from Benbecula. Until she contracts a terminal illness or is horribly disfigured in a car-crash, not another soul has a chance of reading the Gaelic news, and apart from that their only specialised use for me was the odd documentary.

'The Board have no more intention of implementing their minority-language obligations than stuffing raw chillies up their arses,' Fergus never tired of telling me. 'The chillies have it. No contest.'

'Wait till we get our own Parliament.'

'In the unlikely event we do, these buggers'll keep awfully quiet on the subject of the Gaelic in case they're expected to learn it.'

I spent my first morning back clearing my e-mail and writing the script for a piece on the latest hot-spots on the beach beside Dounreay. Then I arranged to meet Roddy for lunch; better to tell him at once, before he turned up at the house with his child in tow.

Through lack of foresight I met Roddy. He stopped to help me when I'd a puncture in a bald tyre fifty yards from the Inverness end of the Kessock Bridge and was regretting the fact I'd been too mean to join the AA. A kind act, to come to my aid, before the politzei rolled up and nabbed me, and I should not malign him. It never grew much more interesting, unfortunately. I reckoned I'd repaid the debt for changing my wheel long before.

I broke the news as gently as possible, then he bitched for half an hour about how I'd made a commitment to him. He dissected a bread roll, and built walls with the crumbs. He blamed me for the fact his son was a neurotic brat. He tugged at his ridiculous little beard. An irritating mannerism; it brings out a disturbing resemblance to Van Gogh - or Robin Cook.

Always washing himself, as if he felt I might have contaminated him. That was the word Van Gogh wrote in his meticulous ledger: 'hygiene', his code for cash spent on Rachel, or one of the other whores. Roddy was another great one for keeping accounts 'for tax purposes'

I swept his crumb-house onto a plate.

'Your feelings are hurt,' I said. 'Your dignity. You didn't love me any more than I did you. We filled an awkward gap for each other, that's all. I have to leave now.' I stood up, realised it was unreasonable to expect him to pay, waved my credit card impatiently at the waiter.

'See?' snapped Roddy, 'because you're such a cold person, you judge the rest of us by your standards. I can't turn it off like a tap. I'm worried about seeing you hurt.'

'Don't be. I'm quite content.'

'You know nothing about this man's background, he's not even here legally. You're in deep shit. Don't expect us to rally round.' I couldn't figure who "us" was. Roddy collects funds for Amnesty International on flag days, wearing a ludicrous baseball cap with barbed wire round it. I shrugged as eloquently as any Russian.

'Callous bitch! What happens to your precious Max when you tire of *him*? I suppose you can have him shipped out at tax payers' expense.' Roddy turned a most unbecoming shade of purple. It clashed with his hair. 'You've made your bed,' he said, choking on a mouthful of water. 'Don't come wheenging to me when you find there's a scorpion in it.'

'And don't come wheenging to me for funds for your prisoners of conscience. You wouldn't know conscience if it bit you on the balls.' Just go, Roddy, before I get too angry with you, and bad things happen.

It gave our fellow-diners something to share with friends afterwards at any rate.

I needed someone who'd be on my side so later that afternoon I told Nick about Max – though not the wedding part. I knew he'd understand, after what happened to his sister, Ruth. She got involved with an Estonian man the year before last, and overnight he disappeared. The builders who'd been hiring him as a labourer got cold feet when awkward questions were asked over a work permit.

Ruth had been away in London on business. She called him to check what had happened, the minute she got back. She'd been with him the night before she left and they'd been making plans to get married. She phoned, and day after day it just rang out. There was no reply when she rang his doorbell. She became frantic, and made his landlord let her in. Some of his stuff was still in the drawers and cupboards. Of Igor himself, not a sign.

Then his phone was cut off. The irritating mechanical voice repeated over and over: this number is not available. Ruth tried the operator, got a human being, got the run-around, and the set pieces that imply you must have an ulterior motive for asking, that you're a stalker, intent on sexual harassment.

She knew so much of the fine detail. All his endearing and irritating quirks, the way he whimpered like a puppy and brushed away imaginary flies in his sleep, the crescent-shaped mole above the cheek of his left buttock. None of that helped. He'd vanished, and though she believes he's still in this country, she's given up looking. He left less trace than snow that's melted.

'She's begun to blame herself,' Nick said at the time. 'She keeps asking what she did to drive him away. It's harrowing, because no matter what we tell her, she doesn't believe it. She doesn't know if he's dead or alive. It'd be easier for her if she knew he was dead. And of course there's no point trying the "official channels". These bastards won't tell you anything. Mind you, Claire and I thought privately that it suited her, in some ways, after the visa ran out. It gave her the whip hand. But I'm sure that didn't really make a difference to the outcome.'

'Well, good for you,' Nick said. 'I hope you have more luck than Ruth. I wouldn't worry about the visa. I always felt Igor would have been better without one from the start. Then they wouldn't have known to come looking for him.'

'It's a secret for now, Nick. You won't tell the others?'

He planted a gentle kiss on the top of my head. Dear, kind, Nick, who resembles his falcons so closely, with his clever eyes and sharp beaky nose. I used to wonder how it would all have turned out if I'd gone to Albion straight from university, and found him before Claire got her talons in him.

When I went in next morning, Anita started whistling the Soviet national anthem under her breath. 'Hear you brought home something more exciting than a painted egg,' she said. 'Bit sudden. Most people make do with a rabbit-fur hat with earflaps. You certainly don't believe in letting the bed get cold. When do we meet him? Does he speak any English?'

Will there never, ever be a man who doesn't let me down?

Next on the to-do list: make peace with Ursula. I couldn't dream of a better neighbour; she's kind, cultured, sophisticated, urbane. Fergus refers to her as The-Dyke-Downstairs, swears he'd be chary about sticking his finger in her to save our street in the event of flooding. I've always felt she's one of those women who are just completely asexual.

I used to envy women like Ursula and Peigi, who can be so complete on their own. But not enough to want to be like them. I need to be needed by a man for my own sake, no matter what Dee thinks.

'He's sweet,' she said, when Max had wandered back upstairs after the introductions, 'but Serena, he's so thin. Maybe he brings out the mothering instinct in you.'

'No one's ever accused me of that before!'

She does a particularly irritating line in knowing little smiles. 'How brave of you to bring home a man you've newly met. Love at first sight. How romantic. But you can scarcely know him?'

'We're being sensible, taking our time. That's why you probably heard me downstairs last night, in my own room.'

'Serena – what if he's a lousy lover? I'm not well-placed to advise you, but it must be quite important to have tried it first.'

Caveat emptor. Certainly different from the comment I'd anticipated.

'It's not the same as trying on shoes, Ursula.' Hate that too. I always feel guilty that they don't fit and buy them anyway. Perhaps she was right, and I did acquire him like something I'd seen in a shop window and taken a notion to have.

'You used to sleep in that room anyway, when Fergus was still in residence.'

I'd moved out of Learmonth's bed soon after we got back from Tallinn. He didn't object at that stage; I believe he was a little in awe of me. 'You're a witch right enough,' he said. Then the rapes. Then the videos. Part of me died in the Estonia after all.

'I was never sure if you knew that,' I mumbled. 'Fergus snored so.'

'Not much deadening between the floors in these old houses.' Ursula laid her hand on my arm, tentatively. 'I used to worry over it and wonder whether I should come up to see if you were all right. I'm not a brave person. Och – don't cry. It'll be fine now, won't it? And in the circumstances, it couldn't be too difficult to get rid of Max.'

'Wheesht!' I wondered how much you *could* hear from upstairs. 'I had to really work on persuading him to come with me.'

Shit! I thought as her eyebrows vanished under her fringe, and back came the cynical smile.

And then there was Dee.

'Are you OK?' I said.

'No thanks to you.'

'Nonsense. It was your own fault entirely.'

'And you've brought that creep's pal back with you? Bit extreme. He was quite cute – but there's a limit. How did you smuggle him in anyway?'

'We got married in St Petersburg.'

'Married? You're not even divorced yet.'

'Yes I am. It was final before I met Max.'

'You never told me,' she said suspiciously. 'That's gross. You must be crazier than I thought. You already tried it once, and it doesn't work for you. Nice warm man on tap when you want it. I'd buy that. However, if the cap fits why use a condom, as they say. You'd sampled it, and it didn't suit you, so why the hell are you trying again?'

As if it was something everyone should have a bash at just once, like sky-diving or bungee-jumping or evening classes in pottery.

'Don't you tell a soul,' I said. 'If Fergus – or anyone else for that matter – hears I'll know it was you.'

Night on night I lay awake in my narrow bed listening to Max tossing and turning. I sobbed silently into my pillow so he wouldn't hear – for him, for myself, for spilt seed, for all the babies that wouldn't be born.

I bundled his sheets into the machine without looking at them. Then I'd lean my brow against the cool glass of the window-pane and remember how I'd sit through Granda's sermons, puzzling over Onan who sinned because he spilt his seed on the ground, for I knew all the farmers in the land did that, it was the only way you could get anything to grow. Granda did it himself. He tore the corner off the neat wee square foil packages and dribbled his seed through his cupped hand into the drills where he wanted carrots and neeps to appear. I had more sense than to take it up with him. Just another mystery that made our beautiful island an unconsecrated desert, brimming over with sin, sin, sin. Sin also lay in communism, cremation, divorce, artificial insemination, homosexuality, Scottish nationalism, British Summer Time, Sunday buses, the cinema, female preachers, women in trousers and anyone who believed in the Second Sight.

'It's not as if I'm asking for anything unusual,' Max yelled, 'I don't want to wear your underwear, or chain you to the bed. I don't want you to take it up the ass. Any other man would have made you quit this caper long ago.'

Don't preach at me about Any Other Man. I lived with him for more than a year, and no he didn't put up with it, he rammed himself in me when ever he felt like it, only this isn't America and if I'd tried to bring a marital rape case against Fergus Learmonth I'd never work again.

'I thought you were different.'

124

'Jesus Christ! Why should you think that? Because you met me in the romantic city of St Petersburg, and it was just like a movie?'

I'd hear him get up in the night, for I'd wake from my half-sleep breathing too fast, remembering another, heavier tread on the steps. I'd hear him enter the bathroom, I'd hear him pee, I'd think: Now he's outside my door. And I'd stop breathing until I heard him climb the stair again.

I used to believe it would get better as I got older. Easier each time. The opposite has turned out to be true. I know it's because I'm more in my own head, and that's the part of my anatomy where the problems start. I didn't need some high-paid shrink to tell me that.

A hundred years ago, even up to my grannie's generation, I could have got away with being like this. In this day and age, when anything's possible, I'm just a freak, an embarrassment, an apology for a woman, the only one in the world who's been left behind. As much of a dinosaur as ever my father was.

In the forest, the very first night, Max should have stretched me out on the mossy ground and done what he wanted, for I loved him so much then I'd have died for him.

We hardly spoke to one another. It was more than the sex. How softly the arguments began, and the love faded, so soft and slow I scarcely noticed. Why won't he make an effort? I thought. It was as irritating as grit in my shoe. He felt it too. Our mutual politeness became more studied.

It's a mistake to expect solidity in a relationship that was welded together by chocolate. I'd introduced my husband to Carla – and Carla's hot stuff.

CHAPTER ELEVEN

Carla Torres is all the things I'm not and long to be. Sexy, generous, warm, confident with men, talented. She's as terrifying as a forest fire or a tropical storm: ruthless, beautiful, and regenerative.

I found her at Giverny, six weeks before I was due to become Mrs Fergus Learmonth III. She flitted past me like an exotic butterfly – scarlet sunhat, conker-coloured hair, turquoise top, jade and peacock skirt – trailing a wake of Opium and a dazzling smile. The elderly bearded man walking several paces behind her gave me an odd look.

'Striking colour-scheme,' I said, leaving him to choose whether or not to think I meant the nasturtiums.

'My wife's from Chile,' he said. 'I'm almost accustomed to it after two decades.'

We grinned at each other in mutual recognition; two dowdy Scottish moths blinking in the sunshine.

They invited me to eat with them in Vernon, and after a single evening in Carla's company I was under her spell. I basked in the attention she drew from every man who passed, and in the smoky warmth of her voice. She insisted that I accompany them to her parents' house in Brittany for the rest of my holiday. 'So that I can make sure you don't do anything daft,' she said.

Had I obeyed, I'd never have married Fergus. She hated him already, sight unseen.

But I fled on the slow train to Nice, to sate myself on Chagall as a prelude to binding myself to a Philistine.

Carla forgave me. 'You must always come to me when some bastard man's broken your heart,' she said. 'I'll put it together again. That's what friends are for.' Lucky she hasn't cut her fingers.

Every component of Carla is flamboyant; her tawny skin, her hair, her laugh, her dress sense. She can wear fuchsia and jade and turquoise all together and look magnificent. Her dark copper mane's always artfully tousled, but she has a dancer's controlled grace, swaying her hips so her progress is syncopated by the tintinnabulation of bracelets, necklaces, ear-rings – a perambulating ethnic crafts shop, but on her it never looks common. Her full breasts undulate and when she laughs – that's often – her entire body ripples. She favours warm, spicy scents and her voice is rich and dangerous; she's retained an exotic, sexy accent despite twenty years as a respectable Edinburgh housewife. The joy of living bubbles up in her like the effervescence in champagne and men get drunk on Carla. Luckily, her warmth's as genuine as her talent.

She's a concert musician, a violinist, though she can play the piano to professional standard too. She teaches music at St Angela's Ladies College and God knows what they make of her; an enormous orange cactus-flower burgeoning in a funeral bouquet.

'Why do you bother to teach if you can afford not to?' I asked her, once I knew her well enough to understand just how wealthy her family is.

'It amuses me,' she said. 'I never do anything unless it amuses me.'

Dougal, on the other hand, is a predictable type – he has a doppelgänger in every traditional University department. He's high in the pecking order in Moral Philosophy, but he'll never make it to Professor now, so he doesn't give a damn who he annoys. He's heavily

127

bearded, pot-bellied, terribly clever and witty, entertaining company, a hell of a boozer. When he was drunk and I was in the post-Fergus doldrums, he'd grope me given half the chance. Possibly he pitied me and intended to cheer me up. It's impossible to imagine him in bed with Carla. He'd bounce off those pneumatic breasts like a melon on a trampoline.

Meeting her altered my life. I'd never had a friend so enervating. Dee talks about sex, but it's never interesting. Carla will expound on techniques for divining the degree of penile arousal in the fully clad male and the freshness of supermarket bread in the same paragraph, and the same supermarket. She has also made a detailed study of iridology and Neuro-Linguistic Programming. Risky to let her gaze into your eyes.

I adore her house, a slice of Bohemia in a drawing room flat in the West End with enormous rooms, ornate plasterwork, and skirting boards half a metre high. The whole end of the main room's taken up with Carla's Steinway, nothing less than a full concert grand. I expect its entry was straight from an Ealing comedy: a crane, a precarious rope sling, the entire window removed. Their bedroom could serve as the set for Victorian erotic photographs – enormous, ornate bed, heavy fabrics, sensual colours: burgundy and deep peacock blue and dark green velvet; an intensely feminine brand of decadence.

('Could double as a whore's waiting-room,' Max observed to me after he'd been given the guided tour. And you would be a connoisseur, sweetheart?)

The strange thing is, Carla and Dougal have never actually married. He had a wife before, and didn't bother with a divorce. 'Doesn't that worry you?' I asked

128

her once, on a day of mortgage-induced-depression. 'If anything happened to Dougal you might lose your home.' She shrugged with that insouciance that makes me want to slap her. 'Then I'd get another.' If I had to name one failing, it would be her inability to even imagine not being able to ask Daddy for another pot of cash. Daddy lives in France or New York as the mood takes him, with his fourth wife, who's considerably younger than her step-daughter.

I was afraid Max would detest her. I'd learnt he despised loud, pushy women in the Anita mould. He loathed blatant use of make-up, and had forbidden me to wear perfume because he claimed it made him sneeze. He adored Carla, from the first meeting, and close encounters didn't have him reaching for the tissues. There was an immediate bond; the ones who could laugh at the Brits. My husband couldn't contain his delight when he found she's a musician too.

They talked of nothing except music. I watched wistfully as Max – who'd told me it didn't matter that I'm a musical incompetent – blossomed in her company.

'Dougal will grow jealous, Carla,' I said.

'He only needs me to keep him warm at night.' She pinched my cheek patronisingly. 'All the while I speak to Max, he's watching you. It's a way of passing the time for him, till he can take you home to bed. You're a stunningly handsome couple. You both have physical beauty but it doesn't compete. You complement each other. No wonder people stare at you.'

Max played on Carla's precious Steinway, more than passably. Because I couldn't read music fast enough to turn the pages for him she would do it, leaning across his shoulder.

Why hadn't I paid more attention at school? Too much time wasted sniggering over the words that sounded dirty. Rubato. Con fuoco. Smortzando. That's what Dee said you felt after a poco troppo vigoroso. Maybe music teachers were formed after the common mould was broken. Ours was the youngest in the school, wore short skirts and was newly married. She looked harassed most mornings. 'A poco prestissimo before she came out,' Dee would whisper. 'She's worried it's going to run down her leg when she reaches up to write on the board.'

Max and I grew ever more distant. He laughed spitefully at my minuscule Japanese garden with its cut-leaf maple in a blue pot, the square metre of raked gravel, the pebble fountain, the mossy rock from Ollasdale, the woven reed panel to screen the shed, the small, luxurious clump of bamboo, and the single metal chair. My friends and neighbours had praised it as a miracle of planning. I'd meant to get another chair, but I couldn't afford a duplicate, so it would have to wait. I wasn't about to spoil the entire effect by getting one that didn't match.

'It doesn't go with the house,' Max said.

'Well, I'd need to have either a Norwegian garden or a Japanese interior. Don't know enough about one, can't afford the other.' I'd hoped he'd smile, at last.

'What's it for?' he asked. For him, function determines form; use confers meaning.

I'd been trying to learn to meditate for the past year. I had pictured him sitting on the ground beside me, his head against my knees, closing his eyes and letting the calm seep into his brain too.

'It's a place of tranquillity,' I said, 'designed to soothe the mind. And I happen to enjoy the sound of running water. It's restful.'

He unzipped and urinated noisily and copiously on the bamboo stems. 'There you are. Running water. You're admiring nature, I'm answering her call.'

I shrieked like a harpy. 'For Christ's sake! You can't just piss where you stand here. This is a civilised country. I suppose you want me to plant a St Petersburg garden, to make you feel at home? Fine. I'll chuck out this lot and plant weeds for you to piss on, and some broken junk. We'll need that too.'

'Not far to look,' he said. 'Just open your shed door and stand back.'

We glared loathing at each other across the three-foot abyss.

'Russians wouldn't have shit like this,' he snarled. 'Why don't you grow vegetables? You can't eat stones.'

'I can get vegetables in the shop. Anyway – there's no room.'

In the midst of my anger I knew he was right. It was a waste. Along with all his training, which he never once mentioned, all these skills mouldering away. I became increasingly obsessed with waste, but I held my corner over the garden. There was more amiss than a row of cabbages would fix.

I pulled out my antidote for the need to raise my voice.

'I'm going for a walk.'

'I'll come with you. We'll walk in your civilised country.'

'Only if you don't talk.'

My legacy from Morag – beyond the earrings and the apple-boxes crammed with matching pairs of ornaments and the knowledge that men are dirty creatures – is the urge to walk, fast and aimlessly, when I'm upset. Not for pleasure she walked once we'd moved to Glasgow, but to exhaust herself, lay ghosts, be excused from feeling. Like a demented gypsy she'd stride out, with me in tow, along the grey hard pavements, to Riddrie and beyond, walking, walking, walking.

We held no conversation on these frenetic pilgrimages to streets where the tenements had run out and there were proper houses, with small gardens and green-painted gates and rows of gladioli or crysanths; flowers of ritual. At twilight we'd set out, after her work, when the house lights were being switched on. Looking into the rooms was like watching a silent film.

That's what drew her, the uncurtained windows where we could observe a family round a table or beside a fire watching TV. We spied on other people's cosy and contained existences; we were hungry ghosts. It wasn't unusual for one of the group to rise suddenly and draw the curtains, as if the intensity of Morag's stare had entered the room, a sudden draught of cold air on the back of a neck.

I still can't catch the damp-earth, funeral scent of crysanths without re-living the panic of imagining a gesticulating man, an Alsatian dog released to chase us.

'Nuts,' Frank would say. 'Your mother's flipped. Gaga. Country folk don't go walks for the hell of it. That's a townie's trick.'

She was still beautiful in these days, coming in out of the mirk like a dark flame, before her face took on the petted, embittered look that marred it long before the cancer.

'What's with the hairdo and the makeup?' Frank'd ask her. 'Done up like a tuppeny whore. Why try to look like that if you don't want a man to get hard for you?'

She lived her entire life through trashy novels and TV and other peoples' windows, and I know less about her past than I do about the characters in her soap operas, for she hadn't such a well-written script. My mother's life has come down to me in snippets from her sister.

I've wondered, since, if she still walked after I'd left, all alone down darkening streets. Did the houses know, the final time she passed? There'll be streets I've walked, the back alleys of Funchal; the palm-shaded paths inside the Kasbah of Rabat, a tranquil side-street in the Musicians' Quarter of Nice, the Nevsky Prospekt - that I've already passed down for the last time, people I've said goodbye to casually, without realising the finality.

'Max,' I said. 'Please, let's not fight any more.'

CHAPTER TWELVE

After the cello joined the family, it had to visit Carla too. Purely by chance I'd noticed it, discreetly sandwiched between Dalmatian puppies and upholstery cleaning services in the Scotsman classifieds. I'd assumed superior instruments changed hands exclusively through dealers. I'd already asked timidly at one of those, and blanched at the figure mentioned. 'You did say a professional instrument, madam?' Cheapskate, bag lady.

The advert didn't specify price, merely a maker's name which was meaningless to me. I called from work and hated Marjorie Adam at first hearing. She suffers from what people who've never been to Edinburgh recognise as a Morningside accent. Coffee mornings and bridge. I could picture her. The type to have a lap dog and chintz-covered furniture and a little woman who comes in to do.

'You're not another dealer?' she asked frostily. The cello had been her brother's. He'd been dead for two years and she'd finally accepted he wasn't coming back to collect it.

'An instrument of this calibre needs to be played,' she said.

I cleared my throat. 'I'm not the musician. It's my husband. We can't afford commercial prices.' I expected her to hang up.

'Your husband is a young musician, starting out?'

'Quite young. He has no work at all at the moment. And no instrument.'

'He's properly trained?'

134

Open College of the Arts, I was tempted to say, a whole year on the postal course.

'He studied at the Leningrad – St Petersburg – Conservatory.' You've heard of that, bitch? Rimsky-Korsakov? Shostakovich? Tchaikovsky?

'Ah, he's Russian?' The lift in her voice pruned at least fifteen years off her age.

So I wasn't the only obsessive in Scotland.

'Why don't you bring him to see it?'

Let her see him, to be more accurate, but perhaps there was no harm in that. The address confirmed my suspicions. Posh retirement flats, that part of the Grange - snobs' paradise. I hadn't realised any of the original houses remained inviolate. Max hadn't been in Edinburgh long enough to lose his innocence, so he was unfazed by the drawing room the size of a tennis court, the plethora of Chinese porcelain, the paintings.

But my prejudices concerning the woman herself hadn't been entirely accurate. Tall and dapper, with what you'd call a military bearing; white hair cut in a severe bob, blindingly smart trouser suit. Deaf enough to need a hearing aid, too bloody-minded to wear one. Just as long as everyone could hear her. Once upon a time, she'd been Reader in the School of Oriental Studies at London University.

Marjorie took to my husband from the first moment. He had eyes for nothing but the cello. It leant primly against its stand, unmarred by speck of dust or finger-mark. Max gazed at it adoringly.

'A Ruggieri. I've never seen such a beautiful instrument. As for playing one... It must be worth....' He rolled his eyes sideways; I recognised he was mentally converting roubles to sterling. 'Holy God!'

I felt the room spin. 'The bow too,' he said. 'It's so beautiful I could weep.'

I could see the tears glittering under his lashes, but Marjorie didn't avert her eyes tactfully. Perhaps she was used to foreign temperaments where nothing intrudes between a feeling and its expression.

'I'm sorry, we're wasting your time, Miss Adam,' I said.

'Please – will you play a little for me?'

He adjusted the spike, drew the instrument into his arms in the way that would always leave me jealous, and ran the bow over the strings.

'I'm afraid it's quite out of tune,' Marjorie Adam said.

'And I'm quite out of practice. I haven't played for over a year.'

He turned pegs deftly, tried a few arpeggios before beginning to play in earnest. I was sure I was dreaming; the opulent house, my Maksim turning out to be a magician as well as an angel. It was, after all, a clump of horsehair applied to a grotesquely expensive wooden box. Pandora's box. The last item left in that was hope.

He looked up at me shyly, from beneath wet lashes. He wanted to please me, though I knew I should have been lying on the floor, kissing his feet. But after a few moments he stopped, swore at himself. 'Never have I needed practice so much!'

It had been a mistake after all. Marjorie Adam was studying me curiously; I forced the corners of my mouth up, but she wasn't fooled. 'He plays well. As skilfully as I've heard in long enough, if it's true that he's a little rusty.'

'So he should be able to find work?'

'As easily as any other classically trained musician nowadays. Not that that's much consolation. Of course, my brother was a banker. He didn't play professionally.'

She and Max launched into a discussion of composers I hadn't heard of, and I'd never seen him so animated. Tcherepnin. A fellow-graduate and a fellow-countryman who'd escaped in the opposite direction from most and gone native in China.

Marjorie produced a file of sheet music. 'Bright Sheng', she said. What's that? Fifty-second hexagram in the I Ching? Apparently not. A very young, very new Chinese composer who uses a lot of traditional material. Why had I smuggled a Russian all the way to Edinburgh to have him learn Chinese fiddle tunes transposed for the cello? I suspected Marjorie was the type who collects obscure composers the way her grandmother might have collected butterflies.

Wrong again. Her great and abiding god turned out to be Bach. And not even CPE, at that, but JS.

'I'm sorry. I'm afraid we're wasting your time,' I repeated. 'We couldn't afford this cello.'

'Stockbridge isn't far,' she said, watching Max's face. 'If I were to lend it to you, would you come here to play for me?'

He looked at me pleadingly. My mind was still running on the bloated state of my overdraft. I couldn't take in what this woman was offering.

'It would be payment enough to hear it played again,' Marjorie Adam said.

At least one of us managed to appear sufficiently grateful. 'You could have sounded more enthusiastic,' Max said once we left. 'And why did you tell her I'm Russian?'

'Sorry - should I have told her you're a Glaswegian with a speech defect?'

'You know what I mean. Anyway - I'm not really. I'm a mongrel. I told you that before. But what harm can it do if I play this lovely instrument?'

'I'm not delirious about the idea of you traipsing back and forth manhandling a cello that's worth as much as some people pay for a house.'

'I won't lose it.'

'It makes you a little conspicuous.' Getting it into the back of the Peugeot made both of us conspicuous.

'You could put a cat-collar on me, with my name on it. If I stray off you can put an advert in the paper. "Lost, between Grange and Stockbridge mid-July, tall thin man, answers to Max, may be timid." Would you offer a reward, Serena?'

'I bet the immigration people offer a reward.' Bite my tongue.

'We have to sort it out. The worst they can do is keep us apart for a while,' he said. 'Better now than later. Get it over with, so we can go on with our lives. It can't be so bad as we've imagined. This isn't Russia. Please God I haven't got you into trouble too.'

'But what if they sent you back after all?'

'You'll come with me. God put us in each other's paths to be together. If it comes to that, we'll go to my mother in Kiev, start a new life.'

Too many mentions of God for an atheist.

'It's not been long enough yet. Leave it another few weeks, so they can't say you only married to come here.'

I hated that cello from the start. The damn thing sneered at me. A Věstonice Venus, with etiolated neck and generous childbearing hips. I couldn't abide watching Maksim in its company. It was as painful as imagining him enjoying another woman. Secretly I christened it Katya-Two.

It's a man's instrument. Women shouldn't play them, evening dresses notwithstanding. I always used to avert my eyes when they showed a shot of the Blessed Jacqueline, with her skirt hitched up and her knees spread in anticipation of sexual congress with a hippopotamus. It possesses the player. Cellists have nothing left over to give humans.

It was meant to be the balm, his music, not a further irritant. But Max adored the damn creature immoderately. 'When I play,' he said, his eyes glittering like a lover's, 'my hands are filled with fire. I can see them glowing, and all the veins picked out the way they are when you shine a torch against the palm. Like a Kirlian photograph. The music beats in my blood. I am filled with ecstasy.'

Then, just as suddenly, he'd be weeping with frustration at his ineptitude. He practised until the fingertips of his left hand were almost raw.

'Harpists used to draw a red-hot poker across to callous the skin,' he said. 'I can understand why.'

My flesh crept at the idea. 'Don't you dare try any fancy tricks with pokers while I'm out.' I dabbed his fingers with surgical spirit, while he winced and complained that it stung. Red-hot pokers indeed. I resolved to write a book called *Surgical Spirit for the Soul*, make my fortune so that Katya-Two could be all his.

I tried harder than ever to understand his world of composers I hadn't heard of. My own pedestrian tastes in music gave me guilt-pangs. I'd hidden my CDs as soon as he was in the house. My saving grace

– in his eyes, never in Fergus's - was my penchant for modern jazz. Even then, there was nothing clever or educated in my interest. I love the mystery of it rather than the virtuosity; the musician as shaman. I grew optimistic that Jan Garbarek would save my marriage. Max should have been a jazz player. It would have suited his temperament. 'That was the only one of Stalin's purges that didn't succeed,' he'd tell me, 'he couldn't kill jazz, because it speaks to the soul. Even camp commandants have souls.'

Max and Carla binged on playing Ravel sonatas while I sat swallowing bile and wondering how to keep the tears from showing. Carla glowed like a de Vianne lamp; her fingernails exuding a tawny luminescence as she flashed her eyes in gypsy-in-silent- film mode and hollered and whooped as if she was having an orgasm. The way the sounds of violin and cello blended was so sexy I could scarcely bear it. On one occasion she roped in a perjink Welsh pianist called Felix she'd picked up at the Usher Hall. Three's less intimate. I smirked to myself all the way home. I knew Max's prejudices better than I knew his history.

'It's all right in a pianist,' he said. 'He keeps his hands where I can see them.'

Ravel left me cold. I favoured cool and orderly northern themes, like the piece they practised over and over, music as delicate as frost forming on a windowpane, twisting a knife in my guts.

'What's that?' I asked Max huskily.

'*Spiegel im Spiegel,*' he said eagerly. 'It pleases you? Arvo Pärt. Estonian composer. That's the last thing he composed before he left to live in the West. His was forbidden music when I was young. He's familiar with exile and homesickness.'

'Because of your lot, presumably?'

He gave a wry smile. 'Because of my lot.'

Vile of me. He'd played it for me, after all.

'Are you so homesick as all that, Maksim?' I asked him on the way home.

'At times. Don't look hurt. It's inevitable I should miss it. I'd scarcely been out of Petersburg in my life.'

He used to say at first we'd take our children there, to see where he grew up, but he never mentioned it any more. A generation earlier and he could have been sent to the Gulag for playing that music he loved so much or for trying to buy the score. Roddy's pals could have written petitions on his behalf. And yet Maksim was nostalgic for it, he preferred his homesick music to Bach. Nostalgie de boue.

He'd sniff the air like a deer, and say: 'Autumn's on its way.' And I knew he was dreaming of St Petersburg, with rain cascading over the pavements from drainpipes that end half a metre up, mud everywhere, buses and trams and trains that reek of damp clothing and hot bodies and houses with too few washing facilities. Perhaps if you don't have to struggle to live, the spirit is sapped. Max found Edinburgh wanting.

'The people here have no sensibilities,' he announced. 'How many of them ever actually looked at a tree? They see any scrap of ground as a building-plot. Look at all the gardens sold to put houses in. Don't they want to have growing things? And look at the houses they put up. They're not homes. That's the only reason you love your house, Serena, because it's worth more than you paid for it.'

We have no culture either, apparently. I'd taken him to Glasgow, to see where I grew up and where I was educated. The underground stations failed to please. And no point in trying to tell him there's anywhere in Edinburgh that counts as a museum.

'I'm lucky,' he said. 'My grandparents were peasants, but they had more culture than that. And they were wise, spiritual people. I didn't grow up believing in nothing. Not like my mother, or your Scottish people who don't trouble to speak their own language correctly. "I should have went there," they say. Why am I worrying? What can you expect in a country where books cost more than people can afford? It's as bad at home now. Maybe if I stay here I'll forget my native tongue.' He bowed his head.

'Let's speak Russian all the time at home then,' I said. 'We'll make believe, like the ones who ended up in Paris and Nice, terribly patriotic and nostalgic and Bohemian. We'll get a samovar.'

Max pretended to laugh, but he kept his face buried in my hair. 'It is my homeland,' he said. 'Even the chaos that's Russia now, I feel the loss.'

'You preferred Communism?' I wanted to understand, even if it meant Frank Stuart had been right.

'Jesus, no. But what's here is no better, and what's at home now. There must be another way. We want freedom to tell all the politicians to go fuck their mothers. It wasn't as bad as they say, you know, the old system. We had education, a health service, yours isn't such hot shit, I can tell you. People had jobs at least, even cellists, I'd have been found a job, wouldn't need to have tried myself. But our problems won't be settled until they bury Lenin. Imagine. A nation where they

142

still queue up to see a stuffed corpse, as if it was a saint's relics.'

'You'd have hated it, not having your freedom.'

'When did Russians ever have that? But it was a game with rules, like chess except they kept changing while the game was on, so you had to be a skilful player. It was exciting. When I was ten I was more street-wise than the adults here. And our spirit was always free. Even in the camps. What use is freedom? It's poisoned my blood and left me twisted. You're wrong to trust me, Serena.'

Without rancour he said it; I put it down to guilt for having left. He'd watch TV reports on Russia with the same fascination people here had for the Gulf War. I averted my eyes because I can't avoid my share of blame. Zhenya was right - we huffed and we puffed and we blew their house down and left them to the wolves. Britain does that to her mental patients too, nowadays, and calls it care in the community.

'Maybe Russia will never be the same again,' I said, without thinking. 'Everyone who can is leaving now, all the ones who can afford it.'

'Russia is immortal. She will always rise again from her own ashes, like the firebird.'

I wish I had that sort of faith. My country will have an identity again, perhaps, but never a sex.

'Rats,' Max went on. 'They bleed the place dry then leave the sinking ship. Same as I did. And there are thousands more who bide their time, dreaming of finding a new Stalin.'

'He was a mass murderer. My father thought he was a saint.'

'At least he got the country up off its knees. Perhaps it's another Stalin we need after all. Another revolution. My country still has its hell to walk through. Who knows? People used to have beliefs. Why didn't you tell Carla we got married?' he added suddenly.

'I did – didn't I?'

'Don't lie. Maybe it's easy for you to forget. Perhaps you want me to do that too. Is that what you want? Fine. Plenty of other women, if I choose to forget.'

'Oh God, stop going on. I'm sure I told her. I'll call her tomorrow and make sure I did.'

That's when I began to keep my eye on my model husband, the neighbour-from-heaven. Men aren't made to be faithful.

The Colonies were built for sociable people. Outdoors there's a communality of living Max settled into as effortlessly as a cat on cushions. He knew more people than I ever had before; he had a fan club. He'd sit in the tiny garden, peeling potatoes for our meal, and people would greet him by name as they passed. I'd press my face to the glass, so I could marvel at his blond head, bent so earnestly over his work. He worked equally meticulously on everything he did, in total concentration. I envied him that facility in reaching the Zen state; I've not mastered it, ever. He's the gannet; I'm the petrel, skimming the tops.

He'd take Katya-Two outside occasionally to practise, and the whole neighbourhood would listen, creeping out silently as elves; he didn't resent that the way he resented being asked to play for my friends. He was making a special effort to avoid fighting with me. I felt suspicion growing on me like a second skin.

'You're so lucky,' the pretty red-haired girl from the next street along said to me, dreamy-eyed. I knew her by sight, never to speak to before. She sounded

144

Irish, and she was the only person I'd ever seen with truly green eyes. I didn't know her name. She had a small child, still in a pushchair.

'Maksim's so talented.' She pronounced his name carefully and correctly and wistfully. 'My husband can't do anything clever like playing an instrument.'

I winced. No other woman was allowed to call him by his full name. That was my privilege. To anyone else, he should just have been Max. And doubtless he knew her name, and her husband's, if there truly was a husband, and her child's. Must order in a few concealed video cameras.

Max always knew when I'd be at home; he kept a careful note of my shifts. Perhaps on the other days he didn't stop at the door when he lifted the pushchair up the steps for her. She was beautiful, in a soft blowsy way, with her tousled hair and her creamy skin, and she made no attempt to conceal her admiration for my husband.

I began to feel the cold more than usual. The nights were getting longer. I couldn't banish it from my imagination: Max with other women. 'That woman in the house with the yellow door – the red-haired girl – what's her child called?'

'The little boy? Charles. She's very particular about that. Not Charlie. Charles.'

'What does her husband do?'

'He works in the butcher's, round on the main street. You must know this. They've lived here five years, since they married.'

'I only know she's a neighbour. I was talking to her earlier today.' I watched him carefully for any signs of alarm. 'What's her name?'

'Bernadette. But she gets called Bernie. I think that's why she's so touchy with the child's name. You hadn't spoken to her before? She knows you.'

'I suppose I never see these people, with being out all day.'

'I would be out all day too if I could work at a proper job, I wouldn't have time to gossip to our neighbours. Then I'd be the same as you, I wouldn't have a life.'

The edge to his voice should have obviated the need of a knife for the tatties.

'I wasn't getting at you.'

'Always, always the tone you use, you're getting at me. I'm doing my best, Serena,' he said sadly. 'Isn't that good enough?'

He wasn't indulging in self-pity. I never knew anyone so little in thrall to that vice.

But he was watching too much TV for his own good. There'd been a Moslem spokesman on the previous night, demanding separate schools, maintaining they'd a right to run their own areas according to their own laws, a state within a state.

'Listen to that,' Max said. 'I don't want to alter this country. I don't want to look different or make my own rules. All I want is to blend in and be the same as everyone else. How come they get to stay? They can shout on TV demanding their rights. I have to hide, we have to pretend I don't exist. This isn't fair.' His voice shook with emotion.

I couldn't argue. No point in telling him again that he'd get sympathy because he looked more archetypically English than anyone else I knew - Rupert Brooke rather than Rudolf Nureyev.

'Your people still love to hate us. James Bond, the hero, always fighting the wicked Russians who want to destroy the world.'

'Och, that's just films. People don't think like that in real life.'

Not a few of my shipmates had been afraid to disembark in St Petersburg unless it was straight onto a bus.

'You'd be surprised. Anyway, everyone blames us for Chernobyl.'

'You were on our side in the war. '

'No one remembers the war. Not that one, anyway. The war people remember is the Russian demons battering hell out of Chechnya and Eastern Europe. All nations loathe us. You ever hear a Finn or a Pole on the subject, any of the Baltic nationals? The Georgians and Armenians as well, damn it. They blame us for the earthquakes. Even Zhenya's people hate us now. Even my own people hate the Russians.'

Maksim laid his head in his hands.

'Compassionate nation, yours. They love it when someone spends a fortune bringing home a stray animal. That was on TV. Some soldier brought back a dog from Bosnia. Probably give him a medal. He's a hero. I don't know why I believed it'd be easier for me in this country.'

Every evening he was home, Max would sit slumped in front of the set, watching in an indiscriminate torpor. Anything, just as long as it wasn't a historical documentary. 'History!' he'd sneer. 'Who wants to hear more lies they've made up about the past?' American cop dramas held a special fascination for him; he classified them as science fiction.

'They pretend there are poor people in America. That's nonsense. You've only to see the audience on the

147

Jerry Springer show. Like Christmas geese. No poor people.'

'As many as there are anywhere else.'

'As many as Russia? I don't think so. Even your commercials aren't for poor people. It's all expensive cars and confectionery. I have seen no adverts for things you need to live.'

Fergus has a theory that all the sweetie adverts are for women. 'We'll know we've reached the end of civilisation as we know it when they show us a bloke giving head to a Bounty Bar,' he says. 'Same goes for the soft-drink ads. The rot's set in when it's an audience of male voyeurs wincing and clutching their groins as he tilts back his head and slides his lips round the Diet Coke bottle.'

Max's viewing went beyond indiscriminate; it went as far as the soft porn junk late at night.

'How can you watch that trash?' I'd ask him, angry that his tastes could be so gross. 'There's no plot, no acting, only bare arses and silicon implants heaving in the air. That's not sexy.' And you get to see the women full frontal and a lot more and a lot longer than you get to see the men. That's the material that's made for male consumption.

Max's eyes would glitter, and he'd chew his beautiful nails, spoiling them. 'I like to remember what I'm missing. You grudge me this? You should watch too. You might get the hang of being a woman.'

That was too reminiscent of Learmonth's antics towards the end. The first time Fergus brought home one of the videos, I thought he'd done it for a joke. I know some women like porn, and it was only that - nothing kinky - but I could never take them seriously enough to find them arousing. I was more interested in figuring out how they'd conducted the auditions for the money shot. Plastic sheeting on the floor, presumably, and a white-coated steward running out with a tape measure and coloured markers, the same as for tossing the caber. It would have had Kinsey wetting himself. But Fergus would already be moving the coffee table out of the way. He made it plain he expected me to join in, there and then, in the middle of the sitting-room floor.

That was when I started taking the bread-knife to bed with me. He agreed to divorce me when he found out.

'What's sexy for you anyway?' said Max. 'A man with all his clothes on? You love nothing better than to get me going, but the minute my hand goes anywhere near my zip, you freak out. As for you undoing my pants! You'd sooner die, wouldn't you, though you know it'd really turn me on? You'd sooner die than make the first move on a man.'

That had been Donald John's first mistake, making me undo his trousers. If he hadn't frightened me so much in the first moments I might have kept my thoughts clear and my hand in my pocket. I'd wanted to confess to the police doctor, because she was kind to me, and gentle. But I was afraid she'd tell, even though she made Grannie wait outside the room (God alone knows where my mother was; not with me, anyway). And when she spoke to her afterwards, in a quiet voice, Grannie raised hers to say: 'He hadn't interfered with her then? The Lord be praised!', and turned to me to tell me I'd been lucky. The police doctor said sternly: 'Can I have a word with you in private, Mrs

MacKenzie?' But I knew there'd be no gentleness waiting for me at home.

CHAPTER THIRTEEN

I had to see Dee in secret, because Max hated her so much.

'He'd have been better off with you,' I said wistfully.

'No thanks. Why?'

Indecently large, self-regulated income; an enormous flat with high ceilinged rooms and good acoustics; a well-stocked liquor cabinet. An accommodating body and a clutch of eggs awaiting reprieve from the freezer.

'You like sex,' I said.

'Mmmm. He certainly has bedroom eyes. So what's the problem? You have a bedroom, I recall, and Fergus's multiple-orgy bed?'

'We have a bedroom each.'

It took her a moment to cotton on. 'Jesus H, Serena – you're not still singing from that hymn-sheet?'

When we were teenagers, she used to enjoy explaining the fiasco to my half of a double date. 'Och, she's like that. Some paedo frightened her when she was wee. She hasn't been the same since. It's not *you* Tom/Dick/Harry. I think you're gorgeous.'

But she's grown up a lot since those days. Become quite the psychoanalyst.

'In the unconscious everything's supposed to turn to its opposite,' she said. 'You should be an insatiable nympho. Trust you to be different. You just lead them on then kick up a fuss. Have you not read Eric Berne? "Rapo" personified, that's you.'

'Stick to your own trade,' I said. 'Crooked teeth are your province, not twisted minds, even if you have read a book.'

'Nonsense. Sex and dentistry have a lot in common. The plugging of a throbbing cavity for purposes of comfort and hygiene. Shall I go on? Shall I expand on the uses of thin rubber coverings during both? I don't know what you can do, Serena. See a shrink.'

'Been there. Got the tee shirt.'

The policewoman who gave me a bath after the doctor was finished with me was an attractive blonde, not unlike Dee. She washed my hair, let me use some of her rose-scented skin-cream, because I'd scratched my face on branches, then found an enormous tee shirt for me to wear. They needed to keep my clothes. She fastened a thin leather belt round my waist, and said: 'Aren't you smart! Wish I was as slim as you. Some chance.' And I wanted to put my arms round her neck and plead with her not to send me back to them, but to have me adopted instead.

Max had eased into a pattern of spending a couple of nights a week in pub called Colquhoun's down in Leith. Katya-Two couldn't keep him at home either. Then the couple of nights stretched to three and four, and he'd come in smelling of whisky, full of artificial love, and try to pull me close, to make me notice him at last. It worked. I'd slap him as hard as I could. He derived satisfaction from that, because he'd won. He'd made me do it. After that he'd either laugh or weep, and how was I to cope with that?

'When life's too much, drinking's the only honest act,' he'd say. I opened my eyes to the fact Max was a drunk. I couldn't claim it was a surprise. That's why they chose Christianity over Islam, because they couldn't do without it. Distilling was just another Western import, like VD and Big Macs.

When the alcohol possessed him, he wasn't Max any more. He was a bumbling idiot, full of false bonhomie, grinning inanely. He'd turned into my father. Frank was just the same – didn't appreciate seeing a woman drinking. Boozing is men's business, same as leaving the house like a shit-heap. Max wouldn't drink in Stockbridge either, that's why he walked to Leith.

'To drink with real people,' he said. 'Real men with real lives and rough hands. Not the beautiful people who work in the media, or in advertising, or in selling houses to other fools like themselves. Posers with their brains in their back pockets. Arse-holes with mobile phones – that's good, isn't it?'

He'd the trick of swallowing air and farting, as competently as any school-kid. He'd produce a hum-dinger, then pretend he was answering it. It was hysterical. It made me sore to hold in the laughter, but I wouldn't give him that satisfaction.

Sometimes a Russian ship would be docked at Leith and he'd come home reeking of foreign tobacco. I'd start in on him again till I knew he was wishing he'd stayed on board and sailed all the way to Archangel. Did he guess that more than once I wished it too, in my heart?

I grew desperate with loneliness, because by then I was afraid of Carla.

Only once I tried the experiment of taking Max to one of Anita's parties. Whatever her shortcomings, she's knowledgeable about real music, his type of music. He was on edge the entire evening. He sipped expensive white wine as if it was hemlock, and threw a tantrum on the way home.

'They despise me. I felt humiliated. Why should I associate with people like these? They all talk to me slowly and carefully as if I don't fucking well understand English.'

'Oh crap, they're being polite, trying to make conversation. More than you do.'

'They treat me as if I'm something dangerous and smelly that needs to be kept on a leash. I'll give them animal. I'll show them I can bite.'

It wasn't their fault. Stress is contagious.

'You're so false when you're with them,' he said, 'your voice changes, your accent. I hate it. I keep looking to see where the camera is. Why can't you be yourself? The way you were in Russia. Spontaneous and loving. That's the person I thought I was running away with, not some actress who only cares about impressing pricks like these. You changed the minute you stepped on the train back to this place. You turned into my mother. Why did you stop being sweet and feminine? I liked you better when we were travelling through the forest together.'

I liked me more then too.

'"In Russia" was about three days,' I said. 'You changed too. You've stopped being brave and independent. You're a spoilt, wheenging child.'

I felt real fear then. I'd known I had to let him have his turn first. That's manners. But, oh God, when we both started –

'Well, go to their parties on your own,' Max yelled. 'The tall man, the English one, the one with a laugh like Founder's Day in the mental home – he's in love with you anyway. He doesn't want me there.'

154

'Nick? Don't be daft. He's happily married. You met his wife. They have a young baby.'

'Babies you get from screwing at the wrong time of month. Happy doesn't come into it. What is it he calls her - "Cleh"? What name's that?'

'Claire.'

'Right. The 'r' is silent, as in asshole. He's in love with you. Doesn't trouble to hide it when he looks at you. You think he says this too – "Don't be foolish, Cleh, Serena's a happily married woman?" '

No. He thinks I'm a happily divorced one with a live-in lover. 'You make it bloody impossible for me to work with them,' I yelled. 'As if it wasn't bad enough already. I need my job.'

'Oh yes, married to a shiftless lout like me, who can't support you, you don't half.'

It was easier to control if I invited a few of them to our house, but no more fun. Social evenings as relaxing as walking barefoot on broken glass. The first time, I made the mistake of asking him to play for them. He wouldn't embarrass me by refusing though I swear I could hear his teeth grinding above the sound of the cello. And he let me have it afterwards. I never met a performance artist who so loathed having an audience.

Other evenings he'd have me in stitches after they'd all left, for he's a superlative mimic, specially of bullshitters. He could produce a very convincing version of me. A squeaky voice and a wee bum-wiggle; that was Serena-on-her-high-horse. I bet he was popular with his drinking pals.

And I was less than overjoyed when I found he wasn't always such a coy performer. He admitted he'd been out busking with three other musicians at the top of the Mound. 'It's brilliant. You should have heard the audience. Didn't want to let us stop. They say when the Festival starts, we can be on the sound stage in the gardens.'

And I yelled and nagged and swore and wouldn't let myself be the tiniest bit pleased.

'At least they're friendly. I can jingle my coins in my pocket. My pocket money. Big joke, eh? Serena's money. They treat me like a man. They don't know I'm the lodger in Serena's wonderful loveless house and I get to sleep in her husband's bed.'

The guilt I felt was too painful, so I nagged him over trivialities instead. I nagged him over leaving his clothes lying about, and burning food in the frying pan so that all the clean washing smelt of it. I nagged him over the size of his feet.

'For Christ's sake, Max must you leave your shoes cluttering up the floor?'

There was so little space in our hallway at the foot of the stairs, and you can't tuck size elevens in a corner. He didn't do it to annoy me. Ever since he could walk, ever since he'd worn shoes he'd taken them off as soon as he entered the house. Dreadfully bad manners to do otherwise. He believes the Scots are filthy people.

'You know I don't like to wear my outdoor shoes in the house.'

'Do you think I want this to be the first part of my home people lay eyes on, your bloody shoes?'

'The streets of Edinburgh aren't exactly clean, Serena. Maybe you prefer that I should tramp dog-shit through the house?'

'You could watch where you walk, or wipe your feet.'

'I'm hot for you,' he yelled, ' I desire you, I want to make babies with you, I want to have you squirm with pleasure in my arms. I'm prepared to wait till you feel ready for that. But all you care about is where I put my shoes.' He hurled them up the stairs so hard he took a chunk out of the plaster.

'Your habits are disgusting. You pee with the bathroom door open. When you bother to do it indoors. You think I want to watch that?'

'I am like some pet you bought on impulse,' he said. 'Oh dear, it's so difficult to house-train it, too much effort. And it costs so much to feed. You could take me back for a refund. Pity the receipt's in Russian.'

'No, with a pet there's always the Cat and Dog Home as a last resort.'

Next day I bought a small wooden shoe rack that fitted on the wall. Max smiled to himself when he saw it. It became a standing joke with anyone who visited us.

'Serena's mosque,' they'd say. 'Where do we perform our ablutions?'

But it was like having a mouth ulcer you can't keep your tongue off. 'It'd help if you'd just try to be tidy. And clean the bloody toilet when you've got shit all over it,' I said.

'Why should I do women's work?' He tossed his head in that petulant way he has. 'The hell with it. I'm the man in the house. I shouldn't have to take orders, put your shoes there, don't light your disgusting cigarettes here. You told me this is my house. In my house I do what I want.'

He picked a hazelnut from the bowl and deliberately and loudly cracked it with his teeth, to see if I'd rise to the bait the way I'd done at first, screeching at him: 'Use the nutcrackers.' 'What did God give us

157

teeth for?' He cracked more and more, specifically to annoy me now. He'd take crown tops off beer bottles the same way. 'You want me to thank you? I came with you, didn't I? You thank me. Come on, bitch, tell me how ungrateful I am. How you rescued me from starving in the gutter.'

'I've never said that. But you weren't far off it, were you? Starving. I could tell from looking you never had enough to eat.'

'I wasn't like all your lot. You can tell from looking at the people in the street here they've had too much to eat.'

'Well at least here you don't normally see a doctor's child wandering round with a wee sign on his forehead saying "feed me".'

'Look at our literature, our art, our music. Nothing you have here can hold a candle to it. You are the paupers. I am proud to be Russian.'

These were the spine-tingling moments when I thought he meant to thump me. But he'd pull his irritating trick of becoming calm. 'We're too much in each others' company. You need some woman-friend you can let this all out with.'

'I used to have some of these, before you scared some off with your abuse and seduced the others. And you've been using my deodorant again. You always leave the top off and your disgusting hairs stuck to it.'

Oh hell, hell, hell. I brought him home to be kind to him and look after him. When did Act Two begin? I hadn't read Mars and Venus. I always made the mistake of trying to follow him when he fled to the cave. 'I don't mean to go on at you. But it's not really quarrelling, is it? Squabbling. It's all about small things. We see eye to eye on the big issues.'

'Couples get divorced over how they squeeze the toothpaste, Serena, not over their philosophy of life.'

CHAPTER FOURTEEN

Our Colonies gardens are beautiful in the twilight, when the sky's sucked the colour from the flowers because it's jealous; an arty soft-focus sepia-tint, rose-fragranced vignette. I'd left the windows open to let the last breaths of late-August warmth come in. Dougal had cried off; new students to be processed. Maksim and Carla were lingering outside. When I left they were dismembering Bartok and half of me wanted to strain to hear if the topic was still the rudiments and theory of music.

They'd lowered their voices, and from my bedroom it sounded like the murmur of doves. They were laughing too much and too low. Carla's laugh always sounds as if she's been told a particularly filthy joke. I couldn't think of an excuse to intrude in my own garden, but the temptation to look was irresistible; I stood well to the side of the window, in case they saw me. Always the same, the wee girl with her nose pressed against the glass, burning with envy. I despised myself.

So sad. I'd thought I'd be the one lingering in the scented dim light with him, giggling and licking scented raindrops off the neighbour's rose-petals, or sipping wine and sharing secrets. Between Carla and Max there was the rapport that's called body chemistry.

Fergus maintains chemistry doesn't come into it. 'Physics,' he says, 'volume, friction, generation of heat. Probably a dash of biology too. You're all searching for the one with the biggest antlers in the hope he'll have an enormous cock and a high sperm-count.'

160

They weren't touching, though they were sitting close, still drinking. I don't know what I meant to do if they'd been in a clinch, or if I hadn't been able to see them at all. I padded aimlessly into the kitchen, away from the sound of that sexy giggling.

'Serena? Carla's leaving now. Aren't you going to say cheerio?' Max pranced into the room, bright-eyed, his face flushed from the wine.

'I'd gone to bed.'

'Why – aren't you feeling well?' He went to the sink and began rinsing glasses.

'Not particularly, as a matter of fact.'

Carla strode in. She doesn't knock. 'You deserted me, left me with only this boy to entertain me. Max, what are you thinking of? Serena's all ready for bed, it's rude to keep a lady waiting.'

'He seemed to be doing all right. I could hear the pair of you braying like jackals.'

She pulled a face and laid a cool, heavily ringed hand on my forehead, a slender unshod foot on top of my bare one. 'You have a slight temperature but your feet are like ice-blocks. Max, take her upstairs at once and comfort her.'

'Don't get too close in case I'm coming down with something. He can have my cuddle as well as his own.'

She was never one to give a quick squeeze. 'Off you go then, and warm the sheets for your man while he drives my car backwards up this damn street.'

I experienced a strong but fleeting urge to ring the politzei and report her as a drunk driver.

Maksim laid his hands on my shoulders when he came in. 'Are you really feeling ill?'

'What were you talking about?' I couldn't prevent the catch in my voice. I wanted a cuddle to make me warm, but he gave me a quick peck on the cheek, then held me at arm's length.

I turned away and started to dry the glasses, mechanically. She used to be my friend, I thought. That too you've stolen.

'Didn't you want me to keep her outside?'

'I don't know why you had to canoodle in the dark with her.'

'Canoodle! What kind of word is that? You think I was screwing her? You claimed you had work to do. I thought you wouldn't want to be disturbed. You said you wanted peace and quiet.'

'That was Dougal.'

'My God, I believe you're jealous.'

'You love it, don't you, the way she leans across you shaking her maracas in your face.'

'The only thrill I get. You never do that do you? Of course, I don't see what you get up to with the men at work. Or your husband.' He selected an apple from the bowl.

One of the four survivors from my set of Edinburgh crystal glasses shattered on the floor. He couldn't possibly know. Anyway, all I'd done was let Fergus kiss me a bit harder than he should when I'd run into him in an empty studio that day. It wasn't as if anything had happened. Max had just struck lucky with a multi-purpose throwaway accusation.

'We're seeing far too much of Dougal and Carla,' I said. 'Too dependant.'

Co-dependants. Willing victims. Collaborators.

'All right, so we'll see more people. It's because you don't invite others.'

'I'm fed up with being the only one who provides friends for company. It's like having to continually think what other people want to eat.'

162

He shrugged and went on eating his apple. 'That's hardly my fault. If we'd stayed in Russia it would be the same. You'd be complaining that it was always my friends.'

I shivered. It wasn't only the night air.

CHAPTER FIFTEEN

I spied on Max more and more. I ogled him from behind the curtain, like a dirty old woman. I watched his bare back as he set up two chairs as a makeshift sawhorse in the garden and began to saw the wood to make new shelves for the bathroom. His back was the most beautiful, erotic object conceivable. It gave me a stomach cramp to see how the muscles rippled beneath the skin as smoothly as an animal's. He'd been training hard, since he found he could use the community centre gym for three pounds a session. He said musicians have to be as well-honed as dancers.

He was the fittest man I've known, and the cleanest, for despite Roddy's obsession with washing, he never seemed wholesome. Because Max couldn't go to the sauna every week, he'd rub himself all over with rough salt, and rinse it off in a cold shower. Afterwards I could feel the heat of his body across the room and his skin was immaculate; good enough to eat.

He'd found an old carpenter's belt in the shed. I'd no idea where it had come from, for Fergus never messed with wood and nails. My new man laboured with utter concentration. He'd never find it demeaning to work with his hands, whether he was sawing and shaping wood or playing Bach.

The belt was too big; it had slipped down over his hip-bone at one side, the worn leather obscenely sexy against the creamy skin at the other. I knew exactly what he was up to. The effect on me wasn't uncalculated. Rough trade indeed.

I used to while away the hours of Peter Mackenzie's sermons day-dreaming about Jesus, and in my imagination, that's how he looked. I never understood why the school bibles showed him as another wimp in a girl's nightie. He must have looked the way Maksim did then, as he worked alongside Joseph and James, sawing and planing and shaping timber, his hair tied back, his elegant, narrow, Byzantine-icon face beaded with sweat, a fine film of dust lying across his arms and shoulders. A handsome, muscular, sexy working man, with sticky resin on his fingers, and the sharp, hot scent of fresh-cut wood on his skin.

He'd a temper too, by the sound of it, flinging the money-changers out of the temple, and all their gear after them. I bet he swore at them. He knocked around with a bunch of fishermen after all. Not noted for their delicate language. A hard edge to him.

Zinging with life, he'd have been, to attract the attention of a woman like Mary Magdalene. She was no cheap tart, she was seriously stylish, and she'd not have wasted her time or her ointment on a lesser man. He had beautiful feet, I daresay, long-toed and elegant Giotto painted hem, just like Max's, and the Magdalene would have massaged the oils into them languorously, bending her head so that her lips and her breast and her arms were drowned in her long, dim hair.

And he'd have sent the disciples away as she began to kiss his toes, and drawn her head up to look in her eyes. 'Mary, Mary, Mary! What are you doing?'

And the tree he'd be nailed to still growing green in a wood like Ollasdale.

Ursula was at my side, steadying me. I'd forgotten I'd invited her for coffee.

'Are you ill? You turned quite faint. You're very flushed. Sit down. I'll make the coffee. Are you maybe pregnant?'

Not that, certainly. A former nurse should know pregnant women stopped falling in a swoon when Victoria died. And not the type of illness a hot drink would cure.

I realised I was losing my mind. Peter Mackenzie's flesh and blood, keeling over from having erotic thoughts about JC. Soon, soon, I thought, I need to take Max to Aunt Peigi's house, where we'll be laid together to sleep in the same bed as a matter of course.

'Your thermostat's faulty, he'd yelled at me that morning. 'You start to get hot, then alarm bells ring and the freezer kicks in. That's not how it's supposed to work. You need to come to the boil, let it happen, and cool down slowly, slowly, slowly. It's exquisite. You have to get this fixed. For yourself. I'm not asking you to change only for me.'

I pushed him away. 'The Australian chakra woman I went to said my second chakra's blocked. About as useful an image as yours. If I knew how to unblock my sodding chakras, do you think I wouldn't?'

'Do you think sex is shameful? Maybe it's because your grandfather was a religious freak.'

And I couldn't tell him, no it's not that. It's just that if I let my body off the leash of my mind, maybe I have to admit that Granda was right, and I did know why Donald John took me to the woods late in an afternoon in July.

'You have to love me first,' I said.

He sighed. 'It doesn't happen that way. Love's not like a thunderbolt. It's like a potato. You have to bury it deep and wait patiently to see what you get when the shoots come up.'

'That's not very romantic.'

'I'm not romantic. I'm a pragmatist. And I'm a man. I have urges, and I need an outlet for them.'

'It's good for you,' I said. 'Freud would have said that's what makes you creative. You can sublimate it all in your music. You should be thanking me. Women have the raw deal. We don't have semen to conserve. If we had, we wouldn't waste it and spill it around indiscriminately.'

'Fuck Freud. What did he know? I never went without it for so long in my life. It's bloody well bad for me.'

Max would watch wistfully as I drove off to work. He loves driving as much as I hate it, and he's the best driver I've ever known, insouciant, skilful, and precise. But he hadn't a valid licence either; he'd have had to fill in forms. So though I'd let him back the Peugeot up the street out of gridlock hell, if we had to travel together he'd sit hunched beside me like a sullen child. 'You're the boss,' he'd say in that petted tone that pronounced me guilty. 'You can drive your car.'

As if that made it all right. As if any of us extract any benefit other than money from work. Though we all pretend we have interesting, glamorous lives, they're as hollow and prickly and desolate as the sea urchin shells on my mantelpiece. Nick with his falcons, Anita with her flute; their lives are plays they act in. Peigi says it's the same in any workplace, but I know it's never as bad. The people I work with have a higher-than-average need to believe in their own importance. That's why they're there.

167

Long before, I'd realised they'd stop talking when I came into the room. In an imperceptible way I'd been found wanting: not our type. Some days it made me angry. More often I had to blink back the tears and fight the urge to run away, drive in the other direction and keep going and have no more times when Anita would ignore me when someone important was being shown round and introduced.

It used to amaze me to read reports of journalists locked away, tortured, or killed for resisting authoritarian regimes. In Albion you'd be trampled in the rush to volunteer as informers.

But I was trapped like a moth in a lampshade. Maksim had a life, and I didn't. He wasted little time on self-pity. He shopped for our food, and was amazed that he never had to stand in queues. He tried to cook for me. He tried – unsuccessfully - to keep the place as clean as I claimed to like. He glowered at the tiny patch of earth that was to have kept us in vegetables. He showed unhealthy interest in the winos on the Mile.

'They drink meths?'

'God knows. Presumably not, these days.'

'Meths, perfume, boot polish on bread. Gorbachev made us experimental. And you can distil vodka from *anything*.'

By the end of August we'd both lost hope, though I forbade myself the thought it'd be a relief to come home and find him vanished, departed, deported, whatever.

'Play me records of some of your Gaelic music,' he said sadly. 'I want to hear some new tunes. I want to understand your culture. It has to be mine now too.'

I put on the CD of Karen Matheson singing *Am Buachaille Bàn*, and watched his face. Without prompting, he latched onto that. 'Don't explain to me what the words mean,' he said. 'I want to have the melody pure in my head.'

Perhaps, for him, I might have sung it again one day. How strange that nearly half a lifetime ago the set piece that won me my medal and my fifteen minutes of fame was the ultimate love-song for a fair-haired man.

'I wish I could play some instrument,' I said. 'It'd be good to share.'

'A musician needs an audience. That's what you can do best for me, be my audience. I play only for you, no one else in the world, because you're the one who can hear me properly.'

'We'd understand each other better.'

'That'll come. I need you to listen to me, as much as I need to play.'

However, I began to regret not getting rid of my old piano before he'd had the chance to tune it. No sanctuary even in my own home.

'You don't mind that I play music with Carla?' he said, casually. The pair of them had had the front off it and twiddled some pegs and had it more or less in tune. 'Carla'. It was a love-word in his husky, throaty voice that was not unlike hers, the rolled 'r' and the rich vowel-sounds. 'Carla'. A caress. Tigers purring after mating.

I tried to smile.

He put his arms round me. 'It's so pleasant to work with another musician again. She's good, it'll help me improve.'

He'd spent half the evening with his face down another woman's cleavage. I wanted him to want to be sexy with me. He held me for a few moments, but he didn't kiss me, and I hadn't the old excuse to push him away.

169

He smiled to himself 'It's OK,' he said. 'I still want you. But it's amazing what will-power can achieve.'

'I think Carla wants you.'

'She has Dougal to console her.' He strolled over to the window and gazed into the darkness.

'I don't know why Carla puts up with him,' I said. 'She's so attractive – she could have any man.'

He turned back to me, with a sigh. 'People stay together for strange reasons. I'm not terribly highly-sexed, by the way.'

He opened his arms to me, and I held him tight, to avoid the pain in his eyes. There were worse demons than the immigration authorities we still had to face.

'Let's go away this weekend,' he said, his mouth against my neck. 'I have somewhere I have to go tomorrow morning, but after that let's go somewhere, just the two of us. You have a tent in the shed – did you even know you had that? We could go to the seaside, camp out.'

'I'd love that. But let's wait till next weekend, when we have both days.'

'We have to make this work,' he said. 'We must make an effort.'

Perhaps he was right. My thoughts had been tending in the opposite direction recently. One of the things that held me back was the thought of admitting Fergus had been right all along.

'Come with me then,' Max said next morning.

He'd to meet someone at an address in the Old Town. He had a map sketched on the back of an envelope.

'You'll easily find it without me,' I said.

'This is a big moment for me, I want you to be there. Aren't you interested?'

'Tell me what it is you're doing.'

'Playing music. This place is supposed to be a recording studio. I have a friend who works in the music industry. He's set this up.'

'Which friend?'

'Johnser. John Seaton. You'll meet him today.'

It was through a pend in one of the un-gentrified segments of the Canongate, where the steep sunlight of August's too harsh for the lean streets. The acrid smell of horseshit hung in the air. There have been no horses there for years. The smell was trapped with all the other ghosts in the dead stones, all the little lost drummer boys the Ghost Tours guides scare the tourists with.

But it wasn't bad once we were inside. Johnser sat me down beside him at the mixing-desks, and then Max and Katya-Two were ensconced in the small glass booth.

The tune; so familiar, and yet so unfamiliar.

'He's brilliant, isn't he?' said Johnser. 'It sounds genuine. Traditional, like. Sounds as if it should have words.'

It took me a minute to compose myself. 'It does,' I said. 'It's a Gaelic love song. It's about a fair-haired man.'

'Could be about Max then.'

I hope not. The one in the song toddles off and leaves her.

What a deadly sickness is love
There's none who suffers it
But feels every day is a week

171

'What's this for?' I said.

'A whisky commercial. Did he not tell you? Likely he wanted to keep it as a surprise. Good that, isn't it? Appropriate. I thought all the Russians drank was vodka, but he's real fond of a dram is Maxie.'

At first I was angry, as if he'd stolen something special from me. But it was my own fault. I'd not explained the significance of that song, and I thought my heart would burst with the beauty of it. It was brief, not more than five minutes; Johnser was beside himself.

'He'll have so much work he won't know what to do with himself. It's a waste to have him playing nothing but stuff written by dead people.'

'Arvo Pärt's not dead,' I said glibly.

Max grinned at me as we walked back to the car. 'That'll bring in fourteen hundred. What did you think of it anyway? It's like a miracle. The inspiration only arrived in the last hours before I was due to produce the goods.'

'Fourteen hundred what?'

'Pounds. Cash. That's what I've earned.'

'That's impossible.'

'It's my share for arranging and playing. Johnser says I can make far more once I get known. He says the sky's the limit.'

'You get too well-known, friend, and you'll find yourself in Saughton.'

'Stop fretting. I have to be able to work, and drive a car, and be a real person. If it means I have to spend a while locked up, too bad.'

'They'd put you in prison, like a criminal.'

'That's what I am. It's not legal to travel with a forged passport. Didn't you enjoy my music?'

'It was wonderful. You're exceptionally gifted. You deserve to make money, but....'

He nudged my arm. 'Don't get depressed. Thank you for coming with me. I hardly see you the rest of the week, with your important work. I want to look at you. Best friends?'

'Anyway, it's marvellous you earned so much.' Too late, as usual with my appreciation.

'Not quite Maksim Vengorov, but I'll get there. It's not only the money either – this is what I love to do more than anything, to be able to get the tunes in my head out there for you to hear.'

Next day, the Diana thing happened, and I hardly saw home for a week. Some faceless wonder from Albion's mother station was yelling down the phone at me : 'What are you fucking Jocks playing at? Don't you know there's little children weeping in the streets down here?' We'd been tardy in cancelling a football match. The Scots can't be trusted to get it right.

The studio was overrun by geeks with orange hair and attitude and Souf London accents. The boss man himself arrived, and I was sent downstairs to collect him. Then Anita met us on the stairs and practically put my eye out with her elbow as she rushed to gush, ignoring me completely.

'Rude, self-centred cow,' I yelled after her, but she was in full flow by then. Didn't even notice.

I walked home weeping with rage, and had to restrain myself from taking a hammer to the TV set. All these stacks of rotting flowers. Grown men blubbering like babies for the cameras. Teddy bears, for Christ's sake.

Max was glued to the screen.

'What the hell are you watching that for?'

173

'Trying to figure out what makes the British the way they are.'

I snorted. 'Your lot and the French had the right idea about what to do with royal families. I bet you'd never heard of her before this.'

'Nonsense. All the Russian magazines wrote about her. They said she was very fashionable and beautiful. I didn't find her attractive. Too much like a calf on its way to be slaughtered, the way she rolled her eyes up.'

'I suppose they'll make her a saint now.'

'The way we did ours?'

We ended the evening in truce, united by our scorn for making saints out of over-privileged people who excelled in nothing but self-pity.

CHAPTER SIXTEEN

By the following Saturday I'd earned my time off. We drove to North Berwick, walked the beaches bent double against the wind, ate fish and chips off the paper, slept stiffly side by side in sleeping bags and pretended to enjoy ourselves. Not strictly true; Max thought it was fine. At least we were spared having to watch the funeral.

'You told me you loved the sea,' he said accusingly next morning.

'Not this one. It's too open. I like the beach, but the open sea frightens me. I like to see the other side.'

'I thought you said your island is far out to the west?'

'It is. But Balvaig's on the side where you can see other islands.'

I'm not from a race that built on hilltops to see the enemy coming. My inheritance is of caves and woodland to hide in, though occasionally we'd turn on our own and smoke them out or roast them. Only the North Sea's chilly, nacreous skies I can appreciate.

'You're comfortable with wide horizons,' I said. 'That's the difference with Russians.'

We watched a couple throw sticks into the sea for a black lab.

'I'd like to have a dog,' said Max. 'A very big one. Something like a Rottweiler.'

What's with these people, that they all want to have drug dealer's dogs?

'We can't have a big dog in town. We'll move to the country, some time. Later. Then we can have a dog. Maybe not that breed though. Dee and I couldn't believe the number of enormous dogs like that we saw in St Petersburg.'

He was looking sad. 'You could reach St Petersburg, if you sail long enough,' he said, eyes brimming.

'You can see it, can't you?'

'Always. Don't let's be sad today, Serena.'

I tried to cheer up for his sake, and to stay happy when he suddenly headed for the water, shedding clothes, plunged naked into the waves and splashed around. I gathered up the trail of garments, and stood at the edge like his nanny, racking my brains to think what I'd dry him with.

He sprawled in the shallow water on his back kicking his legs, so that small droplets landed on my skin. 'Take off your clothes and come in. You said you'd teach me to swim.'

'It's freezing.'

'It's good for you.'

Then he was out, and in my arms while I tried to rub him dry with my cardigan, slippery as a fish, his skin so hot it burnt my fingers. Fire and water. He put his arms round me, and I thought maybe I would have to go in, to cool down. He picked me up, still butt-naked, and ran into the water with me, pretending to drop me, clothes and all. I clung to his neck till it felt more like adultery than marriage.

He wolfed down our cheap café meal with a better will than I'd seen for weeks. It made me smile. No chance of converting him to vegetarianism - he doesn't consider it a meal unless there's meat. The sea air and the exercise had put colour in his face; he could have been a Scandinavian peasant farmer at his dinner, or a Dutch painting, with plenty of vermilion on the palette. Every few moments he made me blush with a glance that was bold and secret.

When he'd come out of the waves, disconcertingly masculine, and snuggled in my arms, and looked in my face lovingly, the way he did the first days, I'd found myself contemplating how it would feel to walk into the water and keep walking, till my feet couldn't find the bottom, take in my death by the mouthful and the lungful rather than wake to another day when there was hostility in his eyes.

'Maksim,' I said, 'when I die don't let them burn me. I want to be put in the ground. Or laid on a mountain for the birds to pick my bones.' You'd think they'd have done that in the Highlands. So many mountains, so little ground you could dig. 'And I don't want dirges. I want a jazz band, and huge black men in white top hats.'

'What a time to think of dying, just when everything's coming right for us. We'll both be put in the ground, in a very long time, in a single grave. They can open my coffin and lay you in my arms. Let's go home now. Talk to me about Balvaig. When will you take me there?'

All the way back to town I told him about the subtle colours that compose the landscape that's the island. If I'd been born an artist that's the palette I'd have favoured over the harsh clear colours of the South. Grey on grey and no two shades of it the same. It makes you pay attention to texture and elusive shadows, to which surfaces hurl the light back in your eyes and which swallow it greedily. And the complicated Art Deco sunsets in peach, terra-cotta, lemon, amaranth, pistachio, with the sea a bolt of silk.

Its geography is sculpted by ice as clearly as any in the Baltic or Scandinavia: mountains which

177

are   damson and slate in summer and autumn, whiter than the wings of gulls in winter; the small scour of Lonemore bay where a child can fish safely from a rowing boat; a scutter of islands, some no more than rocks; the basin of fertile land that cradles the village and its fringe of crofts. And the sea, eternally present to the eyes, the ears, the nose.

Over on the mainland, there's the lushness of Inverewe and its eucalypts. I prefer the severe lineaments of Balvaig's face - a pine branch swaying against the full moon, waterfalls, small clear pools; cormorants on the rocks, wings stiffly extended, waiting for their deodorant to dry; peaceful, deserted beaches, shell-strewn and melancholy; moss in the woods, snow in the high corries on the three Beinns, bog cotton on the moor. Voluptuous touches too: wild orchids among the rushes, and the shameless swollen-lipped shells the sea would dump on the very doorstep of the kirk, like foundlings, to remind us of sin.

A sensual place, though the God of my people abhors sensuality. Having created this harsh, fragile beauty he abandoned it to folk with stones for souls.

'I hope you won't be disappointed with it,' I said to Max. 'There's not so much as a full-time shop in the village now. Just a sort of pub. The school's likely to close any year now. Most of the people are retired.'

They glean a little cash from the tourists; bed and breakfast, boat hire; few more personal services. The good-lifers from the soft south make pottery and driftwood picture frames. Three times out of five they return whence they came after a year or two complaining of the shiftless and xenophobic Scots.

A grim and tenacious people, mine, like Max's. Survivors, frontiersmen. They know in their hearts you cannot buy and sell the land any more than you can

178

own the right to look at the moon, and that the odds are loaded against life being good.

But to hell with it. What's the point of thinking of the past? They cleared better places than Balvaig, and they'll do it again if it suits them, the landowners. They've retained a preference for folk that think like sheep. The place is ruined. System-built bungalows spoil the view wherever you look, and there's more chance of Colchester or Coatbridge than Celt in the voices. The shops in Portmore sell crap as bad as any you'll find on the Royal Mile, and you can't get a decent cup of tea. Balvaig's less of a community now than the Stockbridge Colonies. But there's still a pub. And a fish farm.

'And the rain!' I said to Max. 'It comes like stair-rods down your neck more than three hundred days of the year, from out of a sky that's as heavy as a mucky fleece. Most days you can't see the scenery for mist. When it's not raining, midges like zeppelins come out to firebomb the tender skin under your eyes.'

'Sounds good!' he said. 'In Karelia it's mosquitoes. You think I mind rain?'

I needed him to love it all as I did, irrationally and completely.

He opened a bottle of vodka when we got home, switched on the two dimmest lamps in the sitting room, and LeAnn Rimes *Blue* – the music Max despises, country kitsch.

'I'm glad you came with me to the sea. I wanted to make amends. Forgive me?' He pulled me into his arms. 'Relax,' he whispered. 'We're only dancing close.' I'd drunk so much I was unsteady on my feet. I let myself lean against him and wound my arms round his neck.

'See? It's easy when you relax.'

Fergus used to yell that exhortation at me. 'Relax, you stupid cow, how the hell do you expect to enjoy it if you don't relax?'

I could feel Max's heartbeat. I wanted to have his blood beat in my veins, feel with his feelings, see the earth the way he sees it. Experience me the way he seemed to; desirable, not the broken, damaged freak I am. Have all that swaying, seductive rhythm inside me. I wanted to be Max.

He began to kiss me. Soon he'd stopped pretending what we were doing was dancing. And I wanted that to happen, wanted to feel how reassuringly easy it was still for me to get him in that state.

'It's time, Serena,' he whispered. 'Everything has its time, and this is ours.'

My mind was off in cloud cuckoo land: *I'm not drunk enough yet; I wish I'd on less tatty knickers; I wish I'd time to have a shower; Jesus, I'm as bad as Roddy, obsessed with hygiene. Hygiene and receipts and the way everything has its price.*

As Max pulled me upstairs, my imagination was full of the narrow and unwelcoming bed Van Gogh claimed as his; *La Chambre de Vincent* - a euphemism for the grave that, in the old ballads, a narrow bed - and how a man who was surely a cold fish in his dealings with women used such hot honey-dripping colours, and painted stars that looked like spermatozoa. And never a single one sold. What drove him to keep going? And what was in his deepest mind as he walked to the whorehouse, jingling his coins in his pocket? The Dutch used to be like us, repressed and buttoned down by religion, and now there's Amsterdam. They put Vincent in the madhouse too. Mad, mad, mad, and the blood running down the side of his face from where the ear should have been, and it was her fault, Rachel the whore made him do it, and the blood running down Donald John's legs, and the knife-blade red and sticky on the grass, and the glutinous, swimming-pool-smell mess on my hair and my dress.

'Max – stop. I'm not ready,' I said. But he was already well past the point where the brakes work. His eyes were opaque and bleary as he tumbled me onto the bed, tugging impatiently at his own clothes and mine.

I'd lost control of my lungs and struggled for air, convinced I was having a heart attack. Max didn't seem to notice. 'Wait!' I croaked.

'I've waited so long,' he said. 'I can't wait any more, sweetheart.' And he lunged into me.

I shrieked, he drew away from me as if I'd burned him. I rolled off the edge of the bed, crawled to the doorway and fled to the sanctuary of my own room. I rammed a chair-back under the handle and huddled in the covers, trying to restore warmth to stinging flesh. I heard Max's feet on the stair before my head touched the pillow.

'Let me in.'

I didn't reply, so he put his shoulder to the door, skittering the chair across the room, making gouges we never managed to get rid of in the floorboards. Our house bears the scars too. I rolled myself into a ball, waiting to be raped. Maksim switched on the lamp and stretched out on the covers beside me, sliding a protective arm around me.

'I'm so sorry,' he crooned against my ear. 'I'd rather have died than harmed you. I didn't realise. I should have waited till you were ready for me. Look at me, sweetheart. Oh God – there's blood on your pillow.

181

Are you bleeding, Serena? Should I take you to the hospital?'

'It's just my mouth. I bit my lip.'

He fetched a wet face cloth and sponged my face unbearably gently. His hands were shaking. 'I'm so sorry,' he said, over and over.

'It's me that should be apologising. I let you think it'd be all right. I thought it would, tonight. You were doing what's natural. I'm the freak.'

He stroked my hair, and cuddled me through the covers. 'Should I call a doctor?'

'I'll be all right. You should go back to bed. It's cold.'

'Let me get under the covers then.'

'You won't be comfy. The bed's not long enough for you.'

He slid in alongside me, warm and strong and comforting. 'Serena – do you find my body repulsive?'

'It's not that! You're so big.'

'That shouldn't be a problem, sweetheart. Women are designed to cope with much more than that. Babies. You have to get help with this. I know you wanted it too. You have to see a specialist.'

Fergus had demanded that as a right. 'I already did. She could find nothing physically wrong with me.' She referred me to a shrink, but I only went once. The hell with that.

'But it didn't feel natural. It wasn't like...' Max stuttered to a halt.

'Finish the sentence. Don't you know it's worse when you half-say something? It wasn't like?'

'Well – it wasn't like the way a woman's tight the first time.'

182

I clamped my jaw down on my tears and shrank as far away from him as I could. I wondered if I could bear feeling how I felt.

'It wasn't Katya, sweetheart,' he said, drawing my rigid body back against him. 'It wasn't with her. Jesus, I can't remember the girl's name.'

But he could recall the sensation, the bastard. His body chose that moment to start arguing the toss over control. Wonderful. He could get off on merely thinking of his supreme moment of manhood.

'Shit! I can't help it. Don't pull away from me like that. It's only a part of me, no different from my feet. Our feet are all mixed up together – you don't mind that, do you? What I do have control over is what I do with it. And I've told you, I won't try that again in a hurry. Now, lie still.' His beautiful toes twined among mine. 'Anyway. It was the first time for you once, and it wasn't with me. Was it with your husband?'

I didn't consider that worth an answer.

'Shhh,' murmured Max, stroking my head. 'It doesn't matter. I've no right to ask you that. It's my jealousy talking.'

I did remember the name, though. Gareth. Gareth McTaggart Calder, date of birth: tenth of May 1965, place of birth: Invergordon, eyes: grey, hair: dark brown, weight: seventy-two kilos, height: one metre seventy-nine, occupation: medical student. He was handsome and confident, and he was always laughing. He had an alcohol dependency at twenty-one.

We got stuck in a lift together in the Hume Tower. He had no legitimate business there in the first place. Much later I learnt he'd been on his way to meet another girl from her English Lit tutorial, and that his pals called him Shag-a-Polo.

Not that I lost my virginity in the lift, though the quick poke in a broom-cupboard or a stall in the women's toilets, that was Gareth's style. He had a theory that's what the wee niches in railway tunnels are for. I lost it on the none-too-clean sheets of his room in a tacky flat. Gareth went into the bathroom and produced a used towel for me to lie on.

'Saves washing the sheet. Now, relax. You'll enjoy it. It doesn't hurt.'

It bloody did. Maybe initiation rites have to, or they don't work. Sharp objects driven into flesh. Tender pieces of skin torn or cut. It hurt, and I felt nothing, nothing except relief when he bellowed like a mad animal, and it was over.

Gareth laughed ruefully. 'Sorry. I can usually last longer than that even the first time. But you're so lovely and tight, like one of these Egyptian girls that's been sewn up. God! There's blood everywhere. You must have had a tough bit of skin there right enough.'

I thought that made me his. I believed the duty of love was born of the fact my blood was on his thighs as well as my own. I wasn't so naïve as to fail to recognise him as a selfish bastard. The sort of man who'd be in another town and another woman when I was having his child, then arrive late having weaved round closed snow-gates, bearing filling-station flowers for me and chocolates for the midwife. And I'd have been sitting up in bed trying to look cheerful, with my hair fixed and my make-up done. It'd all start over. He'd probably have given the nurse one in the sluice-room on the way out.

All that I knew intuitively as he broke into my body. Where the naiveté showed was in the belief I

184

could change him. That illusion lasted three weeks and five days, until I came home early to find him in my flat. I'd lent him a key so he could do his washing. That was OK. I'd the key to his flat too, though God alone knows what I was supposed to find there of any use to me.

They didn't leap apart when I blundered into my room. They were locked together like randy dogs, on the new primrose yellow sheets I'd bought for his sake. Gareth slowed on his stroke, turning his head to grin at me. 'Coitus interruptus! ' he said affably. 'Coming in beside us? No? Well, shut the door behind you, there's a good girl.'

I went calmly back to the kitchen, forced open the door of the machine with a screwdriver and threw his washing into the muddy back court. Even the radio on maximum volume didn't drown out their noise. The SAS could have stormed the building and you wouldn't have heard a sound above the racket Gareth was making. I remember thinking how convenient it was that he always hollered: 'Oh baby! Oh Jesus! Oh God!' when he came. That way no one's feelings would get hurt, unless he happened to be rogering an atheist.

And I remember that I wanted to kill him, because he'd stolen the one good thing I had, that I'd meant to save until I got round to finding Sergei Timochenko again.

I banged on the door of my room. 'Don't you dare smoke in my bed!'

That's what did for Gareth in the end, that addiction to the post-coital ciggie or three. It happened the next year, in his own flat. Gas leak. Either that or he and the bitch had been careless enough to leave gas taps on. At least he died before he could qualify as a doctor and damage more women.

So I do remember the name. What I can't clearly recall is the sensation, beyond that it was unpleasant. Presumably that's to do with the way men and women are made differently.

Gareth got me into trouble anyway, the bastard. He got me evicted. After I'd turned him and his floozie out of my bed, I burned the sheets, and regretted it later, because they'd been expensive. But the old bisom downstairs complained to the landlord that I was chucking rubbish out the window and lighting bonfires. I had to pay for the washing machine too.

'I didn't mean to upset you,' Max said. 'I was thinking aloud. You can read my mind anyway.'

'Only the nasty thoughts.'

'You think silently and brood. I blurt it all out.'

Fergus used to get off on making me talk about it. Like dogs sniffing a lamp-post to know who's been there before them.

Max was silent for far too long. I stroked his face. It was wet with tears.

'It must have been painful for you as well, being stopped at the last moment.'

'I'll get by.'

'I suppose you're sorry you didn't stay with Katya, if the pair of you were humping like baboons every night.'

'She didn't treat me as if I'm a leper.'

I pushed him away, as far as I could in that damn bed.

'I'm still here, aren't I?' he yelled. 'Doesn't that hold any meaning for you? Who are you crying for? Listen, when I have to use my hand, to keep sane, you think it's her I picture in my head? Or Carla? No, God help me, I imagine how it'd be to do it with you. Though tonight, that was well beyond the realms of fantasy.'

I tried to slide my arms round him.

'Don't pretend to love me. You want to get me hot for you then push me away. You call that love?'

'I don't want to be this way. But you think of nothing else these days.'

'I never thought about it two days running in my life before. Living in this house with you. I have to see you walking around in your underwear, hear you bathing, imagine you lying in your bed. It's driving me crazy. It interferes with practising my music, getting on with my life. I have to lie in bed alone thinking of it. You never think about sex at all?'

'Occasionally. Not the same way as you.'

'The way most people think about getting knifed.'

'So you've never done without it at all? Must have had an inexhaustible supply of women, if Katya was away so much. How many were there, Maksim?'

'Stop it.'

'Tell me.'

'Jesus, I don't know.'

'How many. Ten? Twenty? Thirty? Hundreds?'

He swore under his breath. 'Do I ask you that?'

'You know you don't have to.'

'I have told you over and over, there was never anyone special for me. There's not one woman in the world you have to be jealous of. And no – I certainly haven't been with hundreds. I'm choosy you know, fastidious. You are jealous of Katya because you think I loved her? I don't say that lightly to a woman, Serena, though I think you've said it to plenty of men. I don't want to know how many. I don't want to know if you

187

told that bastard you loved him. Katya and I were friends, but all that there was between us in bed was sex, not love. She didn't have this need you have to be reassured all the time.'

I could feel his heartbeat, strong and steady; he could choose to be calm when he decided to, damn him. Mine fluttered like a trapped moth. I wanted to snuggle in the warm circle of his arm and make the words stay down too.

'I'm desperate for us to be friends. That's why I'm jealous. You were so close to her. I suppose she's extremely beautiful. Russian women are.'

'Is that why you always wanted to see a picture of her? She was nothing to look at, compared to you. You're the most beautiful woman I've ever been with.'

I sobbed uncontrollably again. 'So it wasn't only physical. Katya was your soul-mate.'

'Tell me what you really want, Serena. What do you want out of life?'

'I don't want to have to spend my life worrying over money and sex and all the rest.'

I don't want to be a dried-up sexless object like Morag.

'I'm trying to find out what you do want.'

'This. Closeness, warmth, trust, companionship.'

It would have been a different wish list three months earlier. Higher salary, a speedy and terminal illness for Katie-Mary so I could be Serena Stuart MacKenzie, the face of Gaeldom at ten past six Monday to Friday. A bigger house. Designer clothes. Furniture from Ikea. Bigger tits. A Jack Vettriano original – probably *After the Thrill is Gone* (even though she has a fag in her hand). Tenderness. But I can't ask for that, because what you ask you don't get.

'You want what I want, in your heart,' Max said. 'A normal life, a couple of kids, a home, not merely a house. It's safe to let yourself love. I won't let you fall.' I knew he was right. I recognised the nostalgia I used to feel, reading the gravestones in Balvaig Burial Ground. *Gus am bris an là.......* Until the day breaks.... Such long, long lives and long, long marriages.

Max's anger is a thunderstorm; afterwards, the air's so calm and sweet. He held me close and kissed me the way he had in St Petersburg, friendly loving kisses, not sexy ones, the best kisses I ever experienced. I wonder how men learn to kiss? I wonder how they learn all the techniques of loving? It's not a male peer-group thing. That's restricted to competitive antics. How do they learn the rest?

'Max, who was the first woman you slept with?'

He groaned and shook me. 'Why do you ask these things? You know you'll get upset if I tell you and the same if I don't.'

'I won't. I want to hear. I need to know everything about you.'

He hesitated. 'A friend of my mother's.'

'The same age as your mother?'

'Not quite. But a lot older than me. She was a very sexy woman who was frustrated because her husband was a drunk and couldn't get it up. She was an expert teacher, Serena. You should be glad of this. What a disaster if I was clumsy and inexperienced. I'm good at loving because of her. When we've sorted out your problem, we'll both be glad of this.'

'How old were you?'

I judged from his silence he was calculating whether to lie. 'I'll answer you, then we'll change the subject. Agreed? I don't want a reaction from you. Fifteen.'

As I opened my mouth to comment he covered it with his.

'I'm sorry,' he said. 'Now I've made a mess of your bed.'

'Doesn't matter,' I mumbled.

'I'll clean it all up in the morning,' he said, sliding out from the covers. I lay still, paralysed by a sense of déjà vu. Fergus lumbering back upstairs from that same room, stopping off at the bathroom to hawk the phlegm out of his throat, while I lay numb, feeling as if he'd spat in me too

By the time I realised Max had only gone to fetch a clean towel to spread over the sheet, I was sobbing with rage, disappointment and frustration. He stroked my hair and crooned my name.

'That was inexcusably selfish,' he said. 'I'm a crude pig. But I couldn't help it.'

'I want to have your babies,' I snivelled.

'You will, sweetheart. We won't risk starting that before you get your problem sorted out. Have you any idea what size a baby is? I was an enormous baby. More than five kilos. I don't want some great, hulking child of mine ripping you apart. I couldn't do it like that anyway. I want to give you pleasure too. Be patient. When you're better, we'll make love properly, we'll make babies.'

'How many?'

'Two,' he said, in the tone of the kind daddy telling a bedtime story. 'A boy first, then a girl.'

We'd all live happily ever after. 'You've chosen the names already, I suppose?' Hansel and Gretel.

'That's something else we have to do together.' But he'd hesitated just long enough. I knew the names were in his head. I'm too superstitious to have asked.

'Don't cry any more. We'll find a doctor who can work magic on you. Now you have to answer me,' he said. 'Who has damaged you so badly? Was it this Fergus? He went on with it, although he knew he was hurting you?'

'I can make myself go numb. It's the first few seconds that are worst.'

Max held me so tight I could scarcely breathe, squeezing all the resentment and fear out of me.

'Tomorrow I'm breaking up that damn bed upstairs for firewood. It's brought us bad luck. I'll buy timber and build a new one, only for us. Your bride's bed. No one else'll ever sleep in it, except our children.'

'We could sell it. It was expensive.'

'Burn every last piece. Cleanse the evil.'

We were both awake a long time. I knew he was in the place I'd been so often; the long white corridor where you can't see the end, and all the doors are closed, and all the handles on the inside. He buried his face against my neck, and slept. We hadn't been apart a whole day since we met, and this was the first whole night we'd spent together skin-to-skin.

By the time I'd had my shower next morning, Max had the sheets in the machine. All trace of it obliterated, as if I'd dreamt it.

'It's better if we sleep apart until you're ready right enough, Serena,' he said. 'I'll miss you, but it'd just be a repeat performance of last night. I haven't as much   self-control as I imagined I had, and it's not fair on you.

That night I helped Max push the first pieces of Fergus's bed into the stove.

Granda said that's the purpose of Hell; to burn up all that's bad in the world and leave it clean.

'You'll burn in hell,' he announced when Grannie brought me back from the police station. He thrust his contorted features close to mine so flecks of spittle struck my face when he shouted. 'Jezebel! Harlot! Accusing a man from a godly family. One of the Lord's innocents. You wanted to corrupt him, and now look what's happened, the poor lad'll likely be shut up with raving lunatics for the rest of his days. You'll burn in hell.' Then his face turned purple, and the veins on his forehead stood out like ropes, and he fell over backwards. Grannie rushed towards us, wailing : 'Oh, Peter, Peter!'

Then she turned on me. 'Wicked girl – now you've gone and killed your grandfather.'

Next day, the doctor gone and Granda quiet in his bed, we heard about Donald John's father. Nobody needed to tell me I was responsible for that too, so I was quite calm. I remember thinking how clever it was of old Mr Munro, to think of pressing the trigger with his big toe, and that it was as well he'd locked himself in the byre, so Donald John's mother wouldn't have to clean his brains off her kitchen walls.

Max held my hand tightly as the flames licked the stove's glass door. Burn up the evil. Lock my imagination in the cold, dark shed.

This must be the problem for people who genuinely have the Sight. No sympathy for the double bind you find yourself in. If you can see disaster coming and step aside, dragging your loved ones after you, you're a witch. If not, you're a fool. Either way, it's all your own fault; you knew how it would be.

The month after I burned the sheets I'd bought for Gareth Calder, another of his rejects was dredged out of the Union canal. I still believe anger can be the healthier response.

Max carried wood home from B&Q the next day, and built himself a passable bedstead. We lived in amicable truce for the next week, even though the advertising agency paid by cheque, and we had all the palaver of making sure they used the correct spelling of "Stuart". 'You couldn't have believed they'd pay you in used fivers?' I said defensively. But Max just smiled. 'I want you to have it anyway. It means I can begin to pay you back for everything. I still owe you for the meal on our first date.'

This is not the plotline I wanted. I have failed, and I don't know how to run this script in reverse.

CHAPTER SEVENTEEN

I had a day's respite to sort out my thoughts because Marjorie Adam had taken over Max's life, and he had time for nothing else. She'd been hell-bent on organising a private recital now that the Festival was well and truly over. Show the organisers how it should be done. With the double doors flung open, the drawing room was the size of a small concert hall. Superb acoustics. Max would be at his best. I used the moments before proceedings got under way to study him. He was trying to look calm, but he was taut as an over-stretched string.

Marjorie had ordered a special little dais; by the time the piano had been heaved onto it, and the chair for the woman who was to turn the music, Max would be squeezed in right at the front. 'Jeez,' I thought when I saw it, 'she doesn't realise he'd be happier behind a curtain, with a bag over his head.' Fireworks display later. I still hadn't learnt when to keep my thoughts to myself. I'd been nagging him earlier about the wisdom of low profiles. 'You're paranoid,' he said. 'Nobody gives a shit how I got here. Marjorie's certainly not bothered. I told her, and all she said was "let me know if you have any problems. I have contacts who might be useful". She's a sensible woman.'

I sat very primly, watching my husband as if he was a stranger. He'd had his hair cut very short. I didn't approve of it at first; too redolent of a Hitler Youth recruiting poster. But tactile, I'd discovered. Crisp and sensual and electric, like running my hand against the cat's fur the wrong way.

He looked delectable in the suit he'd hired. (She'd obviously given him some cash in advance; I hated her more than ever for that. It should have been up to me.) I'd never seen him dressed to kill; it made me smile, to find Max has his vanities too. He'd have nothing to do with a bow tie that came ready-made. He demanded a proper one, and did it up perfectly first time without so much as glancing in a mirror.

He looked particularly Russian that evening. The taut, stubborn set of the jaw, the haughty expression he had when he deigned to look at his audience. I knew he was in a bad mood; seething underneath the calm exterior. Marjorie had chosen the programme. Heated words had been exchanged over the Bach Sonata in G major. 'I can't do it,' he'd moaned. 'It doesn't move me. Bach doesn't speak to me. I'll never be able to do it.'

'For Christ's sake, you're a musician,' I'd said. 'You can surely practise enough?'

Marjorie had parked me on an elegant gilt and brocade sofa right at the front. I wasn't too deliriously happy about being so much on display either. I hated my dress.

God knows why, but he'd been determined I should look the part for Marjorie Adam's damn recital too. I wanted him to help me choose my new frock in my lunch-break that day, the way a real husband might. He was late. I stood in Jenners' doorway, out of the rain, and contemplated how ugly people in the street were. When he arrived, he looked distracted and bored. I bought the first dress that fitted, hardly even looking at it.

Plummy-voiced dames sized him up like a piece of meat. 'A younger version of Nureyev,' I overheard one say. I stored that up to make him laugh later, once he could relax. They could look and dream; I'd take him home, in the back of a taxi. I'd snuggle against him and undo the top buttons of the immaculate pin-tucked shirt, slide my hand against the skin of his chest (which is almost as innocent of hair as an adolescent's), tease him, pretend he was a gigolo I'd picked up.

Carla was there, smiling radiantly at me as she caught my eye. He must have set up that invitation personally, and only when he looked at her did his expression relax. Perhaps she was thinking the same as I was, that he should lighten up the whole caboodle, start with his version of Dvorâk's *Songs my Mother Taught Me*, which he could do dead-pan, with a pained expression and just a smidgin off-key; he'd have his audience helpless.

He gazed straight into my eyes, a serious, long, quizzical look, before he began to play. Once he starts, he forgets everything else, he'd forget me no matter if we'd come hot from an all-day sex session. The tension in his jawline relaxes, his eyes half-close, his head's thrown back, his lips are faintly parted.

I didn't recognise the pianist who was accompanying him, though he obviously did. They eyed each other with mutual loathing. She glared at his back as he fidgeted with the music, fidgeted with the spike, fidgeted with the bow each time, before turning to nod at her over his shoulder. 'OK. Now.' Once, between the second and third movements of the Bach he muttered something to her, and I thought for a moment she was going to stand up, chuck her music on the floor and tell him to bloody well play by himself.

But the evening was a success. They loved him. I was barely aware of what he played in the second half or what cursory exchange we had at the interval.

'Circulate, socialise,' he'd told me. 'Enthuse over how wonderful I am!'

I tried my best, though I was terrified of being lured into treacherous conversation where I'd drown. I veered between feeling invisible and enormous, like a huge, pulsating purple zit. Carla was flitting about as brightly as a disembodied flame, glass in hand, her hair gleaming like a beacon, her sexy laughter floating above the rumble of voices, doing a brilliant job on my husband's PR. The young Nureyev caught my eye from across the room. Marjorie was wheeling him round, while he bared his teeth at old women of both sexes; he looked as comfortable as a Jewish vegetarian in a pork butcher's. I felt I should rescue him. What would the old girl have thought if we'd disappeared upstairs to one of her elegant, fastidious, cream-and-chintz bedrooms?

As soon as we were in the taxi to go home, Max loosened his tie, so that he looked like a dissolute nobleman, but he was distant and distracted, and sat with his arms wrapped round Katya's case, ignoring me. He looked so tired. Poor Max, I thought – he puts so much into the music. I'll massage his shoulders and his neck (for that's where he stores all the tension), and I'll caress each inch of his spine (even his bones are exquisite, he could stretch out on a table and be used as a model to demonstrate anatomy to medical students).

But he stalked so sternly and purposefully to the stair, I didn't dare follow him up. I sat in the kitchen, waiting for him to come back and wish me goodnight, at least. When I eventually crept up to his room it was in darkness.

'What do you want?' He didn't trouble to disguise the hostile tone.

I perched on the edge of his bed. 'You didn't say goodnight.'

'I'm very tired. Goodnight. '

'Why are you angry with me?' I said.

He sat up and switched on the lamp. 'Why did you bring me here? You knew how it'd be, that I'd have to smile and scrape and pretend to be grateful. I hate the West and all you people stand for. I hate it that that old witch throws me crumbs and expects me to sing for my supper.'

'Hardly fair. She paid you for tonight.'

'Why does she ask me to play for pricks?'

'Because you claim to be a musician and she's been generous enough to allow you carte blanche with a valuable antique instrument.' Which he loved more than he loved me. No need to ponder which of us he'd save first in a fire.

He punched the pillow viciously. 'Musician! I don't know who I am any more. Jesus, I was terrible tonight. I should never have agreed to it. That bitch of a pianist! You didn't notice? She played the Bach about twice the proper tempo. It was terrible. Made me sound like an amateur, an idiot.'

'It sounded fine to me.'

'You! What do you know? This old woman, this Marjorie, thinks she can buy me. She told me I could stay over when I want. My own room's all ready.'

'Why would you want to sleep at Marjorie's house?'

'To get away from you.' He'd rolled to the far side of the bed.

'You told that old bitch you want to get away from me?'

'No, she can see that for herself.'

198

'She knows you're a married man, and she asked you to sleep in her house?'

'The invitation included you. But why fight in a stranger's home when you can fight in your own?' He switched the lamp off, turned his back to me and drew the covers over his head. As I stumbled downstairs my ears were singing the way they do when a train passes in the subway.

Next morning he brought me breakfast in bed, and cradled me in his arms, and nuzzled my ear. 'I was vile to you. I was hideously nervous. Too many people. And I hadn't practised enough. When I play badly I'm in deepest hell – can you understand? That's no excuse.'

'Then why let yourself get so stressed-out? You're always telling me to stay calm.'

'I need it. I need to get the adrenalin running.'

'Great. Why should I have to bear the brunt of it? You managed to shake off the stage fright when you decided to play in the street like a beggar. I hadn't done anything to deserve the way you spoke to me.'

'You say you love me. You have to love me when I'm a selfish bastard too.'

I didn't smile for him. That's the benefit of a traditional education, plenty of Shakespeare. *Love is not love which alters when it alteration finds.*

I'd wanted what I imagined he was, the gentle, tender, funny man I ate chocolate in bed with. He was still there, somewhere, but I couldn't separate him from the monster. They're both Max. I want the incredible hunk who doesn't turn into the incredible hulk when I kiss him. But I'm the one who was struck blind for long enough to get us into this mess.

CHAPTER EIGHTEEN

In the Maelstrom of tidying that followed a quarrel, next morning Max found the bag of Simon's baby toys I'd chucked to the back of the shed and forgotten about. He'd discovered that the only safe way to open the door of it was with the foot extended to catch the junk that fell out.

'You're like my mother,' Max said. 'Always hoarding junk. What good will it do you? When the disaster comes, what use will any of it be?'

At the bottom of the innermost layer he found the toys. So he nagged me till I told him Roddy had a child, nagged further till he extracted the brat's name, current age, IQ.

'Why don't you like children, Serena?'

'Jesus! I don't dislike them. Do I have to like other people's? Simon's a spoilt, wheenging brat. I'm sorry for the little sod, it's not his fault, but it's not mine either.'

'Takes one to know one,' he said under his breath, loud enough for me to hear. 'I think maybe children bore you.'

'Did Katya like children? Maybe that's what kept her so long in Odessa, she was nice and cosy down with your mother, giving birth to your own little three-quarters Ukie.'

He clenched his hand, opened it, clenched it again, punched it against the flat of his other hand. It gave me a peculiar little thrill round the point where your heart's shown on anatomical diagrams.

'Why do you jump like that? You think I'm going to hit you? You make me very angry sometimes, but if that's what you want, sorry, you'll be disappointed.'

'What I want? You think women want to be battered? Maybe in Russia, friend, but not here.'

'I'm so afraid, Serena,' he said. 'I don't know whether you can re-kindle a dead fire. Why do you provoke me? You can't make me do that anyway.'

'You think I want to make you? Why would any woman who isn't mental want hit?'

He smiled to himself, not a sharing smile; crippling shortage of these lately. 'You tell me. You're the woman who isn't mental. If you want someone who'll rough you up, you picked the wrong one. You could have brought Zhenya home with you.'

He caught me by the wrists, drew me into our half-empty shed and kicked the door shut. 'Calm down, Serena.' He held me, though I tried to struggle away from him, bite him, and punch him.

'Quit that,' he said. 'I have no fetish about being hit either.'

'You get so angry if I mention her name. Do you miss her that much?'

'I'm angry because I know what's coming. Now you'll start to rewrite history so that she was really my wife and we had five kids. So you'll get depressed and even more jealous. Why won't you believe it was a casual fling? What you had with Simon's father. There's no blame. We're both normal people, we had company. Now we have each other and the rest don't matter.'

The shed sorted out, he made me start on moving the boxes of Morag's ornaments out of the attic. He lifted down a smaller box and opened it before I could stop him. He sat on the floor, the hideous red plush album in his lap.

201

'I'm so sorry,' I said. 'I wouldn't have wanted you to find these. I'd forgotten they were there.'

He flashed a dazzling smile. 'But I'm glad to have seen them. They're beautiful. You look like an angel in your white dress. A very expensive photographer, I'd think.'

He'd been a pal of Learmonth's.

'And you were married properly, in a church? You hadn't told me that.'

Fergus had presumably bribed the minister. I knew Max would have tears in his eyes, and I wanted to lie. I couldn't think of a glib enough explanation for the picture where the colours of a stained glass window spilled over the white satin and velvet of my dress.

'This is beautiful,' Max said.

Fergus took that one himself, with the big Wista eight-by-ten field camera, and he won a competition with it. I got goose bumps recalling how he'd looked at me after he took that, it had made me blush so much I had to go out into the fresh air, while Dee teased me about hot flushes. Really, I should have given it back to him. He'd see it as a work of art, not the dross of a failed marriage. He'd kept the product of the few occasions he'd persuaded me to pose nude. I was terrified he'd send these to Max out of spite.

'I'll put them in the bin,' I said.

'Is this your father?'

'It's Hugh. Dee's father. Please – I want to throw them all away.'

He shrugged and handed me the album. Max has no time for sentiment, but I hadn't realised that till it was too late. What I'd seen as deprivation was simply the way he chose to live. He's all hard edges. Even Fergus gets dewy-eyed over mementoes.

Max hadn't let me hang up the enlargements I'd had made of Edouard's photos. 'Put them away in a drawer,' he'd said. 'I don't want to be reminded.'

'You don't want to be reminded we got married?'

'That I couldn't even do that much right for you.'

I managed to remove a few of the photos I liked before I dumped the gold-embossed album in the bin. It was incredibly vulgar: 'Our Wedding' in fancy gilded script. We'd let Morag choose it, humouring her because that's what you do for the dying.

I was carrying a potted crysanth to my mother in hospital when I met Fergus. I knew she was dying and I was relieved and guilty; I'd feared I'd have to take her into my own home to nurse. I've never been comfortable with illness, the smells and textures of it. It was sufficient that she was in hospital in Edinburgh, close enough to visit.

I had grit in my eye, and I was huddled against the wind-swept parapet of the North Bridge like a reluctant suicide, eyes streaming, nose dribbling, trying to avoid being trampled by the tide of folk bearing their Christmas shopping home, while I scrubbed my face with a disintegrating tissue. A heavily built man stopped beside me.

'Let me look after you,' he said, producing an immaculate hankie – a linen one, and ironed at that. He drew me into the nearest pool of light. At that moment the street-lamp exploded, showering us with glass. The bearded stranger gathered me in his arms and shielded me with his own body. When the glass finished falling he inspected my hair and clothing and the potted plant for stray shards.

'That's disgraceful. The council will hear more than a little about this. Are you all right?'

'You've cut your hand!'

He brushed aside my concern. It was at that point I realised why he looked familiar.

'Come along,' he said. 'My house isn't far away. You can bathe your lovely eyes and I'll put antiseptic on this cut. You're safe with me. I'm Fergus Learmonth, by the way.'

'Yes, I'd recognised you.'

I agreed to go home with him principally because I knew it was my fault he was bleeding, and only partly because he was on TV. His name comforted me too. The name you'd give a loyal and dependable West Highland Terrier.

He raised his arm and a cruising taxi appeared from nowhere, wheeled around and was beside us at once. I was seriously impressed.

'Promise me you won't ever go home with anyone you don't know,' he said, settling me safely in my seat. 'You're too gorgeous to be out on your own.'

In his immaculate bathroom Fergus bathed my eye with Optrex from the cupboard, and a blue glass eye bath, none of your plastic rubbish.

'You have the most fucking amazing eyes,' he said. I shivered with delight over the nonchalant way he could make the ugliest of words complimentary. 'They're the colour of gentians. And it's not contacts, is it?'

'Certainly not,' I said primly. I expect I wrinkled my nose a little.

'Potassium bromide,' he said. 'It gives better contrast in black and white prints. I use this as a darkroom. Look.'

He pulled down the blind, so that every chink of light was blanked out. I felt his breath warm against my cheek as he leant past me to reach the cord.

'Perhaps you'd pose for me sometime? I do colour too. I can just picture you draped in deep blue velvet, with that black hair and pale skin. I do quite a lot of portraits, for competitions.'

Then he made me tea, and fussed over me, while I basked in the pleasurable sensation of surrendering to fate. I'd decided he was handsome, and burly rather than fat. I realised it wasn't love, not then, not ever, not for me. Stoat and rabbit.

'A teacher?' he said in disbelief, as we sipped our Lapsang Souchong. 'What a waste. You don't like children, do you? You don't strike me as a girl who'd want any of her own.'

That was the enchantment. From the outset Fergus gave the impression he knew what was best for me. 'I'm a magician,' he said. 'And I can tell you're a witch. I'm going to change your life with a single tiny flick of my wand.'

He courted me with flowers and flattery and a gleam in his eye which proclaimed I was the only one he'd ever looked at that way. When he photographed me at that stage, it was always fully clothed.

A couple of months later, after a particularly sophisticated party where the other women had eyed me splenetically and Fergus sparkled with wit and affection, I let him lead me to his bed. He was passionate and tender and patient in his lovemaking, as if he was still using his body to shield me from danger. Three months and four days afterwards, suffused in the warm glow of knowing I could succeed where others had failed, I agreed to become the third Mrs Fergus

Learmonth. By that time I was working for Albion Media Group; my future was assured.

Morag survived long enough to attend my wedding, though she was kitten-weak by then. She clearly shared Fergus's view that I was moving up a rung or three.

Eva McCulloch it was, Dee's mother, who said it as she helped dress me for the charade of her husband giving me away – 'I haven't anything blue,' I was thinking. And out of the blue Eva said, as the white-ribboned cars were arriving: 'Serena – if you're not sure, it's still not too late - ' But it had all seemed so official – Hugh in his best suit, the flowers, the three-tiered cake, the guests waiting in their new hats, my mother telling death itself to hang on a minute. How could I have gone in to work the next day as if nothing had happened?

In the battleground that was my marriage, I didn't have time to deal with the fact that Morag was heading downhill fast, nagging me about how other the daughters were taking their parents home to die.

I'm sure Fergus was suspicious. When he said: 'How lucky you were with her at the end, just the two of you alone', his tone was insincere. Not that he cared. He wouldn't have wanted her dying in our house any more than I would.

I didn't let them cremate her, though. Fergus arranged her funeral, down to the garish black and gilt headstone. 'Nonsense,' he said, when I protested. 'she'd love it. Pity they won't let us put one either end. She'd have liked that even better.'

Fergus has always had a sixth sense regarding my moods. He perched himself on the edge of my desk the day after the wedding pictures fiasco, swinging a stylishly shod and moderately-sized foot. I took the board-backed envelope out of my bag.

'Here. I found I still had this. I thought you might want it. You were always pleased with how it'd come out.'

He looked at the photo for a long time. 'Come out for a drink with me.'

'Certainly not.'

'For old times' sake. Damn it, witch, you know I'm jealous. I've never admitted that to a woman before. I can't bear to think of you with him.'

'You can't bear to think of me being happy.'

'But you're not, are you? This gangly girlish-looking blond boy's not looking after you properly. I'm worried.' He laid his hand on my shoulder.

'How do you know what he looks like?' Afterwards I thought: I should have struck him for implying Maksim looks in the least effeminate.

Even Fergus can be embarrassed. 'I popped round one evening to make my peace. I could hear the two of you from outside, well into the yelling stage of an argument. "It's around now that she gets to throwing dishes," I said to myself. "Not a politic time." So I didn't knock. Then he came storming out of the house. I was torn between being tactful and wanting to check you were all right.'

I started to put on my jacket. 'How typical of you to skulk around.'

'What's wrong? All couples argue. We did. I didn't tell anyone. I'd have been mortified if some old boyfriend of yours had turned up while we were bawling abuse at each other.'

'You think the fact you were spying on me is likely to persuade me to come for a drink with you?'

'Don't be cruel. You still belong to me. Emotionally, at any rate.'

Where the hell had all the others disappeared to? Never an audience when I needed one.

'I never belonged to you. Specially not emotionally.'

I switched off my terminal and headed for the stair. Fergus fell into step beside me.

'Darling kitten, I know you were sorry for your Russian. But this is taking charity too far. It's been a dreadful mistake, hasn't it?'

'I wasn't sorry for him. He's a very independent person, a survivor. I fell in love with him.'

'You fell in love with me, once. According to you, it doesn't last.'

'Fergus, we got divorced, remember? After you'd paraded our sex life in public.'

'The lawyer wasn't public. He's very discreet. Handles all my business.'

'I suppose you're on commission. He's a salacious old pig. He was loving every moment of it.'

'I can see you're not happy. Look, he'd be better back where he came from. We can make sure he doesn't arrive home penniless. I don't mind contributing. If we send him off with a couple of thousand dollars he's a rich man.'

I should have been flattered to know Fergus set my value so high. 'He wants to stay here.'

We'd reached the street. I was cursing myself for not having the Peugeot with me that day. No simple or graceful getaway.

'It might be possible to arrange that,' said Fergus. 'Political asylum. There've been a couple of cases lately where they pulled that off if they said the Mafia were after them.'

'I want him to stay with me.'

'You never understood how much you hurt me. Losing you was the worst catastrophe of my life, much worse than my other divorces. Let's be pals, the way we were before he was here. Let's work it out.'

He'd slid his arm through mine. God knows what was wrong with me, I couldn't summon the strength to shake him off. His voice had the silky tone I remembered well; it means he's plotting. He could have taken away my career, quite casually, and my home with it, without feeling he'd dirtied his hands.

I went to the pub with him because I'm a coward, and because of the lethargy that had numbed me like nerve gas. We went to the place where we'd hung out when we were first together, and I spent three hours chattering, laughing at his jokes, and remembering why I'd married him. He lit one of his horrid, sexy cigars, narrowing his eyes against the smoke in the way that gives him an air of Bogart. If we could have lived our lives at parties and in pubs, I'd still have been his wife.

'I'll walk you home,' he said.

'I'll take a taxi.'

'As you wish.'

And he kissed me full on the lips, as we stood on the greasy pavement under the fake antique streetlight. He kissed me passionately. It was soothing and I'd had too many drinks, so I kissed him back. I slid my arms round his neck, and felt how warm and safe that was, the dubious comfort of a familiar body. I let him kiss me with his sexy mouth and his leg pressed between my thighs till he was hot and gasping with desire. Flattered I was, and exhilarated that at least I could still turn him on.

'Come home with me,' he said gruffly.

He'd bought a flat not far from Dougal and Carla's when we split up, even more glamorous than theirs. I'd visited his new home; never his new bed.

'Don't be daft. You know I can't. That's all finished, Fergus.'

'It'll never be finished for us, witch. I need you. Come home with me, I promise I'll be kind to you, I'll only do what you like, I'll give you such exquisite loving you'll forget everyone else.' His stubby fingers were unfastening the buttons of my jacket.

I pushed him off. 'Stop that!'

'What does it matter? Christ, Serena, you're my wife.'

I was so angry I couldn't bite my tongue hard enough. 'No I'm not. I'm Maksim's. I married him in Russia.'

'You couldn't have. The divorce wasn't through.'

'It was. The papers were there when I got home. It's all perfectly legal.'

'But you were only there for a day or two. There's no way it can be done that quickly.'

'They manage things differently there.'

'Do they indeed? We'll see about that.'

I went home to my cold, empty house, showered then had a bath, and sat up to yell at Max when he came in.

When the phone rang, it was only Dee. 'Where have you been all night?' she said. 'Something to tell you.' Suitable sperm donor at last? 'I've sold the practice. I'm moving to London.'

'London? You can't. You can't leave me.'

'Come with me then. There's plenty of work for journalists there too. I'm certainly leaving this dump.

I'm bored. Edinburgh's not the place it once was. It's too small.'

'But it'll be wonderful once we have the parliament.'

'We haven't even had the referendum yet. There seems to be a risk it won't go the same way as last time. That pisses me off more than the lack of decent shoe-shops. I'm a tax payer. I'm a capitalist. I don't want to spend the rest of my life under the thumb of the Strathclyde Soviet Republic.'

'Crap. It'll all be snobs like you. Men in suits.'

'If I wanted Communism, I'd have shacked up with a red. No, I'm off to be one of King Tony's loyal subjects. I'm going to embrace the values of Middle England. Farewell knees-up's tomorrow. Bring Stalin, if you must.'

'But when are you going?'

'Next week.'

'So you've done all this – fait accompli? And you never said anything to me.'

'You're so wrapped up in your own troubles no one tells you anything.'

When I thought about it afterwards, I could see she'd done me a favour. She'd shown me there are elements of my life that can't be put on hold. I either had to get on with it or end it, and I felt my bridge-jumping days were over. I never thought about it much before I met Max, but I had a strong sensation that I too was put in the world to be someone.

Dee has never been a suitable role model. I suspect she'll never marry. She'll be sixty-three and still tinting her hair and painting her nails and sticking her foot out to trip up Mr Right.

CHAPTER NINETEEN

Anita held her hand over the mouthpiece of the phone, face full of concern. 'It's your Russian chap,' she said.

I panicked before ever I heard Max's voice. He'd never ring me on the newsroom number, always on my mobile – and only in a crisis at that. I glanced at its screen. Blank. I'd forgotten to switch it back on after my last interview. House burnt down? Gorby run over? Immigration officers. He was at the airport, on the point of being deported. Unlikely. The haar was so thick they'd stopped flying.

'I had a small accident, Serena,' he said apologetically. 'I tried to get you on your own number. I didn't know what else to do.'

'What kind of accident?'

'A car hit me. Not hard. But I'm too sore to walk home.'

The sob in his voice frightened me far more than the images I'd conjured up. 'Jesus – where are you?'

I could hear traffic in the background. His voice sounded weak and far away. 'There's a church beside me – it's not a church now, I think, it's closed up. It's on a roundabout. I hadn't enough for a taxi. I'm sorry. I didn't want them to take me to the hospital, but I don't think I could get home from here. Let me look at the street sign…East London, I think…'

'It's OK. I know where you are. Phoebe Traquair's church. Stay put. I'll only be five minutes.'

Exactly the same junction where I nearly died in 1996, sitting helplessly in a line of traffic, in the path of a driver whose brakes had failed. At the last moment, his car veered sharply to the right and rolled over onto the other carriageway, in the path of a lorry. He died. I lived. Shaken, but not stirred.

'Can I -?' said Anita.

I shook my head. 'Max got knocked down or something. I'll come back as soon as I can.'

'Don't worry about that. We can cover for you.'

He was balancing himself against a low wall, face the colour of damp putty; it looked worse under the tan and freckles. He made no effort to stand up.

'Where's the car? He just drove off?'

'It happened up there.' He waved his hand in the direction of Leith Walk. 'It was my own fault. I know you've tried to teach me to cross properly. The driver waved me to go ahead, and I didn't go - he was still stopped, so I walked, but he started again at the same time. He was very upset. He thought I was drunk. Someone wanted to call the police. No police, I said. They tried to get an ambulance – Christ, there were twenty people by then, I don't know where they came from. I told them I was all right and walked away as fast as I could.'

He'd learnt the other survival tactics easily enough. Only the first time I'd asked him to post a letter for me had he wasted hours hunting for a blue box. He'd learnt that whatever the size of the shop you put the groceries in your basket before you paid for them. He knew that if you take a parcel to the post office you wrap it first, at home. He accepted the idea that Ursula's not risking robbery or rape because she doesn't have bars on her windows. He got the hang of it that a bus breaking down is a talking point, and that though trains run late it's minutes, not days. But he couldn't get his head round the concept of courteous drivers. 'At home they'd be lining you up for a direct hit', he'd say pathetically.

I sat on the wall beside him. 'Do you remember how we met?'

He started to laugh, then clutched at his side.

'What were you doing over here anyway?'

'I was lost. I was trying to get home. In the fog it all looks different.' He began to sob again, loudly and without control. Passers-by were staring.

'Is it worse, Maksim? Oh, sweetheart, does it hurt more? I need to take you to hospital.'

'No! Absolutely not. I want to go home. I'm such a fool, useless, useless fool.'

I had to support most of his weight to manoeuvre him into the car, and out again at home. I undressed him and laid him on the sofa. The bruise on his right side, from his chest to his thigh, was already darkening and swollen. I prodded him as gently as I could. He winced and yelped. I couldn't quiet my mind enough to work out how much of a risk it'd be to take him to the infirmary.

Ursula. She used to be a nurse. She was home.

'You must take him at once. He needs to be X-rayed.'

'I'm frightened to. Ursula – he's not here legally. He didn't have a visa. I'm sure they'll have umpteen forms to fill in. I'm so afraid if they find out he'll be taken away. Can't you look at him, see what you think?'

She examined him coolly and professionally. 'I don't think you've broken any bones. But really, I can't be sure. You might have an internal injury. You must go to hospital.'

Max sat up, grimacing. 'No chance. You get sick in those places. I'll heal myself. I'm not badly injured.'

'How would I know if it was serious?' I asked her in the hall.

'More pain. Acute pain. Vomiting. Loss of consciousness. He's certain he didn't hit his head?' She pursed her lips. 'Keep an eye on him. Call me if you're in the least worried. I'd come with you. We'd cook up some story.'

I could see what she was thinking: there may be worse neighbours than the ones who merely trade insults and blows along with the body fluids.

I tried to soothe the bruised part without hurting it. I was afraid he'd start throwing up as the shock hit him, or bleed profusely. I've never been good with illness. I wasn't sure I could nurse even the man I had claimed to love. But he was already more like his usual self.

'Kiss it better,' he said, with something close to the old grin. 'Lay your hands on me and heal me, woman. Pray over me, or something. I'm starting to feel better already.'

'You've put on some weight since you came here.'

'I never had so much to eat before in my life. My skin feels different here. I have Scottish skin now. No more shabby clothes. You couldn't understand what a luxury it is for me to be able to put on a clean shirt when I want one. I'm so sorry to cause you trouble when you've been so good to me. Darling Serena.'

Russians and Glaswegians. Hopeless with love-words, because when we say them out loud they sound like bullshit.

'Go and vote,' he said suddenly.

215

'What?'

'It's your referendum, isn't it? Today. You still have time. Go and vote.'

'I already did. On my way to work.'

'You voted for independence?'

'That's not what it's about. It's just for our own parliament.'

'It'll make no difference anyway,' said Max.

'It must make a difference. We'll be able to decide more things for ourselves.'

'No difference. Not unless Scotland finds a new solution. Capitalism doesn't work.'

'Nor does Communism. You should know that.'

'But what do you think will be different while there's still the worst kind of capitalism? As long as money talks loudest, things won't change, except for the worse.'

I grunted something about needing to hope, and left him to fall asleep, while I curled up on the floor beside him.

He was so much better by next morning it was obvious he'd be fine. In his sleep, he'd murmured my name, without resentment. He remembered to be glad that the referendum had gone in our favour.

Within a fortnight, he was as fit as ever and we were able to resume the wordless walks, the slender thread that held us together. He's the only man I ever met who doesn't feel obliged to spoil a walk with the sound of his voice. Until I found *The Living Mountain* in Thin's second-hand department, I believed that we silent walkers were freaks. Now I know better. It's the purest form of companionship which exists.

In the early days Max would often twine his fingers round mine; that ceased, but still if my foot slipped on a stone or if – as happened once at Cramond – we passed a stranger who gave me bad vibes, his hand was there at once to steady me. And he didn't always let go immediately the moment passed. We were more aware of each other than at any other time, on those wordless walks. We'd stand at the summit of Arthur's Seat, drinking in the view, and after a few minutes he'd sit down against a rock in the sun, his eyes shut. I knew as surely as if I could see behind his lids that he was seeing another river. I'd perch beside him and slide my arm round him, his fingers would close over mine, and we'd sit like that, sometimes as long as an hour.

More ways of being happy than one. Peace. This at least must be desirable. No one ever gets to live happily ever after, except in fairy-tales.

Until almost the end of September, he didn't go out in the evenings. He played the cello at home for the two of us alone. I'd sit on the landing, nursing my emotions. I couldn't be in the same room - it'd have been like watching him make love to another woman. Katya-Two nestled between his legs, a part of him, his head resting against hers, as he caressed her with that sensitive left hand that would caress me, if I'd only let it. I couldn't let him see that I was jealous of a cello.

So I'd sit hugging myself to prevent my innards from exploding and shooting from my mouth, turning the floor into an abattoir's dustbin. But there was always the risk the player would erupt without warning, like Mount Saint Helen's, sparks everywhere, uncontrollable conflagration.

'Shit! I'm useless! If I'd any talent I wouldn't have been a pauper at home. I'd have had plenty of money, a big car, a house. I'd have been able to ask you to be my wife with a future to offer you.'

He'd have had a choice too. He wouldn't have had to come with me in order to eat and have clean shirts. 'Nabokov said "in exile one lives by genius alone",' he sobbed. 'I don't have it, Serena. I'm scared. What am I to live on?'

I couldn't answer that. Same old story. Answer hiding in the bottom of a bottle.

CHAPTER TWENTY

Soon after midnight, I heard Max downstairs, fumbling to get his key in the lock. A familiar sound that put an orange mist before my eyes, and the taste of bile in my throat. He'd been drinking more and more, but never to the staggering and dopey stage. Till now. He slammed the door too hard, swore in Russian, started attempting to negotiate the stair.

The special meal I'd made for his birthday was cold and congealed in the bottom of the oven. I'd been tempted to throw the Arvo Pärt CDs in the fire. It was freezing outside, and he was wearing a light jacket. I could hear the blood swishing through my brain, ready to explode with rage and misery, while he climbed the stair on all fours. Animal. Drunken pig. He made it to the landing, grinning inanely, trying to focus on me, and stood up swaying and hiccupping.

'Where have you been till this hour? As if I didn't know. I could smell it from the door. I'm glad you want the police to lift you for being drunk.'

'Is no crime to be drunk.'

'It's a crime to be an illegal immigrant, you fool.'

'No police. I saw no police.'

'Did you walk home beside the river?'

'Yes. Nice night.'

'Cretin. There's not even moonlight. You could have drowned. You can't put one foot in front of the other. There's deep mud at the bottom of that water.'

He lurched against me and I beat his chest with my fists. 'Bastard, selfish bastard. I thought you'd had another accident. You think I want a phone-call in the middle of the night to say you're in a hospital, or prison or something?'

'Shhh, don't be angry, my beautiful Serena. I was quite safe, I wasn't on my own. I was with Tom.'

'Who the hell's Tom?'

'Bernie's husband. He wouldn't have let the police take me away. S'rena, don't be cruel to me.'

He lost his balance and wrapped his arms round me, swaying so we almost both fell. The smell of his whisky-breath made me want to vomit. I pushed him back with more force than I intended and he sat down hard in the sitting-room doorway. I was living a re-run of my parents' marriage.

There was a light in Max's eye as if to say : 'Ah! This is exciting!' He pulled himself up, and tried to embrace me again. And though I didn't intend it, my nails found his face on a reflex; a lucky hit. I drew blood. I slammed into my room, leaving him bewildered, his hand to his cheek. He slumped on the landing outside my door, scratching at the wood like a puppy, blubbering like a spoilt child.

'S'rena, I'm so unhappy. You understand this? I'm so lonely. You won't be a wife to me, I'm not supposed to be here at all, every day I wait to hear the police knock on the door. I know I let you down. I'm so unhappy.'

He struggled to get up, belching alarmingly. I bundled him into the bathroom in time, not meaning to help him, concerned for my carpet. But I found myself holding his head and sponging his face and worrying about his pistachio-and-cream pallor. He retched himself empty, while I held him absentmindedly.

And what the hell did I promise anyway? Not 'for better, for worse'. I couldn't recall the words.

I have no memory, ever, of Morag looking after Frank when he was drunk. Instead she'd bolt the outside door. I remember her standing behind it, in her nightie, holding the big steel poker in case he tried to break in. He was sick on the landing and she left him to clean it up next day.

Kneeling on the cold bathroom floor, my arms round Max's waist, trying to take the strain into myself rather than his gut, because I was still worried about his injury, it came to me that I don't have to be Morag. More than anything that's what had put me off the prospect of having kids, the palaver of stinking nappies, strings of dried puke on every sweater. 'It's different when they're your own,' folk say. 'I don't think so,' I used to tell myself. 'It's no crime to be squeamish.'

So I cleaned him up, helped him pee because he couldn't aim straight, brushed his teeth for him, and discovered I couldn't do it without feeling something – but I wasn't sure whether it was love or pity or guilt. Surely that has to be a part of what love is – cleaning traces of someone else's shit off the porcelain, helping them vomit all the poison out, and still finding them desirable?   I manoeuvred him upstairs and into bed as gently as I could.

'Will you be all right now?'

He clutched my hand. 'Stay beside me. I want you near me. Please. I'm cold and I'm lonely.'

'I'm angry with you.'

'I know I'm a worthless lout, you should be angry, but please stay with me.'

I couldn't have refused him. He was incredibly cold, and that was more worrying than anything else because on the coldest nights Max was always warm. I used to tease him that he was a hot-blooded creature: a shrew or a vole. In retaliation he'd tease me about my feet.   I held him, and tried to weep silently so he wouldn't notice.

'Perhaps you're beginning to love me at last,' he said. I could hear him smiling, in the darkness. 'If you can deal my the more noxious emissions of my body and still cuddle me, there may be hope.'

'Max. Happy birthday.'

He laughed miserably. I'd like to say we both settled to sleep with optimism in our hearts.

CHAPTER TWENTY-ONE

But I lack the talent for optimism. Next day Max had shaken off his hangover by the evening, and we were back at Carla's. She watched me closely in the first few minutes, and enquired after my health. When Dougal began to frame the crass and obvious question, she kicked him – not bothering to hide it.

'Come through with me, darling,' she said after supper. 'We'll try on jewellery, leave these hard drinkers to their man-talk.'

Carla sat me at her dressing table, took off the dusky crimson amber necklace she was wearing and put it round my neck, still warm from her own skin - an amazingly sensual touch.

'Suits you better,' she said. 'It brings out the highlights in your hair. No -,' she laid her hands over mine, 'keep it, it's a present.'

'I couldn't. It's beautiful. And it's old, it's valuable.'

'Your friendship is more valuable to me. You should wear amber for your health. Wear it for your husband. Slip into bed wearing nothing but that and he'll be like a wild stallion.'

I wasn't sure I appreciated her visualisation.

'So much tension in your neck! I'll give you a massage. What is wrong between you and Max? Be careful you don't lose him. He's a sensual, passionate man.'

How dare she speak to me like that? Hinting she'd seduced my husband – then touching me too.

'You didn't want Fergus for sex,' she crooned. 'Don't deny it. I didn't blame you. He was a coarse

223

man.   Why the hell did you marry him?   I wouldn't have let you, if you'd come with us.'

'Dougal liked him.   Anyway, I admit it was my own fault. I've paid for it.'

'This time you picked a good man.   Possibly this is because you chose him before you knew him.'   I tried to stand up, but she kept her hands firmly on my shoulders. 'I blame you for what you're doing to Max. If you don't enjoy sex you should have found a man like Dougal who can't get it up more than once a year.'

'What do you do then?   I hardly think you go without, Carla.'

'It's not my problems we're discussing. I keep myself amused.   But if you can't give Max what he needs, you should give him his freedom,' Carla said, her deft fingers working their way between my shoulder blades.   'You were married so quickly it can hardly be legal.'

'Has he told you he wants that?'

'God forbid.   He adores you.   But it doesn't make you happy, so for both your sakes you should get out of it.'

She put perfume on me, while I was still bemused – not from a spray, but sliding quick, deft fingers down between my inadequate breasts.   'This is the spot to put scent, if you're intent on keeping him, then. Drive him wild.'

Drive him to antihistamines.   She started painting me with her make-up. 'You should wear more eye shadow, kohl too.   Your superlative eyes are your best feature, that and your hair – don't ever cut it. Then it needs a little lipstick to balance the effect.'

I was an easy target: mouth still hanging open. She carried on regardless.   'Max is the type who needs sex.   He doesn't just want it; he needs it to be healthy. I can hardly believe he's not the best lover you ever had. He's well-equipped for it, and I bet he has as much talent for loving as for his music.'

'All this you can tell from looking in his eyes? That he's hot stuff and well-hung?'

'I can tell from looking at his feet.'

'What utter crap.' Though you should look at them. They're nearly as beautiful as his hands, they're so long and supple he should be able to play the piano with them. Very possibly he can.

'No, it isn't. I've made a study, over many years. Maybe one day, I'll write a book. It's one of the most obvious diagnostic signs. That's better. You're almost smiling again.'

I'd been thinking it was just as well she'd never shared this wisdom with Dee. She'd have been locked up years ago for loitering in men's shoe shops.

'As a matter of fact, I couldn't tell you whether he's good in bed or not,' I said coolly. 'You tell me.'

That stopped Carla in her tracks. 'What do you mean?'

'I haven't slept with him. That'd be OK by me, but he says he doesn't want a white marriage. Isn't that a quaint expression? Would certainly make you think twice about talking about white weddings.'

'What are you saying? Serena, you have to sort this out.'

'Yeah, yeah. What am I supposed to do? Dab on some scent to fix it? It's too late, anyway.'

'You can't go on that way. Tell me more.'

'So you can write a book about that too?' This was the woman I'd hoped to confide in, to be able to rest my head against her well-cushioned shoulder and say: 'Carla, he's huge. Enormous. I'm frightened. And why do they always want you to touch it, as if having to look wasn't bad enough. Help me.' I'd wanted to be able to tell her I was so miserable, I'd never had good sex in my life, I wouldn't know what it is, and I was so lonely, and I thought Max was it for me, and now it had all gone wrong again.

'You can't blame Max,' she said. 'He's a man. It's a natural urge. You have to sort yourself out.'

'Just like that.'

'What happened to you when you were young?'

'Haven't you heard Dee going on about it? She usually does.'

'As if I'd waste my time listening to her. Were you raped?'

'Nothing so clichéd. Just a nice, ordinary sexual assault. I was nine.'

The headline above the newspaper photo of Donald John being hustled out with a jacket over his head had said: *Carstairs for beast who subjected schoolgirl to terrifying sex ordeal.*

'He tried to rape me,' I said. 'He couldn't, because I was struggling so much. I managed to get away from him. I hurt him quite badly as a matter of fact. There was a lot of blood.'

Carla put her arms round me. 'Ghastly! But it was a very long time ago – didn't you get counselling?'

'Don't you start. Anyway, it wasn't so much what he did as what happened afterwards. Extremely unpleasant. Blood and gore and recriminations and folk dying right, left and centre. Police and reporters crawling all over the village. For which I got the blame.'

'I wish I could help you,' crooned Carla, rocking me like a child. 'But I'm a musician, not a psychiatrist. I don't know what you need.'

'Not one of them, at any rate. I need a few tips for switching off my imagination for long enough to let Max start, that's all. Well – that'd be enough to be going on with.'

'Oh, God,' she said, 'bodies are complicated things. Heart and gonads and brains all mixed up and cross-wired. It would be so much easier if all the bits were in separate bags like the giblets in a chicken. But there's something I can show you - '

She leapt to her feet and went out to the bookcase in the hall.

'Here,' she said, handing me a book. 'You can't let your muscles boss you around. You have to learn to control them. Kegels. Ugly word, clever man. I bet he warmed his speculum. Read this. It's all about getting the hang of what the muscles down there feel like when they're clenched, then relaxing them, so you learn to do be able to do either without having to think about it.'

'Exercises?' I said dismissively. 'I think maybe I need more than a few exercises to fix me.'

'Well, it won't do any harm. You won't get incontinent when you're old either. Best lesson I ever learnt. It's what they teach women to do after childbirth, in Chile.'

'But you never had a child, Carla?'

'When I was very young, before I came here, I had a daughter. She died.'

'Jesus, I'm so sorry,' I said, sitting up red-faced. 'I didn't know. Is that why you never go back there?'

'My husband disappeared soon after. It didn't take long to accept that he was dead too. Nothing to go back for. There's not a day I don't think about them. But I have to live my life now. It helps, having friends. So you see why it's important to me that you keep the amber.'

'Oh my,' Dougal said when I wandered back through in a daze. 'Serena, you're as delectable as a film star. Come and sit on Uncle Dougal's lap.'

I suppose he copped hell for that later.

I started to scrub at my face as soon as we were in the car. Max moistened the corner of his hankie, carefully removing most of the black circles I'd made under my eyes. I loved him most of all when he was in one of his tender moods. Suppose I took Carla's advice, climbed the stair that night, and slid in beside him naked except for the glowing necklace?

'Have you been talking to Carla about us?' I said.

'What about us?'

'You know what about us.'

He swore under his breath. 'You may not think I have much sense, at least credit me with a little pride. You think I'm anxious to shout that from the rooftops?'

'Then how did she know? Why would she say I'm cold towards you?'

'You are. You never touch me, you never come near me in public. You think I'll embarrass you? Get a boner in front of your friends?'

I wanted to slap the puzzled-Labrador-puppy expression off his face. 'She says our marriage can't be legal anyway. Everyone says that.'

He sobered up at once. 'We did what we did. In front of witnesses. It was speeded up a little, that's all. You're my wife. Carla loves you too. She's a kind person, Serena. A frustrated mother.'

'Jesus! So she'd told you that, after knowing you about half an hour?'

'Told me what?   Serena, don't fall out with Carla.   She's your friend.   I think you need women friends.'

'That's why I have no intention of letting anyone break up the friendship,' I said.

CHAPTER TWENTY-TWO

'Look. Your husband's on the telly,' Max said.

The new series of *Learmonth on the Lookout* had started its winter run; he watched in a fascinated stupor.

'Fergus is a disappointed man,' I said. 'He thinks he deserves to be in London, flying the flag for punters who expect Concorde for the price of EasyJet.'

Lookout would have represented success beyond imagining for some, but it only went out in Central Scotland. He'd been walled up in a provincial tunnel like Henry, the engine who was naughty. God knows who he'd offended in the past, because he's superb at his job, meticulous. Each detail has to be just so. Nick says that makes him a *perfect* bastard.

'He's just an actor,' I said.

'You've a nerve, accusing your husband of being an actor. You can put on a pretty good act. So you regret it, when you see him? He's a TV star, he must be rich.'

'He's a lot better off than I am. Not the way you read in the papers, the hundreds of thousands a year class. Anyway, the best of luck to him.'

'These things signify for you, money, status.'

'You think I'm impressed because his name's in the Radio Times?'

'It's important for you. You need to have luxury, like this house. Better to have a husband who earns a lot.'

I punched a cushion, hard.

'And you loved him,' he went on, 'you must have. Or do you only marry men you don't love?'

'Max!'

He turned to face me squarely, folding his arms. 'What qualities in me did you imagine you loved?' The doctor's son, delivering a bad prognosis.

'You're the one having second thoughts,' I said. 'You started on that the minute we were married. You changed from happy and optimistic to ill-tempered and morose as suddenly as if someone had flicked a switch.'

'I'm trying to understand.' He sounded weary. 'You should have been less impulsive. You admit you burned your toes the first time, with an unwise marriage.'

'Fingers. Burned my fingers.'

'Whatever. Burned your fanny.' He began to drum his own fingers on the chair-arm. I wanted to yell at him to quit fidgeting. 'I want to be able to fall in love with you, Serena.'

'Bit late in the day. That's supposed to come first.' For that I got the dismissive laugh that's almost as irritating as the shrug.

'I've told you before, it doesn't just drop out of the sky.'

'Why did you come with me then? Just to get away?'

'I won't deny I was glad to leave at the time. Your friends have told you this, Serena. If you'd listened to them you would have understood better. "As well this one as another", I said to myself.' He reached across and squeezed my shoulder. 'Jesus, I'm teasing you! I wouldn't have gone with just anyone.'

Memory can swallow a lot. Never that. I'll never forget that he put that into words, these words. 'Sorry it didn't work out for you,' I said.

'Why do you turn every time we talk into a fight?'

231

'*I* turn it into a fight? You're the one who pontificates about the significance of marriage, now you announce quite calmly it was a sham for you at the time.'

'The spark was there. But love needs bloody hard work. You're the one who didn't take it seriously. On a whim, you decided.' Max could become impatient so quickly. 'If you'd met me here you'd not have given me a second glance. You were obsessed with the idea of falling in love in St Petersburg. Any man would have done. You admit you liked me better – "loved" me, as you prefer to say, before you knew me at all. Now you've had three months of living with me, you've changed your mind, the way you did with this Fergus. You want to walk away from the mess, the same as a dog that's crapped in the street. I can't be bothered with the way you decide it's easier to end it.'

I knew there should be humour hidden in this, Max bawling at me, sparks flying from his eyes as he expounded on the nature of love. 'I don't understand what you want me to say,' I said. 'It's you that's changed.'

'I don't want you to say anything. I want you to desire me. In your body, not your head. You wanted the same as me the first night. You were put off by the fact we'd no privacy. I didn't mind that. I found it endearing, that you were so modest. This is OK, I thought. This girl has qualities I can love. She turns me on, and I can be a three-times-a-night man for her, once she's home in her own bed.'

If he could have seen into my mind, and the places I'd seduced him there! It didn't stop at Jenners' doorway; the thick undergrowth beside the Water of Leith just yards along from our street; the giant lily pads in the Tropical House at the Botanics.

232

'I didn't want that,' I said huffily.

'I didn't know that, did I? This Sergei you dream of, this waiter. That was just about sex too. When he stood at your shoulder there it was, right at your eye-level, the cute little fly of his lovely tight trousers. You creamed your panties imagining what was under there.'

'And men don't do this?'

'Of course we do. We'll drop a knife so the waitress has to bend over and we can look down her blouse. Men and women are programmed to find each other's bodies erotic. I can't believe it hasn't happened to you. Don't cry.'

The tide of his anger ebbed quickly, leaving me stranded and gasping for air. He stretched his arm along the back of the sofa and stroked my hair cautiously, as if I was a temperamental and sharp-toothed animal. 'Fergus has another woman?'

'I've no idea. I'm not interested. He didn't leave me for another woman, if that's what you're asking, he wasn't having an affair. Neither was I.'

'You have a lot in common, the same job, the same friends. He's a handsome man. I'll bet he's attractive to women.'

'I'm fed up with the subject of Fergus.'

'Did he beat you? You think I'm going to beat you? That explains quite a lot.'

I've never escaped from the trap of feeling it must have been my own fault. The way people looked at me confirmed that. Fergus has fleshy, sensual lips. 'Thin lips mean cruelty,' I said to myself when I met him. 'He's not cruel then, so that should be OK.' As much garbage as most old wives' tales, like the one that opposites attract, or that if you speak of Old Clootie he'll appear.

When the bell rang at nine that night, I peeked out and saw no unfamiliar cars in the street.

'Someone selling double glazing or Jesus,' I thought. 'Hardly worth answering.' I heard Max pad down the stair, open the door. 'Can I help you?'

'You can let me in.'

Creeping Jesus. I'd assumed he'd be at home watching himself on the telly. I stormed onto the landing.

'What do you want, Fergus?'

'Ah – the angel of the house! I'm delighted to see you too.' He pushed past Max and came upstairs. That's why he's so efficient at his job. He could push past a serial murderer, brandishing a microphone. He doorsteps thugs, and he's never had so much as a bruise to show for it. A powerful man. That's a large part of why I fell under his spell. The others at Albion are hyenas, snapping and yelping over the carrion. The only killing they're brave enough to face is character assassination. Fergus is a true predator, even if he brings down his prey by stealth and cunning, and he nails the real villains. He doesn't bugger up ordinary people's lives just to fill an awkward thirty-second gap in a bulletin. His heart's in the right place. If only someone had snipped the wiring between the lower organs and the brain.

'Why are you here?' I said.

'To check that you're all right, kitten. You look a little flustered. Hope I didn't interrupt hubby doing a spot of interior decorating. Well, perhaps not. How are you? No one sees you now, I hear.'

I retreated into the sitting room and he followed me. I could smell the whisky on his breath from several feet away. Max laid his arm protectively round my shoulders. He'd enough pride to pretend not to recognise him.

'Serena, do you know this person?'

'It's Fergus.'

'Her husband,' said Fergus.

'No, I don't think so. I am her husband. What do you want here?'

'Well, I'm visiting my wife – OK with you, Boris? I want to be sure you're looking after her. She's not one of your Commie women. She's used to better, a decent standard of living.'

'Why are you here really?' I said.

'Social call - remember that, do you Serena? It's what civilised people do. They sit around sipping chilled wine and discussing Schumann. Not that you're up for that, if I recall. You could bring us up to date with the latest opus of the Brothers Gallagher, or the newest thing in diesel-dyke-music.' (This is how Fergus deals with the fact he'd never heard of Melissa Etheridge.) 'Well, witch, how are you?' He held up his fingers in the anti-evil-eye sign. 'Don't glare at me like that, woman.'

'Leave us in peace,' I said. 'You've had your money back, so shift your arse out of here.'

Fergus threw up his hands and flinched.   'I didn't think you were into using words for any body-part below the neck. What's that in Gaelic, now? I'm sure they have a fine word for arse. Given the variety of wildlife and the looks of the women, they probably have thirty words for it, like the Eskimos with snow. Sheep's arse, dog's arse, goat's arse, duck's arse....... Mind you, their sheep aren't such hot shit either. That's why they all emigrated to Australia. Better-looking sheep. What do you, think, Boris?'

Please God, I thought, don't let me laugh.

'Why the hell d'you call me Boris?'

Fergus shrugged. 'That's what you're all called, isn't it? Where's the cat? I never agreed another man could have it. Where is he Serena – upstairs or through in your bedroom?'

He walked calmly onto the landing and opened the door of my room. Gorby had deserted me weeks before to stretch his lanky frame alongside Max's at night. Cats have no mind-crap about loyalty. When it's a matter of extra paw-room, no contest.

'You're not taking the cat.'

'Cuddles up to Boris here does it? I must admit, there were nights I found the idea of the cat's arse seductive, for want of a sheep. I thought the mail order catalogues were all "beautiful Russian women"? Didn't realise they did pretty men too. Just as well you bought the bit of paper before you brought him here.'

'What makes you think buying came into it?'

'I'm an investigative journalist. The thing you pretend to be, witch, only I'm good.'

'Why the hell do you call my wife a witch?' yelled Max.

'Because she is one. Better watch yourself, Boris. Say the wrong thing and she'll turn you into a wood louse. Not a good idea to let her get between you and the door when she has that look about her. Another tip – don't let her play with matches or sharp objects.'

Max stalked towards him. 'Fuck off. Get out of my house.'

'It's your house, is it? Suffering Jesus, madam has certainly climbed off her high horse. I wasn't permitted to call it my house, no matter that it was.'

'This is Serena's home, you're not welcome here. Get out. Now.'

'Look at the state of the man! I know how you're placed, pal. I recognise that frozen, shell-shocked look. All her men have it. Comes with the realisation that the requirement to thresh your own oats doesn't end with the nuptials. Have your cojones docked, why don't you. She'll pay. Anything rather than open her legs. She was like that with me too. You shouldn't shack up with men who need sex, Serena. You should have a government health warning tattooed on your forehead.'

I floundered in the hope Max wouldn't understand what he was saying.

'I think this was your problem. Serena says you were useless in bed, even when you managed to get it up.' Oh, nice shot, Maksim Stepanovich!

Fergus's throat puffed out like a capercaillie's. 'If she suits you, you must have more lead than pencil. Surprising number of long skinny men have little skinny whangers. I'm equipped with a decent-sized one. Too big for her.'

For a moment I feared he was ready to drop his pants to validate the claim. Fergus and his damn knob, specially when he's been drinking. There was a weight-lifting demo with the cameraman's battery-pack that nearly had all three of us arrested in Stirling one time.

'I think your head's too big for you,' yelled Max. 'Perhaps I'll shift it off your neck.'

'She should get herself stretched. They can do that now; there's a clinic in London. Same place does fancy stitchery to make them virgins again, she could have the whole works while she's at it, can't imagine how she managed to lose it in the first place. Required a general anaesthetic I should think.'

Max grabbed him by the lapels. I could visualise it all: the police, the handcuffs, the court case, the headlines next day.

'Maksim – don't touch him. It's not worth it.'

'Oh, I think it gives me such satisfaction it's worth a lot.'

But he didn't hit Fergus. He placed his hands around his throat and shook him, then manhandled him towards the stair. I realised I should be attempting to calm them, the way womenfolk do in Westerns. I grabbed my husband's arms and held onto him as Fergus left.

'What money?' Max said as soon as the door was closed. 'You took money from this creep?' He was so angry I was frightened.

'Ages ago. I borrowed a little.'

'Since you were with me?'

'To get us back here, if you must know. I ran out of cash.'

'This man paid for me to come to Britain?' His laughter came as quickly as the anger had. We both sat on the floor, gasping for breath. It ceased suddenly, as if his throat was cut.

'You told him,' he said.

'Told him what?'

'That you don't sleep with me. That I'm such a pathetic creature I've accepted I'm not allowed to sleep with my own wife. That fat pig knows.'

'He doesn't know shit.'

'You think I'm stupid? You think I don't understand enough English? He knows you don't sleep in my bed: "through in your bedroom", he said. Bugger it, I know the difference between through and up. And all the time, you're grinning at his funny jokes.'

'Oh, nonsense.'

He slapped me so hard I fell over. I sat up and hit him back with all the force I could muster.

'Bitch.' He caught me by the wrists and grappled with me on the floor; his grip was tighter than a vice. 'And is it true what he said, that you wouldn't sleep with him either? You told me it was because he hurt you.'

'He did. And he degraded me. He raped me.'

'What nonsense! He was your husband. Is he a good lover?'

'What do you want me to say? You want to know if his is bigger than yours?'

'His bank account's certainly bigger than mine. I think this is why you let him do it to you.'

I yawned; nervous reaction.

'Bored, are we?'

He started to unfasten my trousers, still trapping both my wrists with his other hand. Right there on my favourite rug, in the place I'd imagined lying cuddling Max, he was going to invade me and hurt me. I twisted my head and sank my teeth in his arm. He released me immediately, and sat with his face in his hands. I felt terrifyingly calm.

'This is where he leaves,' I thought. 'This is how it ends.' I tried to stand up, but he held onto me, gently now.

'Let me go,' I said.

I never wanted a sappy fairy prince. So this is what I do - I fidget and scratch till the Beast breaks through. I have turned into my mother. I'm a woman who drives her husband to rape her on the sitting-room floor.

'Sweetheart, I'm sorry,' said Max, and I could tell without looking that there were tears on his face. 'I don't know what made me do that. I swear on my father's grave I'll never treat you that way again.'

239

I wanted to punish him, and I wanted to hold him and weep with him.   'I'm tired.   Let's talk tomorrow.'

'I need to hear you say you forgive me' he said. 'I hardly know what I'm doing.   Jesus, I'm losing my reason.'

I clamped my mouth shut, but a strangled sob escaped all the same.

'Don't. I won't hurt you any more.   Give me a clue.   What do I need to do to make you happier? You're always sad.'

'You do make me happy.   It's me that makes me sad. Maksim, why did you really come home with me?'

'Because you're brave and beautiful and loyal and compassionate, and you lay a whole night snuggled up to me with your lovely hair round your shoulders, black as a mermaid's.'

'Mermaids have blonde hair.'

'Not my mermaid.   She has blue-black hair like a bird's wing, and eyes like flowers, and a skin so fine I can see right through it, I can see her clever brain and her good, brave, gentle heart.'

I wanted to be able to tell him all the parts of him I loved, his muscular shoulders, his beautiful hands, his elegant toes, the way his hair lies the wrong direction, smooth and sleek as fox's fur above the tanned skin at the nape of his neck, his strength, his stamina.   But the words were strangled in my throat.

'Tell me things,' I croaked.

'What things?'

'I have had one awful, hellish day with Fergus and all that, and I need you to tell me something nice.'

'I don't know what you want me to say. OK?'

'See? You can turn even that into a quarrel.'

He stood up and switched on the light. 'I want to comfort you, but you're my woman not my child. I'm sorry I frightened you. I don't understand what you want any more.'

He slammed the front door so hard the Chagall painting fell off the wall. I sat for a long time, contemplating the shattered glass.

I almost found it in my heart to pray he just wouldn't come back.

CHAPTER TWENTY-THREE

'Serena!'

Maksim had a catalogue of different inflections for my name. This was the mock English upper class one, the one that meant he suspected me of activities not entirely on the level. It had a tinge of contempt in it.

'Phone call for you, darling.' He was holding the receiver in two fingers, as if it had shit on it. His eyes glittered. I knew it was a man. 'Not your husband. Different man every day now. This one calls himself Captain Cunti.'

'Bugger!'

'No, I'm sure he said Cunti. You don't want to speak to him?'

I grabbed the receiver. 'Hello?' I snapped. Then I felt guilty.

'Serena?' Paolo's voice: warm and worldly and affectionate. I conjured up his pleasing face. For the briefest moment I contemplated whether I could forget the bloody Fortuna sailing away while he wouldn't look at me, plus the fact I'd made a few desultory wedding vows Max wanted out of. To hell with that.

'I thought I'd dialled the wrong number. Who was that?'

'That's Max, my husband.'

Silence that could split wood at the other end of the line. 'You told me you were divorced.'

'So I was, then. I remarried. Max is Russian. Maksim Grigoriev.'

'You married the man you picked up in St Petersburg? I thought you were a lady.'

'Where are you phoning from? It's a very clear line.' *Ground control to Major Tom...*

'A hotel near the corner of your High Street and – let me see – North Bridge? I was looking forward to having you show me round, but it doesn't matter.'

I couldn't have felt more guilty if I'd sent him a written invitation. Max was next door in the kitchen performing Krakatoa impressions with pots and dishes. I was sure Paolo must be able to hear, and pressed my hand round the mouthpiece.

'We'd be glad to show you the city. Please – you must come and visit us.'

'You and your Russian husband?' He made it sound like a notifiable disease. 'No, I don't think so.'

'Don't take that tone. I didn't ask you to come.'

'No, you didn't. It's my own fault. They tell me I should have come a few weeks back for the festival. I see I didn't need to catch the comedy shows to get a laugh.' He hung up on me.

'Boyfriend in town?' said Max, coming into the room, 'Kapitan Polo Cunti. You made a date with this man before the ship sailed?'

'You know I didn't. I've no idea know how he found my number. I never gave it to him.'

'Passenger list.' His tone was less hostile. I looked up. He was holding out my Prada jacket. 'Wear this. It looks good on you. Go to him.'

'I don't want to go to him.'

'Go to him, Serena. He can buy you lunch if you hurry. Handsome man, good job, plenty of cash, crazy for you. What more do you want? He can take you out to a smart restaurant. Italian. One of the good guys. They don't need visas. Fill in a form. You can

243

probably get it in the greengrocers. As simple as buying potatoes. He can make you happy.'

Don't tempt me Max.

'I haven't time to argue now. I have to go to work.'

'To hell with your work. Call in sick.'

'I can't do that. It's not fair on the others.' Every week there was a new batch of rumours that Albion was being taken over. We were all shit-scared for our jobs. 'I'll come home early. We can talk.'

'I'm leaving you,' he said. 'I'll leave you for some other man to pick up. A man with a good job and no balls. I'll find a woman who doesn't just want to talk.'

'Stop it. We can work this out.'

He put his arms round me and sighed. 'Act like my wife. That's all I want.'

'I do. I nag you all the time.'

Max abstained from smiling, but he kissed me before I left.

'Nice wee job for you tonight,' said Anita, at teatime. 'You're needed at Linlithgow. It's the memorial service for the brat who was murdered. Starts at eight. Candle-lit vigil - the punters love that. The whole country's still in sob-mode after the Di thing. You've loads of time. You can go in the Volvo with Dennis.'

'You can't justify sending a reporter as well as a cameraman. All it needs is a read. I'm not going. It's too late. God damn it, it's Friday. It's dark. It's freezing. It's October. Why can't Nick or Drew do it? They covered the murder.'

'Kiddies aren't a man's thing. You look the part, sweet and funereal in that navy blue rigout. Possibly you could shed a tear or two? I'll tell Dennis to make sure he catches that.'

Terribly preoccupied with form, Anita. She has a theory that the bereaved should always have the manners to indicate dress code in the funeral notice, so that she doesn't risk the embarrassment of turning up in black to a fuchsia-tee-shirt-and-shorts one, or vice versa.

'I've hardly been home before nine once in the past fortnight,' I said. 'This is the weekend.'

'Getting restive, is he? Never mind. I'll switch you to day shifts every day next week, put someone else out. Come on, Serena, it's not as if you have kids you have to get back to. The men do.'

'I have a home to go to, just as much as the ones who've bred successfully.'

'And you have a job that needs you to put it first,' said Anita.

'Stuff your job. I'm sick of your job. It's not as if there's an interesting story around anyway. Why can't we be as honest as they were years ago? "There's no news today, so here's Elgar's Cello Concerto"? No, we mould it and shape it and pretend we're alchemists converting thin air into nuggets of news. I'm sick of being in your secret society, Anita. And you can tell Roger that too. Tell him he can bloody well sack me.'

I logged on again, typed out a resignation letter and handed it to her.

'Don't be so stupid. Take this back.'

I ignored her. She tore it up and put it in the bin.

'Take a candle. You want to show respect.'

'I can't hold a candle and the mic. I'll burn myself.'

'Look in the canteen for an empty jam-jar to put it in. Tie string round the top – didn't you ever do that when you were a kid?'

'Why do we have to cover it at all? This is sick. You're always saying we don't have the luxury of covering human-interest crap, like the papers. This isn't news.'

'There's bugger all else around tonight. If we don't have input from this end, we can all kiss our jobs goodbye. You knew when you came here it was no nine to five set up. We go where the news is when it is. That's the Albion philosophy.'

'I'm not wasting my time doing this. It won't get used. I'm sick of this place thinking it can fuck up my life and not use the product.'

'The Beeb'll have a camera there. They won't have time to cut it for the Nine, or even the regionals. You can get back here and have it cut for the Ten. Brownie points for Albion.'

'Media hype. The papers put the parents up to doing it so they can have a two-page spread.'

'Kit yourself out with a candle, there's a doll. I'll give you the money for it. I wonder if you should take a wee posy too?'

It would have been fine to work for someone I trusted enough to say I had a marriage to end. 'For God's sake, Anita! All right, I'll go. What do you want? I'm not talking to the parents.'

'There'll be a token worthy there from the politzei. Do a "what lessons?" line. And that minister, or some other professional do-gooder's bound to show. "How it's brought the community closer", da-da-de-da. How a few more of the lazy sluts of mothers take note of where their brats are after dark now, that sort of junk.

This is your piece. You decide. Use your initiative, for Christ's sake, if you have any.'

'Who writes your script? Your pal Fergus?'

'Fergus is no friend of mine,' she said, too quickly. 'You're the one who married him, poor little cow.'

'Is that what you all say about me? That I'm the poor cow who was daft enough to marry Fergus?'

She shrugged. 'I'm not aware that "we" discuss you. But since you ask, yes, most people are sorry for you, that it didn't work out. I wouldn't have married him.'

'He wouldn't have asked *you*.'

We glared at each other, then laughed. All the years I worked with her, that was the closest to a conversation we'd ever got. I called home to tell Max to tape the late news, so I could keep it and watch it when I'm old and wonder who I am and where that stranger's gone. I let it ring for ages. No reply. I went to Linlithgow, and carried my night-light in a jar, and laid it in the park where they'd found the small, broken body, and tried to work out how it'd feel if it had been a child I'd known, Bernie's kid, or Roddy's, and felt nothing, nothing, except resentment.

So I cornered the faceless wonder the police had sent, and laid into him on why kids were still getting abducted and raped and murdered in broad daylight while he and his cronies sat on their arses gawping at monitors and counting their brownie points for promotion.

Then I went home, to offer Max his fare home, plus the cash he'd earned that was still sitting in my account. No hard feelings. We'd both been over-optimistic.

The house was in darkness.

CHAPTER TWENTY-FOUR

While I waited for Max that night, the first emotion was anger. I'd wanted to end it properly, handshakes and consolatory words and some semblance of dignity.

Is fheàrr teicheadh math na droch fhuireach, as my Grannie would say. Better a good retreat than a bad stand.

It was only when I heard Ursula's clock strike one that I began to worry. I'd found Colquhoun's number in the book and tried it soon after midnight. There was no reply. He could have been at Marjorie's, but I was confident he'd never have gone there without saying, or carried out the threat to stay over. I didn't dare ring her at that time and risk giving her a heart attack.

So I rang a friend with a strong heart. Dougal's surprised, sleepy voice said: 'No, haven't seen him since the last time you were over. Carla's not here. She's taken a gaggle of kids to a concert in Glasgow. They're staying till tomorrow. Are you all right, Serena?'

I fought against the picture in my mind, trying to control the waves of nausea. Maksim and Carla in bed together. Too tame for them. Somewhere semi-public and risky. In a women's toilet, with her legs wrapped round his waist so only one pair of feet showed, and he had to stifle his mouth against her neck. Another little pastime to amuse her.

I wandered round the house, trying to gauge if anything was missing or different. All his best gear was still in the wardrobe and the chest; the sweaters

248

and sexy Levi 501s I'd bought him. I drew comfort from the coarse denim, held it to my cheek. I decided to look in his shoebox of mementoes for clues. There was only one photograph left; Max and Zhenya in uniform. Apart from that, nothing but an army logbook. His diploma from the Leningrad Conservatory was still on the wall in the gilt frame I'd bought for it.

But I knew from the start Max travels light. He could pack a bag in ten minutes, and if he wanted to vanish he'd leave a cold trail. He's not thirled to possessions the way I am. He comes from a rainy country, yet he's never owned an umbrella. When Dougal lent us one, I had to show him how to put it up.

When I move on, I'll have to spend weeks contemplating the future of my possessions. Bags for the Cyrenians, boxes of things to be sold, others to be stored. A large van; the plangent cries of Gorby imprisoned in the plastic carrier which he loathes.

I'd perceived Max's former lifestyle as squalid, so I failed to notice that he was happier in one small room. His temperament would suit life on a boat, or in a cave. A single pan for cooking, a pair of jeans, a bucket to wash in, furniture picked up from skips. He recognises that clutter is anathema to art and empty rooms gestate inner visions. 'Humble living does not diminish,' he used to tell me. 'It augments.'

I'm not the one who married a pauper. My sole talent's for losing significant others.

Daddy's gone away to live elsewhere.
Will he have another wee girl?
I've no idea. He's just about irresponsible enough.

In destructive testing; you crank up the stress till it shatters, you don't stop short.

I huddled in the armchair, my duvet round me, jolting fully awake every few minutes, imagining I heard footsteps upstairs. Then I took a notion to look inside the stove. The passport cover was still recognisable, though he'd made sure the inside was completely burned. There were several sheets of paper, letters perhaps, which disintegrated into dust as I tried to extract them. Only one had writing and print I could decipher. It was our marriage certificate.

Around ten to two, I heard Ursula's door close, and ran downstairs. 'I don't suppose you happened to notice what time Max went out?'

She looked distracted. 'Max?'

'It's just that he hasn't come in, and he hadn't mentioned he'd be this late.'

'I haven't been here since early afternoon. My aunt in Falkirk's died.'

'God, I'm sorry. I didn't mean to disturb you.'

She smiled wearily. 'It's all right. She was over ninety. She'd just gone in her sleep. The police came for me, because the neighbours hadn't seen her for a day or two. They couldn't get in, so they came here. Now that would have been about two in the afternoon – and I know Max was here then, because they knocked at your house first. They weren't sure of the address. I could hear him moving about, though he didn't answer the door.'

We gazed at each other.

'They were uniformed ones too,' she said. 'Surely Max didn't think - ?'

I'd meant to ask her to walk along the river path with me, to see if we could find him. Not tactful, in the circumstances. I decided to risk walking alone. In less than ten minutes I spotted him heading towards me, unsteady on his feet.

'Come for a walk with me,' he said, clutching at my arm.

'It's the middle of the night.'

'You like to walk. There are friends I want you to meet.' He gave me a wobbly smile, and his eyes gleamed like an animal's.

'I'm not interested in meeting a crowd of drunken bums. Max – we have to talk.'

It was an exceptionally fine night, though freezing. I walked beside him, back in the direction of Leith.

'Talk to me then,' he said.

'It'd be easier if you were sober. Why did you destroy our marriage certificate?' If you were meaning to come back.

'They came for me,' he said. 'I'm so worried I'll get you into trouble.'

'They were looking for Ursula. Her aunt died.'

'That's what they'd say. I know they were looking for me.'

He had a bottle of vodka in each pocket, the genuine product, not a Western imitation; it began to dawn on me who these friends were. He kept offering me a swig, but I only pretended to drink. The first bottle was three-quarters empty by the time we'd reached the area where my gentle river's hemmed in with dank walls and becomes a caged, vindictive beast.

'Let's turn back here,' I said.

'Just a little further. They leave tomorrow, or the day after. I want you to meet them. I'm bursting for a pee,' Max said, heading for the edge of the dock.

'For God's sake be careful. If you think I could go into that water to save myself, never mind you - '

He grinned inanely, fumbling with his zip. 'Hold it for me,' he said. 'The way you did once before. I love the feel of your hand on it. It's gentle, not like other women's hands.'

I turned on my heel, disgusted, and started to walk back along the path. When I heard the splash, I thought: Well, there goes the full bottle, please God. It was such a gentle little splash.

I turned to check he was following me. It can't have been more than a minute later, I'm sure of it. The path was completely empty. It took a moment before I could bring myself to look over the edge. Suppose it was true what they say, suppose Max's beautiful hands were breaking the surface for the third time, reaching towards me, pleading? But the dark water was smooth, not a ripple. It wasn't possible that he could have fallen. It hadn't been five minutes. I've read it takes five minutes, at least, and Max is young and fit.

He was hiding, to tease me, playing his irritating trick of being able to sober up instantly. Frank was just the same. Perhaps it's a skill men acquire in the army.

'Max!' I called softly. My voice echoed off the walls. I called again, a little more loudly. 'Max – stop fooling around. I'm going home.'

A flashlight shone in my face. They were on the opposite bank, two of them. I could make out uniforms, but couldn't see if they were police or security guards. I shaded my eyes.

'Lost my dog!' I called. 'Max! Max! Here boy!' I tried to whistle, but my mouth was too dry. I turned and walked away as fast as I could without running.

I sat up for the rest of the night. Surely he'd have had the sense to lie low for long enough for them to move on, then leg it home? When it got to five, and still no sign, I phoned Fergus.

'What do you want me to do about it?' he said. 'Bloody hell woman, you wake me at this time with an idiot phone-call – you expect me to care?'

'I have to find out what happened to him.'

'What are you trying to tell me – that you pushed him in?'

'Of course I didn't. Fergus – I don't know what to do.'

'Nothing,' he said. 'That's what you do. Are you listening, Serena?'

'I can't do nothing. Suppose he did fall?'

'Hell, witch, I still hanker after you, but I can't sort out all your messes for you. You sit tight and keep shtum. He's probably perfectly all right. Even if he did take a dip, he'd just have swum to the nearest steps, feeling puzzled. If he was that drunk, he wouldn't even have noticed.'

'He can't swim,' I said in a small voice.

'Nonsense. All rats can swim. Now – stop this. Go to sleep for a while. I have to go to London again today – bloody hell! It's nearly time to go to the airport – I'll call you when I get back. Now, kitten, concentrate – listen to what I'm telling you. If the politzei nabbed him, you'll hear soon enough. If he fell in and drowned, there'll be a body. They don't just lie at the bottom, you know. Not unless it's well weighted-down – you didn't, did you? Shush. Stop wailing. Just kidding. Serious again. Who else have you told about this? No one? Good. How good a look at you did these cops get?'

'I suppose they could see it was a woman. Not much else. I had my hood up. Dougal knows I was

253

looking for him last night. And Ursula. I'd spoken to them before he turned up.'

'But you didn't meet anyone while you were with him?'

'There was no one around at that time.'

'OK. So this is the story. He wasn't there when you came home from work, and you haven't seen or heard from him since. If anything turns up, I'll say you were with me most of the night. Do you understand, Serena?'

'Yes,' I said obediently. 'But Ursula knows I was here.'

'Right. Then I was there with you, till around half-four – OK? You left me snoozing in bed while you spoke to her, then came straight back.'

By eight-thirty I was in the newsroom. No one else was in - Albion doesn't work a Saturday morning shift unless there's something juicy on the go. I scanned feverishly through the overnight police releases on the wires. A handbag snatch in Oxgangs, and six cars vandalised in St Mary's Street. I rang their information room: 'Just doing the check-call – anything fresh with you? Not much of a haul for a Friday night. No interesting arrests? Nothing over Leith way?'

'No,' she said suspiciously. 'Why – what have you heard?'

Surely if he'd been picked up, they'd have told me by now anyway? Unless he'd been stupid enough to deny all knowledge, as he'd always promised he would.

I rang A&E at the Infirmary. I rang the ambulance service PR guy. Everywhere I tried, I drew blanks, as I'd known I would.

'She's not home yet,' said Dougal. 'They're due back at noon. Hasn't there been no sign of Max at all? Look – are you sure you don't want me to come over? You must be worried sick.'

'I'm at work. I'm OK.'

I went home, just in case he decided to turn up anyway.

'Why didn't you call sooner?' said Marjorie. 'He must have had an accident. You poor girl. Shall I drive over? Is there anything I can do then?'

I almost broke an ankle when the phone rang. 'Loved your Wee Lorraine piece last night!' Anita bawled into the receiver. Jesus! Was that really only yesterday? 'The way you nailed that sanctimonious geek and shaved his balls for him. Communication Officer! What do they know about communicating? Roger saw it too. He's been bending my ear about why I don't use you more often for a piece to camera. Why indeed, Serena, when you look so good? With you it doesn't matter that it puts a few pounds on. '

'It turned out OK then?'

'I thought you might not have had a chance to see it.' I could tell she was smiling. 'I taped it for you. Hey listen – what we were talking about yesterday. I really hope it works out for you this time. It wasn't your fault with Fergus. He's a bastard of the first order. I was married once you know, and it didn't work out. It's not for everyone. Are you still there?'

'I'm a wee bit preoccupied,' I said. 'Max has gone AWOL.'

'Shit! Is there anything I can do?'

'Not really. I'm just telling you.'

'You've got my home number, haven't you – and my mobile?'

255

Never would have believed I could find Anita's throaty voice comforting.

Carla didn't phone.   She turned up on the doorstep.

'Right – you've obviously checked that he's not had an accident.   You'd had a quarrel?   He's gone to stay with a friend then.   Give you a fright.   Men are bastards.'

Then she studied my face and became ferociously angry. 'My God – you thought he was with me did you?   Bad enough you believe I'd steal another woman's husband – but that you'd believe I'd steal yours. I'm hurt, Serena.   I've been your friend a long time. I'm wounded to find you think I'd stoop that low.'

'I told you before, he was hardly my husband, except on a piece of paper.   And he's burnt that. Anyway, I knew he wasn't with you, though I admit   I did wonder at first.'

I told her the whole story. 'Fergus says I should keep quiet about having seen him. He says Max couldn't possibly have fallen in.'

'Of course he couldn't. Even people who can't swim don't just drop like a stone.'

'I wish - '

Carla stroked my hair.

'I have to apologise to you,' I said. 'I suppose you're the first woman I ever knew who's normal.   I mistook that for something else. I'd give the earth to be like you.'

'No you wouldn't.   You just need to learn to be like yourself.'

'Forgive me?'

'Nothing to forgive. Shit happens, between friends. Now – where could Max be? Who else does he see?'

I walked, just in case I found him en route. I still hadn't given up hope. Colquhoun's pub was a time warp. I hadn't considered the possibility places like that still survived, exactly the sort of place my father would have drunk in. They could have gone boozing together, Frank and his Russian son-in-law.

'It's Max's wife,' said the barman. 'He didnae come home last night. Anybody seen him?'

Wide-eyed stares, shaken heads all round. 'He wasn't here yesterday,' said one man. 'I was looking forward to our game, but he didn't show up. Kasparov, we all called him.'

What a cliché. I was mortified that I hadn't known, he'd never shared that with me. Worse, he never shared it with Dougal, who actually plays chess. I used to enjoy watching Max as if he was a stranger. No game, it had been.

'He didnae turn up for his work last night,' said the barman. 'I wondered. He's never done that before.'

'His work? What sort of work?'

He looked at me in amazement. 'What sort of work does anyone do in a pub? Clearing tables, washing glasses, cleaning the toilets. I thought you said you were his wife?'

'I didn't realise he worked here.'

He laughed. 'It figures. He always wanted paid in kind. He got the odd tenner too.'

One of the old boys laid his hand gently over mine and lowered his voice.

'You must be worried sick,' he said. 'He'd told me a bit about how he came to be here. I don't think any

257

of the others know. Johnser might. John Seaton. All Archie knew was that he always wanted paid in cash. I'm sure he just thought Max was on the dole. Archie – give John a ring.'

I told him my neighbour's aunt had precipitated this, electing to die without cancelling the milk.

'He'll be lying low for a while then,' he said. 'He's got a phobia about uniforms. The bobbies used to come in here, you know, just put their heads round the door, and Max would do his Houdini act. Disappear before your eyes. Even did it a couple of times when the Sally Army came round. Anything in a uniform.'

Johnser arrived, breathless. He was almost as upset as I was. 'You look dead on your feet,' he said. 'Do you want to go home? Have you got the car? I'll drive you.' He went with an unerring accuracy that made me irrationally mad. I knew then who'd been responsible for the days when I used to come home from work to the certainty that Max had been smoking pot. (He used to smile gently at me and say: 'A friend had some.' Then I'd get very angry and yell that I wasn't out working my butt off so that he could slum around with his pals smoking dope.) ·

That's where I'd gone wrong. Separating him from Zhenya. Max never really had much time for women, I think. He's confident enough in his own sexuality to prefer the company of men, the world that's closed and full of mystery to me. I could never have understood him.

All of Sunday I sat beside the phone, willing it to ring. At midnight, I changed the message on the answering machine to say: 'If that's you, Maksim, please leave a message. I love you. Come home.'

Then I realised Peigi might call and hear that, and I hadn't warned her, so I phoned her and almost made her ill with nerves, getting her out of her bed at that time.

I lay down in the big bed, on Max's sheets, surrounded by the scent of his body. I lay on his side of the bed, nearest the door, where he could have protected me from mice. I slept fitfully for several hours, then went to work at mid-day wild-eyed and bedraggled.

Fergus was perched on the corner of my desk, hair newly cut, tremendously pleased with himself. He'd on the dark grey suit I've always particularly liked; I was vulnerable enough to find that made me weepy.

'Got a minute to talk to me?' he said. 'In private.' I followed him meekly through to an empty studio.

'Anything new?' I shook my head. 'Well I have some news. About me, not your Russkie. I wanted to tell you before it's all round the place. Prepare yourself for a surprise, kitten.'

'You're getting re-married?'

He gazed into my eyes. 'That's not a bad idea. But what I wanted to tell you was that I've finally got it, Serena, what I've worked for all these years.'

'Early retirement?'

He laughed, caught me up in his arms and whirled me round.

'London, and an absolutely obscene amount of loot. I'm off in a fortnight.'

'Congratulations, Fergus. No matter what's happened between us I could never say you're not brilliant at your work. You deserve it.'

'Kiss?'

259

I gave him a desultory peck and attempted to extricate myself, but he held me tighter, burying his face in my hair. 'Come with me.'

'Och, why do you ask that? You know I can't.'

'Of course you can; this Russian thing was nonsense all along. I'll have a considerable amount of pull there – I can get you any job you want. Or you can stay at home and write, the way you've always wanted to, my own darling little Colette.'

I tried again to push him away. 'I wasn't your wife even before Max. There was the small matter of a divorce.'

'I was your first husband, that's what counts. I've changed. I'll do whatever you ask, if you want me to put myself in the hands of a trendy shrink I'll do that for you. I'll never hit you again. You used to make me so angry and frustrated I didn't know what I was doing. I've learnt to control that. If it's important to you we'll have another wedding - they'd probably be happy enough to do it again in a church, in the circumstances. I suppose we should, so you'll get my pension. You're bound to live a lot longer than me.'

That gave me a jolt. Fergus looking boldly in the eye of mortality - where did that leave the rest of us?

'It's too late to think like that,' I said.

'I love you, witch, I need you. Come with me and we'll have the most wonderful life you could dream of.'

He was familiar with the worst of me, my warped unfeminine body with a mind to match. His soul's as black as my own. I was almost ready to believe we truly do belong together.

'Take one of your other wives,' I said.

'It's you I want, it's always been you. I need you.'

He was holding me so tight I could hardly breathe, and I could feel he had an erection like a prize stallion.

The therapist he'd made me go to while we were still together asked me if I had rape fantasies. That's what irritates me about career do-gooders, pretending to be professionals when they can't even tell the difference between fantasy and near miss.

'Women stopped having these with my mother's generation,' I'd told her. 'Even Nancy Friday admits that. And I bet a lot of the ones in *My Secret Garden* were lying anyway. Attention-seekers.'

But I couldn't keep my mind off the idea that Fergus could have taken whatever he wanted there and then, no one would even have heard me scream, with the double-soundproofed doors. He must have noticed me looking at the door, and thought I'd seen someone through the porthole, for he relaxed his grip enough for me to wriggle free.

'I'm not coming back to you, no matter what, ' I said. 'Help me find Max, Fergus.'

He does a strong line in theatrical laughs. 'You want me to have the docks dragged? Oh, don't start again. There's no way that happened. He's just taken himself off. It was on the cards, wasn't it? Not many men are going to put up with it as long as I did. Are you sure you don't know more about this than you're letting on? I wouldn't blame you, you know.'

'You have the contacts. You're always telling me how good you are at finding out stuff. Find Max for me. I need to know he's all right, nothing more than that.'

Fergus looked at me artfully. 'If I do that for you, will you spend the night with me?'

I didn't answer, but he shot off, eyes gleaming. I never mistook Fergus for an angel, but I swear I could see the tips of the wee horns poking through his curly hair. I thought it would take days, and he'd have forgotten. But he was back within three hours.

'Not a word nor a sign of your precious Russkie. Not arrested as an illegal or deported or picked up for chasing skirt or fished out of the water. But there was a Russian ship in Leith Friday night. She sailed on Saturday. The Chaika. Home port Murmansk, and that's where she was supposed to be headed. They had to get a freebie from Mathers Mechanical to patch up the engines and the pumps so the safety lads would let them sail. Bob says he has no idea how far they'll get before it breaks down again. Murmansk in a oner – that he doubts. He says they hadn't enough fuel anyway. Might make it home for Christmas. But I imagine that's where your precious Max disappeared to. Now – the arrangement we made. Will I pick you up here after work, or don't you want the others to know?'

'What arrangement.'

'Tonight. I want it tonight, Serena.'

'Och, that. I never thought you'd take it seriously. Jesus, Fergus, you didn't believe I'd sleep with you? I never agreed to that.'

'You didn't refuse either. You were cuddling and necking with me till I was ready to burst, and you were hot for me too.'

'I was never hot for you, Fergus, if you want the truth. '

'You always were a nasty lying little bitch. You'll regret it, though God knows it'll be a relief never to have to cajole you and bolster up your puny ego

262

again or to play house with you. You don't want to be anybody's wife, do you, you just want to play-act. With your pine furniture and your naff pictures and your Scandi-sodding-navian décor. Because you want everything painted in battleship colours doesn't mean anyone else appreciates it. Go to assertiveness classes, why don't you, if you can muster the confidence to walk in the door. Then maybe you'll be able to choose a pair of knickers without taking them back six times or conducting an opinion poll. You'll be able to make a sodding decision when you have to.'

'I've made a decision. I'd sooner cut my throat than spend the night with you.'

'You'll regret it. I promise you. If that bastard's still in this country, I'll have him shipped out to Siberia before he can blink.'

An ordinary life is all I ever wanted. A place where I can see the other side.

I decided it'd be politic to call on Bernie to ask if Tom had seen him. Her face crumpled with concern. And this woman, so much younger and more competent than me, brought me into her home and gave me coffee well-laced with brandy, and was thoughtful enough to chase her child to his own room and speak to him sternly when he tried to come out.

'He's had an accident,' she said, without hesitation. 'But you've tried the hospitals, of course? He'd never leave you. That's all he ever talks about, you, and your work, and the children you'll have together. He's so proud of you. I don't think he was with Tom on Friday. Wait and I'll phone him to see if he has any bright ideas.'

The rest of that week, I worked like an automaton and slept like a zombie. I chanted his name inside my head like a mantra as I dozed off. I'd wake, wondering if I'd dreamt him too.

'Where would someone like Max go?' I asked Carla. 'Where could he lose himself?'

She shrugged. 'If he's still in this country? London.' No hesitation. I felt she knew what she was talking about. 'But you know, Serena, I think it's likely he did leave on that ship.'

'Why would he do that without telling me?'

'Because he realised it would never have worked out for you two,' she said gently. 'You looked wonderful together, but you weren't well suited. You need a man with a gentle temperament.' Carla let me cry myself dry.

'Well, you're right anyway,' I said. 'But I know Max isn't far away. I can feel him breathing.'

His breath was soft on the nape of my neck, the way it was when he used to draw my hair aside and nuzzle me there while I stood at the sink washing dishes.

Carla looked at me pityingly. 'If he wanted you to find him, he'd have left clues.'

'I have to have a last try at finding out what happened to him. I made him come here. I'm responsible.'

In the circumstances, the last person I needed to see was Dee. But Marjorie has friends who still live in London. It only took a single phone-call and I was on my way south for a long weekend on the cheap. Carla was right - one of the few times I'd seen Max really happy in Edinburgh was when he hung out with the buskers on the Royal Mile. Winter makes it easier to find them. I haunted the underground, going from one station to the next, listening for the sound of a cello among the Bob Dylan wannabes. Time after time I was sure I heard him, but when I traced the music either it was a stranger or there was no one there at all. Hide and seek.

Then I'd have to gallop to the nearest Ladies and splash cold water on my face, and glower at myself in the mirror till the floor stopped heaving. Sometimes I had the urge to bang my head against the glass and keep banging till one or the other shattered. I managed to stop myself. Madness is all in the mind. All you have to do is SNAP OUT OF IT. Pull yourself together.

I felt numb, disoriented, the way you do when you're wakened suddenly from a bad dream. I was viewing everything from a distance, voices sounded as if they were at the end of a tunnel. I had become invisible.

I wouldn't have been able to recognise the sound of Max anyway. Not like Jan Garbarek - I can pick out the sax he's playing within the first seconds. Amazing the number of TV soundtracks that use him. Royalties must be good. But I didn't have long enough to study what was distinctive in Max's playing.

I felt calmer when I went back to work, though Anita still cast worried glances in my direction when she thought I wasn't looking.

'You want some sick leave?' she said. 'You're entitled to it.'

'I'm not sick.'

'You're due some leave. Take it.'

'I don't want to.'

'It's not a request, Serena. I need my people with their heads on straight. You're in no fit state to

265

work. Why not go and see your relative – your aunt is it? – in that god-forsaken place you come from?'

When I went in that day, I'd been toying with the idea of resigning once and for all. I'd psyched myself up to it. I broke into a cold sweat of relief. I suppose the square peg feels the bruises for a while too, till its shape re-adjusts. I *can* be good at this; I can have a career. I don't need to live the rest of my life hemmed in by Fergus's prejudices.

'You're right,' I said to Anita, 'I think I'm beginning to get the hang of this job, at last, but you're also right about this – I do need a week or so.'

I had no intention of going straight to Balvaig. Carla was totally unsympathetic.

'Love at first sight's for people with their heads screwed on straight,' said Carla

I glared at her. She shrugged. 'What are friends for, if they can't tell you the truth?'

The Scots should learn to shrug more.

'It doesn't happen like an explosion, Serena. Remember I told you. It's more like a fire in a haystack.'

'It's an explosion for some people. Carla, I'm not heartless,' I said. 'But I really, really want to be with someone I can be happy with.'

'Accept it,' she said. 'He doesn't want you to find him. It's not only that he hasn't been in touch, he's covered his tracks as carefully as any criminal. I was wrong about him, I can admit this freely. He's not a good man. He's a wicked, thoughtless bastard, to do this to you.'

Max used to say that, about himself. He said it was a consequence of growing up in a disintegrating country. 'It's affected us all,' he'd say, 'even the young people. You can't twist and distort a sapling and expect it to grow up straight and strong. I am not a good person.'

But in the street I still found myself waiting to see him come hurrying through the crowd, his collar turned up against the rain, his shoulders slightly hunched, eyes searching for me too, my fine-featured mate amongst the river of lumpy, dour, uncooked-pastry faces, the only figure in colour in a black and white film, like the cute kid in Schindler's List.

I booked my flights to St Petersburg for the next week.

To keep myself busy, I piled up the boxes of Morag's ornaments. By good fortune rather than foresight I took them to Phillips instead of the PDSA shop. I'd never heard of Clarice Cliff or Susie Cooper. Bizarre meant nothing more to me than a good description of the garish colours and awkward angular shapes. Some of the Art Nouveau trinkets were pretty enough – a few of these I kept. I was appalled to find I had more than two thousand pounds to show for an empty attic and mantelpiece. All these years I'd despised her taste, and she'd left me what would have been a small fortune to her.

One more major task to accomplish. I couldn't bring myself to weep as I hauled it up the front steps. I'd lost the capacity to feel anything. My nostalgia was all for what felt like the memory of a fairy-tale.

'You might as well sell it, Marjorie,' I said. 'I don't think he's coming back. I can't ask you to keep it on the off-chance.'

She was in tears. 'I won't sell it. It'll be here for when he comes home.'

Amazing. Losing Max has been the most liberating experience of my life.

'Why don't you go over to your aunt's for a couple of days?' said Ursula tactfully, as I added to the heap of black bags for the bin-men. I know she believed I was losing my mind along with my clutter. She'd agreed to look after the cat again, but she'd not hidden the fact she was with Carla on this: I was making a mistake.

'I will. Once I'm back from Russia. I'll go to Peigi's for Christmas, I've been promising her for years I'll do that.'

'What if Max turns up while you're away?'

'Then let him in, if he doesn't still have a key. He has my mobile number. He'd always try that first.'

As futile as the scientists hunched over radio receivers, waiting for messages from outer space.

Gorby twined contentedly round Ursula's ankles, delighted that he didn't have to be put in his travelling-basket.

CHAPTER TWENTY-FIVE

I didn't break the news to my aunt till the morning I was leaving. 'I'm taking a wee trip to St Petersburg, Peigi. Just a few days.'

'What immediately?'

'I won't be long. Then I'll come to Balvaig for Christmas.'

I needed to know if he'd made it home. I needed, just a little, to know what some of the other people in Max's life were like. I needed to know if I could manage it, carving my own path as a single woman, and that he wouldn't be back in two days or two months or two years so it'd all start over. I needed to be certain he meant what he said about releasing me.

It was surreal to be back beside the canals and the bridges. I'd always wanted to see it under snow, but there was only a thin scattering. I had a week's leave. I booked into a cheap hotel and went to Max's flat. Maria answered the door.

'Hello!' she said. 'Isn't Max with you? We heard you'd set up home together. Zhenya came to take the things he'd left.'

'You haven't seen Max?'

'Not since June.'

'Where does Zhenya live?'

She shrugged. She had no ideas on who else or where else I could try. I'd been telling myself it was a forlorn hope that I'd find Zhenya. Yevgeny Kutozov, and I hadn't the least idea if that was even his real name. Needle in pin factory. I caught sight of him the very first evening I was looking.

'Kuzkuz!' He laughed and plucked me off my feet to swing me round. 'I never thought to see you again so soon. Where is he, then?' He gazed expectantly in the direction I'd come.

'Gone.'

'Oh God, don't cry. Let's find a quiet place to sit. What are you saying - is he dead?' I shook my head. 'Is he ill?'

I hugged him. He felt like the first slice of normality since the night I last saw Max.

'He went away. I thought maybe he'd come back here.'

'No one here's seen him,' said Zhenya. 'I'd have heard.'

'His mother – do you know where she is?'

'Kiev, I think. I don't know exactly. Some hospital. He'd never go there.'

'Has he any other relations or friends he might have gone to?'

He shrugged. 'He was like a brother to me. He'd couldn't come back and not tell me.'

Zhenya bought me a meal, and walked round the town with me all of the next day. He grew maudlin and damp-eyed. 'I wanted so much to take both of you to see the white cranes,' he said. 'I've dreamt about that, how we'd go for a long journey into the forests, just the three of us.'

I could scarcely believe it was the same man. I used to blame him for being a bad influence on Max. Maybe I'd had things the wrong way round. I told him about the Chaika. I gave him as much information as I'd been able to glean about when it had sailed from Leith, and the prognosis there about how many stops it might have had to make. I asked him to find someone in Murmansk who'd know about ship movements.

'I couldn't manage to go there myself,' I said. 'I wouldn't have a clue who to ask in any case.'

Carla and the others were right. He didn't want me to find him. But Zhenya's his friend.

I wrote down my addresses for him, in Edinburgh and at Peigi's house.

'Please, I really have to know that he's OK,' I said. 'You'll let me know?'

'Give him time. He'll come back to you. Time's different for us. It doesn't run in a straight line.'

'It's all right,' I said, patting his hand. 'I don't think he wants to come back to me. I just want him to be safe.'

I understood at last. Zhenya has lost so much more than I have, because he knows what he has lost.

'The girl who sometimes stayed with him – Katya. Do you know how I can find her?' I said.

'She's from Odessa. She went home, I think. I didn't hear that she came back.'

'Do you know her other names? Or an address?'

'I can find out.'

Yekaterina Vladimirovna Pustina. He'd found an old address, and the name of several people who'd know where to find her. He'd have travelled with me, but I was desperate to be alone. It was hard. A day and a half on a dirty and uncomfortable train, thank God I'd had the sense to book a berth, and that it was three other women I shared with, though I had time to regret that I hadn't accepted Zhenya's offer of company. I was hauled off the train at the border, for by the time I'd decided to go, there hadn't been time to get a visa. They took my passport, and they questioned me like a

271

criminal for twenty minutes. Fifty dollars it cost me, to have the privilege of visiting Ukraine for three days. I spent the rest of the journey trying to compose myself, just in case.

'I won't make a scene,' I decided. 'I'll be completely calm. I'll wish them both joy.' It took only hours to track her down.

'She married,' said the elderly violin teacher whose name Zhenya had given me. 'Quite some time ago. Possibly ten months. She lives on Rosa Luxembourg Street. She has a young child.'

My heart started beating far too fast. As I climbed the stairs to her door, I kept having to stop and catch my breath. It was a smart building. Katya and I stared at each other. The baby in her arms was tiny, though it had a good head of fuzzy black hair. 'Mitya,' she said proudly. 'Dmitri. He's almost four weeks old.'

The flat was large and elegantly furnished. She was so proud of it, I had to accept a guided tour. The kitchen was well equipped, even down to the huge American larder fridge. In the sitting room there were elaborate chandeliers, and expensive rugs on the newly refurbished parquet floors. ('No one would want to marry me,' Max had said. 'I have no money, no prospects.') Katya said her husband was a 'businessman'. I didn't want her to elaborate, and she was clearly happy to leave it at that.

In the corner was an antique carved wood music stand, and a violin lying on a chair beside it. I'd have liked to ask her to play for me, but I was afraid. So much of what Max used to play was originally scored for the violin.

'Zhenya Kutozov gave me your address,' I said. 'I think you used to know Maksim Grigoriev?'

'Max? I haven't seen him for ages. So – you're a friend of Grishkin's? You speak excellent Russian. You are part-Russian?' She had the same knowing, gap-toothed smile as Maria. A pretty face, though she'd run to fat before she was forty. Maybe a lot of it was because she'd given birth a month before.

'He was living with me in Scotland for a few months. You say you haven't heard from him?' My mind floated up to the ceiling, so that I could observe myself talking calmly with this woman who'd shared Maksim's bed.

'Not for a year. No – it must be more than that.'

'You used to be his girlfriend?'

'This isn't his baby,' she said, not unkindly. 'I can see in your eyes that you're wondering that. Look – he's the double of my husband.' She fetched a gaudily-framed wedding portrait. The baby's features were a miniature duplicate of the swarthy man at Katya's side, almost embarrassingly so. I used to imagine how it'd be when I bore Maksim's children. They'd be scale models of him, and people would look in the pram and laugh slyly and say: 'No prizes for guessing who *his* daddy is.'

'Grishkin will come back,' said Katya. 'He always does, eventually, like a tom-cat with his ears torn.'

'How long did you know him?' I asked huskily.

'Me? Oh, since we were students. He'd be around for a while, then off again. It wasn't a love affair. I was a convenient place to leave his bag and take messages for him.'

'He had a cello, while he was in Edinburgh. He got a loan of one. I called it Katya. Just for myself, I never told him.'

'You were jealous? Heavens, there's no need to be jealous of what was between me and Max.' Her smug pussycat features creased in a smile.

'Do you know where his mother is? I heard she'd gone back to Kiev. You don't know which hospital? Or whether she uses her own name or her husband's?'

She shrugged. 'Yulia. I never met her. There can't be so many hospitals in Kiev. I don't imagine he'd have gone to her. He hated her, and his father.'

That drew me up with a jolt. 'I thought he seemed to admire his father. Maybe people always speak well of the dead.'

'His father's not dead, is he?' she said. 'What happened?'

'Was he not killed in a car accident ten years ago?'

'No!' Katya started to giggle, then thought better of it. 'He's not dead. Just dead drunk, most of the time. He used to find Max and try to tap him for money. I don't think he'd had a job for years.'

I liked Katya, no point in denying it.   'He's a thoughtless bastard,' she said. 'But he won't stay away from you long. You are very beautiful. You have a good job?'

I shrugged.

'Grishkin can't commit himself to anyone or anything,' said Katya. 'He'll be thirty in a couple of years, and he behaves like an adolescent.'

'A year,' I said. 'Surely? It was his birthday in September. Twenty-nine?'

'No, I'm sure he's the same as me. He'll be twenty-eight now. He's a drifter,' she added, a little sadly. 'It's his background. Nobody loved him.'

'His grandparents did.'

She looked vague. 'Perhaps.'

That was the answer then. Two people starved of love – what did we imagine we could give each other?

'Listen – you're not pregnant?' said Katya. I fancied she settled back a little in her chair when I shook my head.

I couldn't bear any more.

I stood in the street feeling giddy, gazing up at the sky and taking great gulps of air as if I'd been reprieved from a death sentence. It was a big risk I'd taken. If Maksim had been with her I'd have wanted to harm both of them. I looked up at Katya's window. She was watching me. I waved to her almost cheerfully as I turned to make my way to the station for the Petersburg train.

It was only hours later, as we trundled through the flat, darkened countryside that could have been anywhere, bland and tasteless as watermelon, I remembered that I'd meant to try to find another dark-haired native of Odessa. I pulled a face at my reflection and leaned my forehead against the cool, grubby window.

I hadn't thought of Seriozha for weeks. He was like someone I'd known in a previous existence. And Max was right about that too. I'd only wanted him for one thing after all. If I'd gone back and married him, it would have been just as much of a fiasco. Max and I are more alike than I cared to admit before. I'm growing up, at last.

White cranes are practically extinct. The chances of seeing one are slight. The chances of seeing two dance together are not computable within my lifetime. As bad as believing in fairies.

CHAPTER TWENTY-SIX

'It's great to have you back,' said Anita, as I turned up for the late shift.

I gave her the first genuine smile ever.

'There's a lecture at the university medical school this evening – I'd like you to interview the guy who's giving it.'

She waved a press release.

'Is there nothing more interesting than that on the go?' I said.

'It is interesting. He's a world expert on female sexual dysfunction.' She sniggered. 'And wouldn't it just be a *man* who's an expert? Very non-PC to even call it that in this day and age, when you have to be so careful. It says here he's qualified in both medicine and psychiatry. Smart-arse.'

God preserve me from all of that crew. That so-called psychotherapist I went to! (I know it's not the same, but anything that starts with 'psycho' might as well start with 'pseudo' as far as I'm concerned). She was goggle-eyed as she explained that there are about two dozen different varieties, and totally humourless when I said I was sure I had most of them. I expected her to give me a sorority badge. Something along the lines of the Isle of Man emblem, but with three pairs of crossed legs. I never went back.

Wonder if I could just attend the lecture, as a civilian so to speak?

I glared at Anita. Not the first genuine glare.

'It's quite trendy,' she said pleadingly. 'There's not a lot else happening. We'll need it for the morning. Look on the bright side. Maybe he'll be the saviour of half the women in Morningside. Go for it.'

'Why the hell do you think I should be the one to interview him?'

'Well, can you imagine Nick doing it? Having a man to man about women who're not up for it? Now that would be totally OTT in terms of non-PC.'

'But why should *I* be interested?'

'Because you're a journalist.'

'He's probably in the pay of some drug company.'

'Probably. That's for you to winkle out.'

'What's his name?'

'Dr Danny de Bourka.'

'Poser. I hate it when they do that. Pretending they're Norman knights rather than Celts. I bet his granddad was happy enough with plain old Burke.'

'That's my girl,' said Anita. 'Look – there's a pic of him with the press release. Kinda cute?'

The man in the picture had dark curly hair, tidily cut, perfect-looking teeth, the kind of ears that lie flat to the head, and neat wee gold-rimmed glasses. He was kinda cute.

'Taken about twenty years ago when he was in his prime,' I said. 'I know his type.'

'He's probably been at university for about twenty years,' said Anita, still studying the presser. 'Dublin, Oxford, Harvard. Jesus Christ. Give him a hard time. Lay it on him, girl.'

I put up my hair, applied some make-up (not to Carla's standards, I freely admit), collected the cameraman, and went off to give this creepy know-it-all the hardest time possible.

Never let it be said that I don't admit when I'm wrong. The picture was recent, and the good doctor was an interesting and knowledgeable guy, easy to talk to, not one of the type so puffed up with their own importance they're fit to bust a gut. Funny too, and it's hard enough to make me laugh these days. I was glad I'd gone fine and early to get the interview. I sent Dennis off with the tape to let Nick edit it for the morning, so I didn't have to go back at once. I don't often skive.

Anita and Roger were beside themselves next day.

'You really are getting the hang of this,' he said. 'The men love you because you're a sexy wee thing, and the women love you because you look like everyone's perfect daughter.'

Then they told me about the job going in London, on the mother ship, for a health correspondent.

'We don't want to lose you,' said Anita, 'but it's a super chance. Throw your hat in the ring anyway?'

Carla was unhappy about it, I could tell, but she put a brave face on it.

'It's just what you need, and it's not a chance you can pass up. We can visit you. As long as you promise to keep away from that creep Fergus. When would you have to leave?'

'Not till February. We'll spend all the time we can together once I'm back from the Christmas trip, how about it?'

She looked at me speculatively.

'You've met a man?' she said.

'Och, nonsense. I'm just pleased to think maybe I'll have a real career at last, rather than just a job.'

Carla smirked.

CHAPTER TWENTY-SEVEN

A stranger would easily miss the village road's sharp turn off the main route that funnels the caravans to the street lights and chip shop at Portmore, or the lush, improbable plantings of Colonel Crichton's garden just beyond Balvaig on the road to Red Point. There's a hairpin bend into a cantankerous bridge that smashes exhausts and guards a narrow ferny road. Baby burns vanish under the tarmac in an impotent gurgle and the roadside rocks drip diamonds of water in the hottest weather; sweat on Gaia's face. In summer the ditches are full of yellow flags. Through low-grown stands of birch and rowan and gorse the road twists, past unfenced rushy fields and bedraggled, uncooperative sheep, out of sight of the sea till it swings abruptly to the right, climbs steeply and tops the brae. The bay's laid out below like a postcard, and beyond that the wide sweep of Loch Olla hugged by its headlands.

The October after Donald John showed me the fairies, Alan Mackay from the village took me out on his fishing boat one evening. He'd none of the daft superstitions about women or rabbits. A minister wouldn't have been encouraged to step aboard, but that was a personal preference, one my father shared. Coming back into the loch, the engine slowed to walking pace, Alan pointed to the scattering of light-filled windows against the dark braes. The gilded sky was at our backs, and the sea bright; dusk had settled on the land. The points of light reminded me of fallen stars, or tiny candle-flames to draw moths. The loch was filled with the keening of eider duck, and the air was a spider's web against my face.

'God's own country, if there is a God,' Alan said. 'Wherever you end up, Serena, this'll always be your home. Hold to that, and you'll never know poverty.'

I've only to close my eyes, for that picture to come up, the small lights that signify home as night falls on Balvaig and Lonemore and Douglastown.   I knew who I was then better than I do now.

A little past the first cattle grid beyond the village, there's a pair of improbably grand gateposts, built by my great-grandfather, with a neat blue and white signboard:
MacKenzie
Kingdom
Fortress MacKenzie. By the time I reached it darkness had fallen. The taxi driver from Portmore looked dubiously at the potholed track.

'It's all right. I would know my way down with my eyes shut.'

I could hardly wait for dawn, for the panorama of rock and sea and minuscule islets. The landscape that possessed me. Was it aware too? Did the stones and the trees and the burn sigh and think: she's home? I scarcely saw it, the way you can't see your own face without a mirror, that's why it had been so important to show it to Max - so I could learn to see it again myself.

Autumn's best there, the season of metals, when everything, even the moon herself, turns to gold and copper and bronze. I'd missed the best of it. The leaves were sere and faded. Grey upon grey upon grey.

Kingdom hides till the last minute. It's as dour as its builder, Peter Mackenzie's father who raised the house with his own hands, upon the thin sour ground his ancestors had wrested back from the moor, high above the machair. 'The last to drown and the first to burn,' Grannie would say. It doesn't turn its shoulder to the hill but faces the wind, its two dormers like eyebrow raised in perpetual questioning.

It's roof was never marred by a TV aerial for the old man condemned it as the devil's own work, and Peigi says she'd rather have a good book. On either side of it, two Scots pines, wind-sculpted into oversized bonsai, their trunks salmon-pink and silver, heartbreaking in a rosy dawn.

The original croft house still stands, a black house, its thatch replaced with corrugated iron. In Ollasdale wood, Granda once showed me the stumps of the trees cut for its roof-timbers. My folk were like Max's. They built their homes from the materials they could carry home.

We have our own stretch of shore below the steep fields, and an ancient rickle of stones we optimistically call a jetty. Granda used to clear the boulders and the slimy brown sea wrack from there. After he died no one bothered. I dislike paddling there for fear of what's lurking in the fronds, and the sensation of small fishes darting against my legs.

There's an islet you can reach dry-shod when the tide's out, not ours strictly speaking, but no one else ever bothered to claim it. It's perhaps thirty feet by twenty. The Green Isle of the Great Deep. Hours I spent there as a child, building play-houses with white pebbles marking out the rooms and the glutinous green seaweed we called mermaid's hair for carpets, never lonely. On the seaward side is the incongruous wreck of a wooden structure – too fanciful to be called a shed, but we don't go in for gazebos in Balvaig. I didn't go near; its ghosts didn't want company. I asked Peigi about it, more than once, what it had been. 'Haven't a clue,' she'd say, lightly. 'It was there before my time. Something to do with the fishing, I suppose.' Fishing! What nonsense. I hate it when she won't tell me secrets.

I'd lie on my isle, looking up at the sky through birch-leaves or the green and gold bishop's croziers of bracken shoots, and I'd imagine I heard the laughter of another child, till I became fixated with the idea that I was to blame for a forgotten accident. A drowning in shallow water, a fatal stumble, a smothering.

Mammy, did I ever have a wee brother or a sister?

God, no. You were quite enough, thank you very much.

But still I'd search furtively in the photo drawer for the faded, creased snapshot of the smiling, toothless baby I'd murdered, by accident or design.

Then I'd forget and go back to catch grasshoppers in my hands, and butterflies, the tickly sensation of the frail wings, the fairy-dust from them on my skin. No man ever invaded me or hurt me there.

You can see the fish farm from my island now, it's tucked in against the north shore so that it fades into the background, because the folk who run the Balvaig Inn made such a fuss.

Peigi was in a fluster with waiting. 'You've a face on you as white as bone.'

'I've not been sleeping.'

She regarded me sadly, this spinster who'd probably never been with a man, but spent her days patiently collecting the shards of female relative's marriages. Fragments of conversations I must have heard in the days before they thought I could understand:

'What did you marry for Morag, if you don't like that side of it?'
'Everyone marries. Most women don't enjoy it.'
'Most women? You can't judge the world by Mammy. Men want it – you knew that. Women have to get used to it. No good'll come of it. He'll go with other women.'
'I wouldn't care. I wish he would.'
'As long as his pay-packet doesn't.'
'I wouldn't have done it, except for her. You think I was going to be lumbered with a kid on my own?'

And more than once Morag had said something else I didn't catch; what etched it in my memory was the look Peigi threw me, big-eyed and scared.

My aunt has been the exception to the MacKenzie rule on inappropriate names. Margaret. The pearl of great price. She's still a good-looking woman. Her hair's fading to a stylish silver, sweeps of it at the nape and the temples, she's kept it long, and she wears it swept up, like an Edwardian lady. She was always the beauty in the family. Not a conventional, easy beauty, hers. Good bones. I used to take comfort from the fact I've inherited that at least, and Max was the same. Our children would have had these elegant cheekbones too. We'd all age gracefully; enough scaffolding there to keep the face from collapsing no matter how old. What a waste of good genes.

We both went to bed early, relieved to be able to stop pretending. I wouldn't have been able to start telling her what was wrong, because I've never spoken to her on any topic remotely connected with sex, any

284

more than I could to my mother. I don't believe the MacKenzie women have the knack of it. Who could Peigi and Morag have talked to concerning men and loving? Certainly not Grace Robertson, their mother, or the terrifying grandmother, the Seer whose husband never laid eyes on her except clothed from the neck to the ankle.

Peigi told me once she'd been deployed to give her wee sister a pep talk before she was married, on the grounds that she was a teacher and she'd read a book. She seemed to find that funnier than I did, but it wasn't till I found Morag and Frank's marriage certificate I realised why. It was dated November 1966; less than six months before my birth. She must have been hot for him once.

I slept in the room I was born in, with its minute gable window framing a glimpse of hill and sea, like stained glass. I stood by the window brushing my hair, listening to the familiar voice of the burn, looking at the moon-path on the bay. When I was a small child they found me down there in my nightie, up to my knees in silvered water and bawling my eyes out because I couldn't walk on it, and it turned to lead in my hands.

I gazed at the reflection in my small age-spotted mirror and I found I didn't recognise her. If we hadn't mirrors and cameras we'd have no idea how we look. We'd all be happier. We'd recognise ourselves from the reflection in our man's eyes. I'll never let an outsider have Kingdom. I'd rather break everything and burn the place down. No one's to look in my mirror after me; the shaman destroys his drum. I might have made an exception for my own daughter.

I left the lamp on, as I had at home too, since Max was gone. But I woke again in the small hours.

Too much light. Lamplight and moonlight and the outside of the window plastered with the furry brown bodies of moths. I rose and switched it off. Mine would be the darkened window after all.

Mornings were the worst. Max loved that time best of all, never happier than when he was up early and had a purpose to his day. He would have been out of doors at daybreak, sawing wood, planting a few fields of tatties.

Even Kingdom's small scrap of beach made me nostalgic. In summer, a solitary pair of wild swans used to settle there. The cob would stand guard over his mate as if she was the most precious object in his world; they never seemed to have young. Then one year he arrived alone. He'd stand on the same rock, as if he could conjure up her memory by being there. He became more mellow and tame. He didn't hiss and raise his wings when we took him a handful of grain.

'His mate must have died,' said Peigi. I wept for pity.

Another season the same. Next year, there was another pen with him.

'That's not his wife,' I said. I was judgemental, even as an eight-year-old.

'He's found a new one. Isn't he lucky.'

'How do you know the first one didn't just find a new husband?'

'I don't think swans do that. Not the female ones anyway. It's men do things like that. Women keep the faith.'

My aunt had sounded bitter. She glared at the swans.

286

But I thought he looked wistful. He didn't love the second wife as much. It's just that birds need to be in pairs, like shoes and ornaments and people.

'Can you keep these here for me, Peigi?' I said, when I finished unpacking my case. 'I couldn't bear to have them at home.' I'd put all the photos, and Max's Leningrad Conservatory certificate, still in its frame, in a box.

'So this is Maksim? Such fair hair. Shall we keep it with the others in the album? Here's one of your father,' she said. There they were, the two of them, squinting into the sun, arms round each other's waists, both laughing, young and carefree.

'That's not Morag, is it? That's you, Peigi. I haven't seen that one before,' I said, accusingly.

'I've been rearranging them a wee bit. He was a handsome man.' A saw-edge to her voice.

'Your brother-in-law.'

'Not when that was taken. That was before he married Morag. He was at school with me, you know. Another Free Kirk family. Amazing how we were the wild kids. Reaction.'

You couldn't make the mistake that the people in the picture are not a couple. 'Except you, Aunt Peigi?'

She gave a twisted smile. I glanced at the date scrawled on the bottom of the photo. October 1966.

'Morag had another boyfriend when that would have been taken,' she said lightly. 'Tom McGuire. Glasgow Irish. She wanted to marry him, but he was a Catholic. You can imagine.'

She'd clearly forgotten that I'd seen the marriage certificate.

'Is there not a photo of him?'

'Even Morag wouldn't have dared bring a picture of Tom McGuire into Dadda's house.'

'What did he look like?'

'Not unlike you,' said my aunt calmly. 'Same colouring. But then, so had your mother.'

Silence lay heavy on the room.

'So she stole your boyfriend?' I said.

'She didn't steal. I gave. I was used to having to give Morag whatever she asked for. "Don't be so mean," Mammy would say to me, "you'll get it back." I suppose she was their favourite because of the time she nearly died of the meningitis.'

And did she get Frank back when Morag tired of him? And when was that anyway? Was she ever not tired of him? Is that why Peigi went away to Canada? Because she was tempted to take her toy back? What happened in the years Mammy and I lived here and Peigi was teaching in Glasgow, where Frank worked?

'And what became of this Tom Maguire?'

'Haven't a clue. We never saw hide nor hair of him again after your mother married Frank.'

A truth too horrible to dwell on took root in the back of my mind.

'He never tried to get in touch to see how Morag was?'

'Not that I know of. Why would he?'

What is she playing at? Telling me half a secret, then challenging me with those steely blue eyes?

My aunt unfolded the yellowing newspaper cutting from the Free Press.

'Where's my medal nowadays?' I said.

'Safe in my drawer through the house. And do you still never sing, Serena? I often wondered why not.'

To spite your precious sister. She never took the least interest in my singing, till I won my Mod medal. Afterwards, she'd nag me the whole time to do my party turn. So I shut up and haven't sung since.

'Do you remember however early you woke in summer Grannie would be at work in the garden already, singing in Gaelic?' I said.

Psalms, love-songs, everything under the sun while she forked in manure or kelp, or fed her hens. I was hoping Peigi wouldn't remember what I'd sung for my solo. 'A very emotive rendering from a young woman of nineteen,' one of the judges said while I'd smirked to myself. Am Buachaille Bàn, indeed.

In the early days Max used to tease me that we'd have the only children who started school already speaking Russian and Gaelic as well as English.

More pictures of Frank, a few more. He was handsome right enough when he was young, a real hunk, with his laughing eyes and wavy brown hair, eyes the colour of ripe hazelnuts.

'He was a good man, your father,' said Peigi. 'Just foolish, and too fond of the drink. He had a good heart.'

I still have a clear memory of that day, the year after Morag and I moved to Glasgow. I came home from school and let myself in, and stood in the hall, listening to my mother screaming like a vixen caught in a trap. I raised the courage to push the sitting room door ajar, then I ran across the landing.

Within minutes the house was full of neighbours, a couple of policemen arrived, and my father was red in the face yelling: 'Rape? This apology for a woman's supposed to be my wife. As for you, you

289

nosey wee bisom......' But he didn't dare hit me in front of the law.

Morag was even angrier with me. 'What a showing-up, you silly wee bitch! I'll never dare show my face to that woman again.'

'Dee says you do that with no clothes on. You were both dressed. I thought he was just murdering you.'

The next week, Frank moved out again. My mother never tired of telling me that was my fault. And now this. I used to think Max was a stranger. Now I don't know who I am.

'Well, what are you going to do next?

Peigi doesn't give up easily. 'You're not going back to that fat pig Fergus?

She was furious because I'd had a postcard from him. A view of Tower Bridge and the message : *Come on in – the water's lovely.* She understood neither why he'd sent it, nor why it made me angry, but the London association made her nervous.

'Of course not.'

'Or this Russian, this Max – what if he turns up?'

'He won't,' I said, decisively.

'Why do you feel you need a man anyway? And why do you forever imagine you need them for *sex*?'

She's always asking me questions that have no solution, sound-of-one-hand-clapping stuff. My aunt, the Zen priestess. When I have the answer to that one:- Enlightenment. What do I need a man for? Why do I require the same lesson over and over? What have I ever needed one for, when it was clear none of them ever had a need for me, other than the one that's crass and obvious? Except one.

'I often wonder if any of the women in our family are cut out for it,' Peigi said. 'Even my own mother. She should never have married. All these miscarriages. And she hated sex. Maybe we should all have been nuns.' She gazed pensively out of the window, then walked around the room with folded arms.

'I think you should stay quiet on your own for a good long time. You've a new job most women would kill for. You've just newly divorced one man, and you have a future before you.'

'I didn't divorce Max,' I said, too quickly.

My aunt gave me a withering look. 'I was meaning Fergus.'

'I'm not my mother,' I said. 'And I'm done with beating myself up because she didn't love me and neither did Frank. I've had a couple of false starts, I admit, but I want to be married. To the right man, one who's there for me. God, I'll soon be thirty-one.'

'Don't give me the old "biological clock" nonsense. And you're just going to work your way round the world till you find the right one, are you?'

'If I have to.'

My aunt shook her head in despair, but she was smiling too.

'Peigi – do you remember Donald John?' I said.

Her face closed like a clam shell.

'Did they ever let him out?'

She shook her head. 'He died there years back. He'd have been about fifty.'

'Remember the police found the knife in the grass – did they never take prints off it?'

'Well, I'm sure they did, in the circumstances... Why wouldn't they? I suppose his prints were on it, I think he'd picked it up, I believe he had it in his hand when they found him.

'Mine would have been too.'

'It wasn't the first time he'd tried to take a child away, you know. He was a paedophile. It just got hushed up because of his father.'

'He didn't threaten me with it. And he didn't cut himself. He didn't have a knife at all. It was me. I took Granda's knife from the kitchen, the one he used to open mussels for bait. I had it in my pocket. You see what that means?'

Peigi stared at me.

'It means I must have known. In the back of my mind.'

'Don't be daft. You were just a wee girl. You might just have taken it for devilment.'

'Do you think I should tell the police? I lashed out at him, and I certainly knew what I was doing then. I meant to cut it off, if I could. But the blade wasn't long enough. Should I tell?'

'Of course not. If you did it in self-defence, what difference does it make? Why did you never tell me?'

'You weren't there. No one was there except Grannie and Granda, and no one asked me about the knife. No one noticed it had gone. Granda didn't have time to notice. I was going to tell the policewoman in Oban, but I was frightened I'd be put in prison. I never told anyone, till now. Morag wouldn't let me talk about it afterwards. It was as if I'd done something so bad it couldn't be mentioned.'

'You carried that burden all these years?'

Peigi was weeping by then. So was I.

'Maybe he'd not have been arrested and put away if I'd confessed. Then Granda wouldn't have had a stroke, and Donald John's father wouldn't have shot himself.'

'That lad had been in and out of mental hospitals since he was a teenager. And the father too. He'd some sort of religious mania. That family would have come to a bad end no matter what.'

'Granda said it was all my fault.'

'It was my fault,' said Peigi. 'I was to blame for trying to sort out people's lives, then leaving you with the likes of my father and my feckless sister.'

'I think I'll go for a walk, Aunt Peigi,' I said.

I'd half-meant to walk inland, the mile or so to the Fairy Loch. It was too soon. I'd lived it in my head over and over, sitting beside Max on the heather, looking down on the loch with the tiny islet where they sacrificed bulls to Mourie a millennium after the saint they'd replaced him with was dead, ageless water, tiers of wee lochans, scraps of lapis-lazuli sky dropped on the moor, glints of sun on wet rock, prayer-flags of mist on the hill. And the wreckage of a plane scattered across it like confetti, the plane his namesake died in. Frail rocks that'll be dust one day, when there are no more stars to see.

The island's stark beauty terrifies the tourists from the soft south. A few days of sunsets and benign weather make them say they'd love to live in the West. They lie. Off they go on the ferry after their fortnight, and rare the ones you ever set eyes on again. They never find the winter that falls overnight, when you wake to find the three Beinns covered in pristine white icing.

Max would have valued it as I did, as much for its small imperfections, like the crescent-shaped silver scar he has on his left side, just below his heart, the one

293

he'd never talk about beyond saying it was almost his ticket to heaven. He would have loved the juxtaposition of hardness and fragility, the flowers that'll come in spring, the small bright blue butterflies of summer. The shells on the beach at Ollasdale which are the translucent lilac of babies' fingernails.

That's all gone. No more MacKenzies at Kingdom after my time.

So I climbed the hill behind the house instead, and leant against a rock to watch Hector McCrae at his over-late winter ploughing in the field to the north. Primitive people used to roll on the ground in autumn to take its fertility into their own bodies for safe keeping till the spring. They asked permission. Now the ploughs gang rape the soil, the seed's sown by cold metal so the earth's holding out on us. That's why it never happened with Fergus, and the seed was left for the crows to get.

I picked idly at the grey and ochre lichen. Lichens thrive best in places where other life falters. A mutual dependence of algae and fungus, intertwined metabolic processes. It was the same with my ancestors, in this island and on Skye; mutual support wasn't optional.

In the forest, Max had told me lichens signify pure air. I'm so selfish I'd never really thought what that must mean to him. Such a huge country, so much pollution, rusty subs on the Neva, right in the middle of town. Not a good place to raise children. But he used to look so wistful when Bernie wheeled her pram down the street, and when I teased him about helping her up the steps with it he laughed: 'just getting in some practice'.

And if I'd been a normal woman, my body could have been carrying within it at that moment the tiny clump of cells that bore the imprint of features, a personality, quirky characteristics: my slightly crooked pinkies, Maksim's incomparable toes, perhaps his amazing talent that'd bloom against all odds, like a flower bursting through concrete. Would he have left me then?

Would it have had brown eyes or blue? It makes a difference to how you see the world, they say, specially in the spectrum between blue and green. I couldn't see colours clearly at all, without Max. I rolled on the hill's stony lap, howling in misery for want of my man, for want of his baby.

Then I pulled myself together. No. My children will have both parents. And I need a man I can admire as well as lust after. The sad part is, I never managed to find Max's admirable qualities once we were back in Scotland. I brought out the worst in him, just as he did in me.

The sun was setting as I got home, the sky copper-peach with a vivid green flash across the horizon. Only seconds it lasts, the emerald drop, which is supposed to bring luck. It helped me reach a decision.

My last duty before I left. In the old burying ground, I pushed open the creaky gate, held onto its hinges by nothing more than rust and faith. I ran my fingers over the inscription in both languages, that was so familiar I saw it in my dreams:

In loving memory of Flying Officer Prince Maksim Michaelovich Chaliapin, born 22 April 1922, died March 15th 1944. 'He sought the stars, and found in them his heaven.'

I laid my bunch of scarlet Dutch hothouse roses against the stone, sheltered from the weather. I knew in my heart it would be the last time. That's one illusion that's done me more damage than any other.

CHAPTER TWENTY-NINE

I had to blink hard before I could believe my eyes when I stepped out of the hotel this morning. A gaggle of kids – the eldest what, maybe ten, twelve? - had set up a stall directly opposite St Isaac's, in the bitter cold, and draped it with plastic to warm a mini-hothouse with their breath. They were selling pot-plants, and the ploy had worked, passers-by were stopping to look, and to grin at the incongruity of it. Pot-plants! But already my hand was in my pocket.

The building where they lived burned down, they told me. Part of it had been deliberately set alight to show off new fire-fighting pumps, but the pumps didn't work, and the ordinary fire engines took too long to arrive. They came home from school to see mothers, baby brothers and sisters, aunts carried out on stretchers, unidentifiable cuts of charred meat. So they ran away, because they didn't want to be taken to the orphanage where children's bodies are sold to friends of the management. They hid, then crept back to the basement, which was still habitable, once it had dried out. After a council of war, to see what they could live on, they stole a packet of coleus seeds, and started their nursery. In the smoky darkness, along with hopes, they have germinated a new generation of plants with gaudy leaves.

What do winter tourists want with plants? Clever kids! They'll get the money anyway, just as they have from me, and their stock won't ever deplete. Such beautiful children. From the southern republics, I should imagine. Dark curly heads and lustrous eyes, smiles that flash like bunny-tails, voices shrill and tense as startled birds. They were wary, watching out (as I am too, I confess) for anything in a uniform (and there are so many, even now).

Perhaps they won't outlast their plants. Free enterprise. I didn't know whether to be angry or optimistic. Tomorrow morning, I'll find them again, if they haven't been moved on, because I think I know where I can find the name of the local doctor who runs refuges for street-children.

I've strolled round the city once more. This time, it's different. My steps are purposeful. The Neva's starting to ice over, and the streets glint and glitter with frost. All the Summer Garden's statues are sheltering in their miniature wooden houses. Oh yes, it's still every bit as lovely as the postcards, the loveliest city on the planet, and still they come in busloads to see it sparkle, and hold their breath, and wipe their eyes: 'The cold! The beauty!'

I believe I'm starting to get better, though I'm grown-up enough now to realise I'm not out of the woods yet. I can tell myself : I am in Max's city, and I stay clear-headed, though I can't forget that it holds his heart in a way I never did. This is where he'll be if he's anywhere, back among the unbroken white of midnight streets, radiant islands, snow-carpeted bridges and cool high rooms with tall windows. But I'm also learning that Max's St Petersburg isn't the real one, any more than the Catherine Palace is. The truth is somewhere in between, and it's a less depressing truth than I perceived before.

I tried to give him what I thought he wanted – memories, security, sentiment. But his needs all along were more basic : a woman to cook and clean for him, and to be there for him in bed. A replay of his parents' marriage, with more sex thrown in. He never wanted to be my companion. He wanted what I couldn't give. No one's to blame. Mistaken identity.

Already I'm forgetting details like the precise timbre of his voice, and the script of the last real conversation we had. These are matters of importance. There must always be someone to record the final words. *Diminuendo al niente.*

Several times, since I've been here, I've spotted him ahead of me on the street, his lanky, elegant frame and his pale hair, and I've run after him, only to find myself having to apologise to a stranger who looks askance at me, as if I'm a madwoman. These are the moments I wish I could turn it off like a tap, the way Roddy said.

And, of course, I've realised, too late, that probably the consequences of Max making a clean breast of it to the authorities in the UK wouldn't have been anywhere near as serious as we'd feared. There were already thousands of Russians living quite openly in London by 1997. Fergus is right. I'm not any kind of investigative journalist. He is though, and he obviously knew perfectly that I'd vastly over-estimated the risks. He was just winding me up, and I fell for it. Again.

Maybe it would have made no difference anyway. Maksim. I think I fell in love with the name rather than the man. Elegant and urbane and beautiful. The name for a fairy prince with hair like flax. It took longer to see there's a coldness in it too. Maksim. A brittle, evanescent name, a pattern of frost-crystals.

I've thought a great deal lately about words, how we betray each other with words, and judge each other, how a single one can cripple a relationship that held promise and pull the plug on hope and burrow deeper than bullets and burn more than fire. The same language furnishes the words for Mein Kampff and the Duino Elegies.

I've seen Zhenya again. The Chaika made it home to Murmansk by the end of January, but Max wasn't on board. They denied all knowledge of him, but Zhenya thinks they were lying. Apparently they only made it as far as Aberdeen on the first trip, were detained again there for a month. I am angrier about how he has betrayed Zhenya than I am about how he has betrayed me. I made him take Max's money, for safe keeping. He'll need it once he gets back.

I am a free woman. I have made no promises I need to keep. My passport's secure at the hotel, and all I have in my pocket as I stand on the bridge they named for Pyotr Schmidt, is some change and a hankie and a photograph.

And a print-off of the latest email from Danny de Bourka. The paper's disintegrating from much folding and re-folding. Cheeky bugger sent me a Valentine's card last week. Too sure of himself by half, as Anita said.

He's still on a lecture tour in America, but he's coming back to London soon. He wants me to visit him there. I haven't told him yet about my promotion. It's to be a surprise. Eighty per cent of our relationship has been based on emails and expensive phone calls, but already he's planning our holiday. He says he wants to take me to his aunt's house, since I'm another swan freak.

'Swans! When I was a kid, I used to nag all the time to visit my aunt in Galway, because her house looks out on the Corrib, and there are hundreds of them. I loved to watch them landing, with their big feet

down like a plane's landing gear, throwing up spray. And they'd fight, they'd stand right up on the water and go at each other like avenging angels, defending their space.'

I'll never see the white cranes dancing. But swans are good. They don't come out of a fairy tale, they're real and available, and I won't need a miracle to be able to watch them scrunching up the water with their enormous feet. I understand now why my swan at Balvaig took another mate.

And yet Carla's right. The spark's never enough if there's no fuel, but the fire in a haystack arrives by magic. The heat builds and builds and builds until it's unbearable. Then the flame comes, and before you know it the whole stackyard's gone up, and there's a blaze that's visible from the neighbouring county. So it's possible she was right about other matters too. Perhaps it is as worthy to live sensibly ever after.

Tomorrow afternoon, I'll go home. Alone.

Lightning Source UK Ltd.
Milton Keynes UK
UKOW05f1043040913

216501UK00001B/14/P